YESTERDAY'S INN

YESTERDAY'S INN

A NOVEL

Robert Geoffrey

Also by Robert Geoffrey

A Letter to My Son

ISBN-13: 9781536887532
ISBN-10: 1536887536
Library of Congress Control Number: 2016913047
CreateSpace Independent Publishing Platform
North Charleston, South Carolina

For my mother:

Thank you for making our yesterdays happy days.
It isn't always easy.

Contents

Part 1:
Summer Wind

CHAPTER 1

An Ill Wind

THE TWO STOOD ON THE edge of a bare, rocky escarpment, surveying the rolling hills of forest that stretched below and away as far as their eyes could see—a world and a vista that hadn't changed for centuries and would hopefully never change. At first glance, the forest gave the impression of being exclusively pines, but John knew that that was far from the truth, because he had had the pleasure of witnessing the fall colors many times and had seen the evidence of the leaves fluttering on strong autumn winds, marking the end of another New England summer.

They stood quietly for maybe five minutes, breathing hard after their strenuous climb but not speaking, just admiring the panorama and listening to the silence. Finally, John broke his gaze into the hypnotic distance and took a look around the clearing where they stood.

"What do you think, David?" he asked after a moment. "Do you fancy stopping here for the night? I would guess that we only have maybe another hour of light left."

"Sounds good, Dad. It will be nice waking to the sun rising over those peaks," David responded, casting his eyes to the line of hills in the east.

With this thought in mind, the two walked down the ridge for a few hundred yards and found a relatively flat area partly under the cover of a couple of ancient pines but with an unobscured view of the distant hills for their morning enjoyment. David tested the ground to make sure that there was sufficient earth over the rock to accommodate at least some of their tent pegs, and then the two took off their hiking backpacks and performed a ritual of stretches and groans.

John and David had been hiking and camping in the Vermont national park for three days now. This was their fourth summer of taking a week or so of father-and-son bonding—starting when David was sixteen and strong enough to carry his share of the load. They both enjoyed the freedom of the outdoors and felt invigorated by the exercise and the simple life for a few days—a time for thinking, interspersed with the occasional conversation. To some extent, they were very similar in their outlooks and did enjoy each other's company. Although they had been hiking for three days, they had intentionally taken a somewhat circuitous route to make sure that they were no more than a day's walk from their car—in case either had an accident and they needed to get back to civilization.

On their first trip, they had stayed at camping areas and hiked out during the day. But they had come to realize that when they hiked off the beaten paths, there was really nothing to stop them pitching a modest camp in these remote areas—it was more back to basics, and they enjoyed the isolation. They were not entirely sure whether they were permitted to camp in these out-of-the-way spots, but they did not harm the wilderness, did not build fires, and felt somewhat safe with regards to the wildlife—so they did not spend too long worrying about it. They camped and enjoyed nature.

John was still relatively fit at sixty years old, but his once-dark-brown hair was mainly gray, and his eyes had a lot more lines at their corners than they had even ten years ago. David was a good four inches taller than his father, was a good-looking young man—having just turned twenty-one the previous month—and still had the youth and zest for life that time had started to take from his father.

Camp consisted of a small, light two-man tent, one whole end of which was a zippered door opening that, weather permitting, they left open so that they had cover over their bedding but could enjoy the night sky. Apart from the tent, they had a couple of sleeping bags, a small propane burner, sufficient freeze-dried meals, along with some enamel plates, mugs, and utensils, and some basic toiletry items.

On this early evening in mid-August, John set about pitching the tent while David went back to a stream that they had passed a little earlier to fill up their water container. He had the younger legs. Once David had returned from the stream, they set about boiling the water and then hydrating a couple of plates of beef stew and making mugs of coffee. Although the meal did not look particularly appetizing, the two weary travelers were famished, so it tasted good to them, and they devoured it appreciatively. After they had cleaned off their plates, they relaxed, backs against a couple of trees, sitting on their rolled-up sleeping bags and sipping the still-piping-hot coffee while John tuned their small radio to a local news station. The sun had been set for maybe fifteen minutes by now, but the refracted light was causing the long streaks of high clouds across the evening sky to glow a deep-red color. John lit his evening cigar, and the two sat peacefully admiring nature's production.

The tranquil sky and light breeze belied the information that was coming out of the small transistor—and that had been filtering out, with increasing prominence, over the last three or four days. What had started out as a possibility had grown over the days into a probability and now into an almost certainty. An August tropical storm had successfully transitioned into hurricane Jasmine, which had then elected not to take the option of proceeding out into the Atlantic Ocean but had instead opted for a path that was going to take her across Block Island and then up Narragansett Bay into Providence. From the sound of the forecasts, Rhode Island and Massachusetts would bear the brunt of the storm, but the forecast was now predicting relatively high winds and, more ominously, prolonged heavy rain over the Vermont area, as the storm was expected to stall as it got into the region. John and David had listened to the developments over the last couple of days but had not discussed them too much—hoping that the hurricane would take an alternative path. Now they were coming to the realization that the weather was inevitably going to get a little messy in approximately thirty-six hours. The sky told them that all was calm and nothing to worry about, but their radio was telling them a different story.

"What do you think, Dad?" David voiced as the news loop started to repeat itself.

John was looking up into the calm evening dusk. "I want to say that it will be OK, that the news folks are hyping up the storm—I want to say that, but deep down, I think that we should heed the warnings and maybe seek better shelter."

"Hard to believe that it is really going to be bad up here," continued David. "Do you think that we would come to harm out here?"

"Oh, I'm sure that if we hunker down in the tent, we would be OK," John confirmed. "But do we really want to spend maybe twenty-four hours cooped up in there—along with our backpacks and the rest of the gear?" He nodded toward their tent, which was only about four feet wide by maybe two-and-a-half-feet high at the highest point. "It's one thing sleeping in there for a few hours—but lying there not even being able to sit up might get tedious, in addition to getting very damp."

"Point taken," conceded David.

"Maybe the easiest decision to make tonight is to agree that we should listen to the updates in the morning and make our decision then."

"Sounds like an OK plan."

They continued their appreciation of the summer evening, not having concluded anything definitively, but in reality both knew that unless there was an unexpected and dramatic change of events overnight, come the morning they would make their way back to the car with some urgency.

It was a good night—the type of night that John appreciated. They had sat and watched the evening turn into darkness. They had listened to the stillness of twilight evolve into the rustles of the night animals and the calls of the owls, and had wondered aloud if the animals knew that bad weather was on the way and that they had better hunt well tonight.

John had appreciated his cigar very much that night—he always thought that a cigar added to the peace of a peaceful time.

Finally at around a quarter past ten, the two campers had crawled into their sleeping bags and lain back to watch the thousands of stars in the black night sky until sleep slowly stole their consciousness.

It was a night with no worries.

The day dawned as they had hoped. They awoke at about five thirty and could see the hills to the east glowing yellow and orange as the sun started to rise behind them. John went off to take care of his morning rituals, and by the time he got back, David had put some water on to boil and was standing by the radio, listening to the latest update.

"So how does it look?" John asked.

"No real change," David confirmed. "Sounds as if it will come ashore in Providence late this afternoon, and we should start to get heavy rain late tonight or early tomorrow morning."

"Still difficult to imagine," John said, looking up at the clear blue-gray sky.

John brewed the coffee.

"Start to pack up and begin heading back toward the car?" David inquired, knowing the answer.

"Probably best if we finish our coffee and then make tracks—no point in leaving it too late and getting soaked."

They took their time enjoying the coffee and the view, but by seven o'clock they were packed up, backpacks on, and starting to head back down the way that they had climbed the previous afternoon. As always seemed to be the case, the route back to the car turned out to be easier and shorter than they had envisaged, and they got back to the camp-ground, and their car, by around three o'clock in the afternoon. As they came into the camp, it was very noticeable that the number of occupants had decreased to about only 25 percent of those who had been there three days ago. Evidently only some hardy souls were going to stay and ride out the storm. The weather was still fine, but throughout their trek back, the relatively clear skies had been steadily invaded by an increasingly dark blanket of cloud that had started moving across from the southeast and had now covered the entire sky.

"It's coming," confirmed David, looking up as they reached their old Jeep Cherokee.

"I'll start to load the gear into the back—if you want to use your phone to try and locate the most promising area to find a hotel for a night or two," suggested John.

"Will do." David seated himself on the front passenger seat with his legs outside the car and started to search for hotels in the vicinity.

After five minutes or so, David had reached a conclusion. "If we head toward Burlington up to the north, probably about fifty miles or so, there are a number of the bigger chain hotels, so we should get a room with no problem," he announced. "What do you think?"

"Sounds good to me," agreed John. "Shouldn't be any need to reserve a room—see which one appeals when we get there."

It was almost four o'clock by the time that they actually pulled out of the campsite parking area and headed north, John driving and the blanket of clouds getting noticeably lower.

There was no real urgency, so John took the smaller back roads rather than cutting across to the more direct main road. David nodded off almost as soon as they were under way. They had been on the road for about fifty minutes and, according to the signposts, were approaching a small rural town that John calculated must still be some twenty miles from their intended destination, when he pulled over to the side of the road.

David woke up with a start and then, after a few moments of collecting his thoughts, asked, "Are we there?"—clearly a little puzzled, because they appeared to be at the crest of a hill with nothing but a country road both in front of and behind them.

John had rolled down the driver's window to get some fresh air.

"No—we are still about twenty miles away, I would guess," confirmed John. "Sorry to disturb your snooze, but I just passed a sign for an inn and was wondering if we should take a look."

"Where?" asked David, looking around.

"Just back around that bend behind. I'll turn around, and you can take a look."

And with that John performed a three-point turn and went slowly back around the gentle bend in the road.

"Just there on the right." John motioned to David, pulling over before they reached a small roadway.

David looked ahead at what appeared to be pillars marking the entrance of a private roadway and an elegant white wooden sign hanging on short black chains from a post that was also painted white. In old-style black lettering, the sign announced "Yesterday's Inn" and in smaller lettering underneath, "Guests Welcome."

Both looked to the right, but any view was blocked by an unbroken line of trees.

"Did a Yesterday's Inn crop up when you searched?" John asked.

"I don't think so. But to be honest, I am not sure if inns and hotels would show up in the same search. I was more looking for brand names that I recognized."

"What do you think? Should we take a peek?" asked John.

"Nothing ventured," David said. "Why not at least take a look?"

And with that John turned in through the two old, weather-beaten stone pillars and started to follow the paved driveway into the wall of trees, mainly tall conifers, which stretched away in a line on either side, effectively barring from the road any view of what lay beyond.

CHAPTER 2

A Refuge

THE DRIVE ANGLED SLIGHTLY DOWNWARD and, once they had entered the tree line, curved first to the right and then slowly to the left, still surrounded on both sides by the trees, which, although spaced well apart, had created a deep carpet of pale-brown pine needles. The twists and turns of the drive explained why any view of the inn was obscured from the roadway above. After driving for approximately two hundred yards, John pulled over to the side as they emerged from the shade created by the woodland and caught their first view of what they presumed to be Yesterday's Inn, with its surrounding outbuildings and pastures.

What lay before them was a sort of bowl-shaped terrain that stretched for maybe a quarter of a mile across from where they stood and what looked to be a little further in the lengthwise direction. Nestled close to the bottom of the bowl was a large Victorian-era house, painted white with dark-blue or black shutters, and even on this warm August afternoon, there was smoke curling up from one of the number of chimneys that adorned the multiangled roof.

"Well, what's the verdict?" John looked at David.

"It looks appealing to me," David responded. "At least it looks like a more pleasant place to relax, for a couple of days or so, compared to a nondescript motel room."

"Agreed," said John. "Let's go down and see if they have any rooms available. I am suddenly looking forward to a long, hot shower."

Having reached a conclusion, John slipped the car into gear and continued on down the driveway, which headed gradually downhill, initially leading to the left across a large area of open green field, before sweeping round to the right, near the bottom of the hill, to head toward the large main building. At first the drive was bordered on the right-hand side by an old dry stone wall, as it passed across the field, giving way to a rustic split rail fence as the drive curved to approach its destination. From their elevated approach, John and David could observe some of the various other structures they assumed were part of the property.

They saw the driveway terminating in a large paved circle, from which a wide flagstone pathway led up to the front entrance of the inn, and a small stone-covered parking lot, maybe big enough to accommodate ten or so cars, set off to the side of the circle. A separate, narrow gravel roadway led away from the paved circle up to a large dark-red colored barn, set a hundred yards or so to the left of the main house and slightly elevated, as the terrain rose out of the bottom of the bowl on the far side. The barn had bright white timber accents and appeared to be well maintained—in contrast to many similar New England structures that had sadly fallen into disrepair over the years. Directly in front of the barn, at the low point of the property, was a good sized oval shaped pond, with at least two ducks cruising slowly across its surface.

Further around, to the right of the barn, open lush pastures rose gently and largely unobstructed from the area where the inn was situated at the bottom of the property up to the distant tree line on the side opposite to John and David's approach. There were what appeared to be horse stables toward the bottom of the pasture behind the inn—an L-shaped building with approximately six stalls facing the back of the inn and three further stalls along the shorter side facing over toward the barn. Immediately above the stables, an area of the pasture was fenced off with wooden ranch-style fencing, presumably as a paddock for the horses.

Scanning around to the right of the inn, from John and David's vantage point, there was another dirt roadway that led to a few smaller dwellings—cottages—it was hard to tell exactly how many because there seemed to be a few joined together in a row and then a larger one standing alone farther up the hill. The farthest cottage, or house, appeared to be at the end of the dirt road, almost at the top of the rise to their right and was partly hidden by a copse of trees. This dwelling was presumably a part of the inn's property, but John and David could not be sure.

The Cherokee crunched onto the stone parking lot, and John parked alongside the row of five cars already in residence. The two weary campers climbed out of the car, stretched appreciatively, and looked up at the low dark-gray cloud arranged in swirled bands across the entire sky. A steady, warm breeze was blowing out of the east—although only a breeze, it somehow felt ominous to John and David because they knew that stronger winds would be following.

"I think that we made the right decision," David observed.

John nodded. "Let's walk on over and take a look. We can come back for our bags once we know that they have rooms."

The travelers headed along the flagstone pathway bordered by a well-maintained lawn on the right and a landscaped flower garden to the left. Three stone steps led up to the inn's entrance, which consisted of a covered porch, complete with Adirondack chairs, extending for maybe twenty-five feet on either side of the large dark oak door, complete with black forged iron fittings. The door, although obviously a heavy structure, opened easily and quietly into a cool slate-covered entrance hall.

John and David stepped inside and looked around what was the reception area. The room had oak-paneled walls and ceilings with a pair of wide French doors on the left-hand side, leading to what appeared to be a restaurant or bar area, and a large, solid wooden door on the right that was ajar but not sufficiently to see the room within. On the wall opposite the entrance doorway was a large, polished, wooden reception desk on the left side, while to the right a wide, forest-green carpeted staircase led up to a turn, after about eight steps, and then disappeared from view. Arranged against the wall, between the reception desk and the staircase, five old suitcases—three in various shades of scuffed brown leather, with further leather reinforcements riveted to the corners—were stacked, in the order of decreasing size, on top of each other, and two larger cases, with wooden strengthening bands around them, stood alongside. To the right of the stairway was a large antique wall clock with a wooden case and a pendulum swinging rhythmically behind a lower glass door, the gentle steady ticking invading the quiet area—it had watched a lot of days pass. Completing the decor was a wooden coatrack, including an umbrella stand, just inside the entrance door to the left, and two sizable paintings, one on the wall above the arrangement of the old suitcases and one opposite the reception desk adjacent to the one window in the reception hall, a small bay window looking out onto the front porch.

There was nobody in the entrance hall as John and David arrived, although there were sounds of activity coming from the room on the far side of the French doors. In no rush, John took a stroll over to take a look at the large picture situated above the suitcases. The painting was of a 1960s diner in a small New England town on what appeared to be an early-fall day. John stood looking at the scene for several minutes, the details and the atmosphere captivating him—the focal point of the picture was not the diner itself but the car park, which was in the fore-ground, filled with cars that he had not seen for a long time, and people enjoying the day, captured in time. It was the cars that depicted the time frame as the 1960s—when cars were cars, as his father used to say.

"Hello, gentlemen! How can I help you today?" asked a jovial-look-ing man, maybe in his midsixties, emerging through the French doors and bringing John back from the diner.

"We were hoping that you might have a couple of rooms—maybe for two nights," David volunteered, looking over at his father to see if there was any disagreement.

"Shelter from the storm, so to speak?" suggested the man, who then continued without waiting for any answer. "That shouldn't be a problem. I have a few rooms available. Would one with a queen bed and one with a full bed be OK? The rates are one forty and one twenty."

The three men had drifted over to congregate in front of the reception desk by the hinged trap that permitted access. "That sounds good to me," John offered, "as long as there are nice, hot showers."

"No problem there. All have en suite facilities, although once you see the rooms you might want a long bath instead—old deep tubs," the man confirmed. "I'm Bill, by the way. Welcome to Yesterday's Inn."

"I'm John, and this is my son, David."

Hands were shaken all around, and Bill lifted up the counter flap in order to go behind the desk.

"If you could just fill in the registration book, for both of you please, that would be great," Bill said, turning the large bound book and placing it on the heavy leather desk pad that adorned the desk along with writing paraphernalia and a brass "Please ring for assistance" bell.

While John and David completed the entries in the book, Bill turned and took two keys off a wooden key board on the rear wall. There were twelve hooks for twelve rooms.

"Here you go, gents—room numbers three and five, both on the second floor of the house," Bill announced, sliding the keys, complete with brass tags embossed with the room numbers, across the desk pads.

"Thank you," David said. "Pass me the car keys, Dad, and I'll pop out and get our bags."

"Thanks," John said as David was crossing to the front door.

"Do you want a credit card of some sort?" John asked, turning back to Bill.

"No—no need from my side. You trust me that the room is worth one forty a night, and I trust you to settle up before you leave. I like it that way," Bill replied.

"A refreshing approach—but not common today. Do you own the inn, Bill?"

"Yes, I'm the owner, as such, but run it with a few colleagues."

"How long have you been up here?"

"Oh, bought the place eight years ago now," Bill replied, nodding and looking around at what he had bought. "It has been a very good eight years."

"Looks like a very comfortable place," observed John, looking around the reception area. "A place where you can relax."

"Thank you. I suppose that is all that I am really aiming for," nodded Bill. "I wanted this to be a haven from the everyday, so to speak."

As if to reaffirm Bill's sentiment, the old clock gave a deep chime to indicate that another half hour had passed and another five thirty had arrived.

"What are you hearing about this storm?" John asked, continuing with the small talk until David came back with their bags. "Do you think that there will be a lot of damage up here?"

"It will blow quite hard tonight, and probably a good long day of rain—but we should be OK," Bill answered as the front door opened, and David, along with a strong gust of wind, came bustling in.

"Thank you," John acknowledged, taking his backpack off his son.

"No problem. It's getting windy out there," David commented, and then turning to Bill, he asked, "Which room has the full bed, Bill?"

"That would be room three—top of the stairs and turn to the left."

David picked up his room key and passed the key to room five over to John. "I don't know about you, Dad, but I am starting to feel very tired."

"Definitely in need of a good shower or soak—it has been a long day," John confirmed.

"If you gentlemen are feeling hungry later, we have a restaurant area across in the bar," suggested Bill, nodding in the direction of the French doors that he had appeared through earlier. "It isn't what I would call gourmet, but it's very tasty and mostly homemade."

"I have been hungry since we got up this morning," David declared. "What time do you serve until, Bill?"

"No real set times as such, but I do try to let Annie leave by around nine o'clock, so if you want her home cooking, you should try and come down by around that time. Otherwise, you will have to settle for my own culinary attempts." Bill chuckled.

"We will be down long before that," John assured him. "What do you think, David? See you down in the bar around seven?"

David looked over at the ticking clock. "Sounds good to me."

And with that the two weary travelers started over toward the stairway.

"We'll be back in an hour or so," John confirmed over his shoulder as they started up the stairs.

"You relax," Bill called over to them as he headed back to the bar to continue with whatever task he had been busy with earlier.

CHAPTER 3

A Pleasant Port in a Storm

IT WAS ACTUALLY NEARER TO quarter past seven before John came back downstairs to find the French doors of the bar now opened wide and the muted sounds of conversation and eating coming from within. The barroom was an appealing place, John thought, as he entered, a room that seemed to invite you to unwind. On the left, as he came through the doors, was a long bar that curved around at the far end to form an L shape, butting up against the wall. The bar itself was made out of thick, polished dark wood, accompanied by a brass rail toward the bottom, to rest your feet on, and adorned on the barkeep's side with four wooden and brass handles with which to pull draft beer. The customer's side was populated along its length with dark-red leather-topped bar stools, one of which was occupied by David, who was browsing through the morning newspaper and sipping on a pint of dark ale.

Set back a little from the bar, there were a few small circular tables and chairs, again with well-worn leather seats, apparently intended for guests to sit and enjoy drinks. Over to the right, windows, interspersed with glass doors, looked onto the deck outside and ran along the full length of the room. By the windows there were a total of ten wooden farmhouse-style tables of various shapes and sizes, complete with place settings for dinner. Five of the tables were occupied by diners, mainly couples, and one table of four. Outside the evening was getting dark early, due to the heavy cloud cover, and the trees could be seen swaying in the wind, which had become steadier and much stronger. The room lighting, which was starting to take prominence over the fading daylight, consisted of wall lights and small lamps on the dining tables— providing a very friendly ambience.

"Did you take a quick snooze?" inquired a smiling David as John approached the bar.

"I easily could have done so," John admitted, "but actually, I took Bill's advice and soaked in the bath and, to be honest, just didn't want to get out until the water started to cool a little."

Bill strolled over from where he had been serving one of the dining couples. "Would you care for a drink, John?"

"The local ale is very good," David commented.

"I'll take a glass of the same, then, please, Bill," John decided as Bill went behind the bar.

While Bill was slowly pulling the beer, John asked David, "Did you give your mom a call and let her know that we are safe and sound?"

"I did try a couple of times," David confirmed, "but I couldn't get a signal—probably the weather. I'll try again later."

"Sorry—there really isn't any cell service up here," Bill informed them as he placed the freshly drawn beer on a beer mat in front of John, "but feel free to use the phone on the end of the bar. It's there for the guests, albeit not too private."

"No cell coverage—that must be inconvenient," John remarked as David went around to the wall-mounted phone at the end of the bar— an appliance that looked to be fifty-plus years old but did at least have faded white push buttons and not a rotary dial.

"Only initially," Bill responded, watching David investigate the phone in the cradle, "but I don't have a cell phone anymore and, to be honest, do not miss it one bit. To tell the truth, it is somehow refreshing to be outside and know that nobody can get to me, to bother me. Things can wait. To my mind it is actually one of the attractions of the place that you come to appreciate."

"Do you hear that, David? You can actually survive without your device!" John teased. "The world doesn't end."

"Never mind that. Do you have Mom's number, to save me going upstairs to get it out of my contacts?" David asked, still bemused by the phone.

John gave the number to David, who proceeded to punch it into the keypad and apparently got through to his mother.

"Appreciate the use of the phone," David thanked Bill after he had finished his brief call and as Bill was heading back to attend the dinner guests.

"Everything OK with your mother?" John inquired.

"She's fine," David assured him. "The storm hasn't affected the city too badly, but she was wondering how we were faring—so a good job I called."

David and John enjoyed their beers for maybe fifteen minutes and then made their way over to a dining table next to the window so that they could watch the developing weather outside. It felt good to feel safe.

"Here you go, gents," announced Bill as he delivered two menus. "Annie has everything on the menu, and there are four additional options on the blackboard over there. We try to keep it relatively simple, so you will see the main courses listed and then a separate list of side dishes—so you can mix and match just as you want. The price of the main course includes as many sides as you want to try—only the size of the plate limits you," he joked. "Oh—and because this is your first visit, I will point out that you will find peas on the menu."

Both John and David looked at him quizzically.

"For many years, it annoyed me that you never see peas on a menu—ever. Sometimes I would even ask if it was possible to get them. But no, you have to eat asparagus or some vegetable medley. I suppose that the same can be said of other vegetables, such as cabbage—but I like peas, so given the opportunity, I included them."

"Good for you," John said with a laugh, "sticking up for pea lovers."

"Another drink?" inquired Bill.

David and John both nodded their approval.

Bill had been accurate in stating that it couldn't be described as a gourmet menu—or at least the dishes all had straightforward names that did not need any explanation or translation.

In due course, David selected a pork chop with some roast potatoes and applesauce, while John picked the pot roast, mashed potatoes—and yes, the signature peas.

While they ate, the rain really started to come down harder and maybe at a forty-five-degree angle. The wind was now steady rather than gusting. Because the wind was blowing from an easterly direction, which was roughly the direction that the front of the inn faced, the rain was actually being driven away from the rear of the inn, leaving the deck at the back relatively sheltered. But the large barn and the horse stables were getting lashed with the driving precipitation.

"Hope the horses are battened down," observed David as they ate and watched the storm.

"So how was the food?" asked Bill as he was clearing away the dishes a while later.

"Mine was excellent," commented David, with John nodding his concurrence "although to be fair we are comparing your food to Dad's rehydration of dried meals using boiling water." David laughed.

Bill smiled broadly. "Anything else for either of you?"

While David was consulting the list of desserts, a lady emerged from the kitchen, taking off her apron as she walked over to Bill, looking around at the dining tables that were now empty except for John and David.

"The rain has let up a little—so if it is OK with you, Bill, I will take advantage and head off home."

"No problem, Annie," Bill assured her. "Do you want me to run you home?"

"That's OK. I have the car, and the weather isn't too bad at the moment. Do these gentlemen want anything else?" she asked, smiling across at the two remaining guests.

"This is John and David—and this is Annie, who makes my kitchen a kitchen." Bill introduced them. "And if they want anything, I can cope— even I can cut a slice of apple pie. You get off home, and be careful."

"Good night, then." Annie smiled as she headed toward the doorway. "See you in the morning for breakfast."

All three wished Annie a good-night and then turned back to the task at hand.

"Just a coffee—if you have one," requested John.

"And I've been persuaded by the apple pie—if that was on the menu," David added.

"There's always pie," confirmed Bill. "Anything on it? Maybe cream?"

"Sounds good to me."

"If you fancy sitting out on the deck, I'll bring it out there," suggested Bill. "It should be sheltered, and the wind is still warm."

John and David were intrigued by the thought of sitting outside in a storm, so they decided to at least take a look. There were Adirondack chairs and smaller wooden tables arranged along the length of the deck, and a middle-aged couple was situated farther down, sitting and watching the wind and rain whip past the end of the inn. It was somewhat eerie being outside—it felt somehow illicit—but it was quietly enjoyable. In good time Bill brought out the coffee and pie, and the two sat quietly, watching the storm blow—slightly in awe of nature.

Around nine thirty Bill came back out onto the deck, having apparently wrapped up his kitchen duties, to check if anybody wanted a nightcap. Not surprisingly all four guests thought that alcoholic beverages, of various descriptions, would be a good idea to round off the evening.

When Bill returned with the drinks order, he was accompanied by two brindle-colored Border Terriers, who trotted once around the deck and then descended the few steps down onto the lawn below and out into the blackness.

"Rip and Riley," Bill explained to John and David as he placed their drinks on the table. "They like their fresh air and a stroll before bed, seemingly regardless of the elements. Mind if I grab a drink and come out and sit with you for a while?"

"Not at all," John encouraged Bill. "It is quietly exciting, sheltering out here."

Bill went inside for a few minutes, reappearing with a tumbler of whiskey in one hand and an unlit cigar in the other. As he was seating himself in an Adirondack chair alongside John and David, Rip and Riley bounded back up the steps onto the deck, checked that Bill didn't need them, and then lay at the edge of the deck, looking out into the darkness, transfixed, like all the other deck occupants, by the wind and rain.

Having first verified that neither John nor David objected to his smoking, Bill proceeded to light his cigar, and for a while, the three sat sipping, puffing, and contemplating.

It was David who broke the silence after five minutes or so.

"What do you think, Dad? Do you think we made a good choice? Or do you wish we were huddled in the tent, somewhere out there in the woods—bedraggled and trying to avoid being blown away?"

John snorted a laugh. "No second-guessing from me."

"How long had you been camping for?" Bill asked the pair.

"We were about four days into what was intended to be a week in the wilderness," David explained. "We have been doing similar trips for about five years or so. This is the first time that we have been rained out and had to abort the camping."

"A beautiful area to go hiking, though," Bill confirmed. "You can get away from the world out there."

"Are you from Vermont, Bill?"

"No—not originally. I was telling your father earlier that I bought this place around eight years ago, but before that I was born, brought up, and lived in New York and Connecticut. How about yourselves? Where's home?"

"I originally come from Rhode Island but similar to yourself, Bill, ended up across on the western side of Connecticut when it was time to start a career," John said.

"And what did your career turn out to be?"

"In the newspaper business. Started out as a reporter, covering a variety of local issues, but migrated into sports reporting, which was my real passion, after about three years, and wrote for two of the New York papers for about twenty-five years before moving into freelance sports reporting about ten years ago. I write for a number of publications, to some extent can pick my assignments, so I have the luxury of traveling to mainly enjoyable locales and being able to work from home when not on the road."

"And are you in college, David?"

"That's me, Bill. In my second year, and hopefully going on to be a vet, if things work out."

"Were you in the inn business before coming up here?" John asked.

"No—I had never done anything like this before. I had spent my working life as an architect with a few firms, both in the city and up in the Connecticut area. In truth, I didn't come up here to get into the inn business—I just wanted to be contented again."

John thought about this statement.

"Why up here, though? Why so far off the beaten track, out in the woods? Don't you miss some of the conveniences of a more urban area? An architect in New England would sound like a fairly good life. How do you mean you wanted to be contented again?"

Bill took a long sip of his whisky, followed by a pull on his cigar, and reflected before answering.

"Oh, I suppose that I had just grown tired. Grown tired and saddened. A sort of deep-down sadness that grew in me over a number of years and that I couldn't shake. I suppose that I wanted the world to change, but I knew that was a pointless wish. The whole world wouldn't change for me, so I thought, why not try to change my little part of the world? Don't sit and bemoan the fact that you don't like what life has become—go and make your life what you want it to be, so to speak."

Bill paused, looking out into the black night, nodding and remembering.

"Sounds a bit dramatic. What do you mean 'you wanted to change things'?" John asked.

"More and more I found myself longing for a world that was fast disappearing—not just reminiscing but really aching for that world again. I would find myself saddened, and sometimes a little angered, I must admit, by the world that was increasingly forced on me. Daily routine life would cause me to reflect back to a time that I couldn't really find anymore. More and more I wanted the life and the world that I used to know. I wanted to know it again—I just so, so wanted to embrace it again. Then one day I came to the obvious realization that the world I knew wasn't coming back—in fact, it was disappearing faster and faster—so I could either lament what life had become or I could try to find peace somewhere. Find my peace of mind."

Bill stopped, looking over toward John and David to see if his brief explanation satisfied John's query.

"Sorry to maybe ask the same question, but what were you tired of, Bill?" pursued David.

Bill thought about the question for a few moments, as if trying to remember.

"What was I tired of? I should probably leave that for another day, if you are really interested. If I got into it now, I'm afraid that I could ramble on for hours." Bill paused. "What was I tired of?" he repeated, staring into the wind of the night. "No, let's not get into that now, but maybe I could put it more in terms of what I wanted back. I can try to describe that, David, but I am not sure that it will strike a chord with a younger person—no offense intended."

"None taken," David assured him. "Just trying to understand."

Bill collected his thoughts before offering his explanation.

"I had become very cynical, and I wanted contentment again. It will probably sound a little weird, maybe a little eccentric, but bear with me. In a nutshell, I wanted the world to be simple again. I wanted the simple pleasures of life back, and I wanted to be happy again, without the advertisers of the corporate world telling me that I must need more, must need a newer version, shouldn't be satisfied. I so yearned for the joy that I had known, the joy that had been taken away. You could say that I didn't appreciate progress, because, to me at least, progress did not make my life easier or simpler. Quite the reverse—progress forced everybody to live faster and spend an awful lot of time doing things that they never had to bother with before. Spend a lot of time having to understand things that never troubled me in my younger years. I can do without progress—to a very large degree. Yes, in simple terms, I wanted to be happy again."

David and John looked a little taken aback for a moment.

"Sorry if I rambled on—but you did ask," Bill pointed out.

"So you bought an inn?" John asked.

"I didn't set out with a clear plan as to what to do, but over time, and through a few experiences, the thought started to germinate—the world wasn't going to go back to the way it was. But why couldn't I at least carve out a little niche in this world and make it what it had been, to some degree at least—the world that I remembered and wanted? And then the thought took root and I rationalized—why not create something that others could share, if they so wished? So the idea of an inn took shape—an inn, a period of time, a way of life that people could come and visit and share if they wanted to...where they could go back to their younger days or just days that they wanted to visit."

John looked around, peering back through the windows of the welcoming dining room.

"I appreciate that the inn is a very friendly and peaceful setting, but how is it different?" John asked.

Bill smiled. "Don't worry. There is nothing strange or weird about the place—nor is there anything particularly strange about me—at least I don't think that there is. I just tried to avoid a lot of the trappings and perceived conveniences of modern-day existence. Enjoy life—don't try chasing what you think you should be enjoying."

The three sat quietly. The wind had increased in strength, with occasional fiercer gusts that created a whistling noise through the distant tall trees surrounding the inn. The rain was continuous and twinkled as it caught the lights shining out from the inn, lashing past almost horizontally on the way to its destination, which presumably would be the pasture out in the blackness.

After a while the other couple rose, said their good-nights, and made their way inside, into the safety of the inn. Rip and Riley stood and stretched and disappeared down the steps—reappearing maybe a minute later but this time stood patiently peering up at Bill. Bill looked down at his watch.

"I know, boys, a quarter of eleven and you want some supper," Bill said. Then, looking toward John and David, he declared, "I think that I had better head in. Are you two all set?"

"Yes, I think that we will be going up—for the first comfortable sleep in a few days," John said.

With that the three men got up slowly—because of the reclining angle of the Adirondacks. Bill went and collected the glasses from the far table while David picked up their own dishes, and John held the door open. Rip and Riley jumped inside.

"Thank you for a pleasant evening," John said after they were all inside and Bill was battening down the doors.

"No, thank you—both of you," Bill replied. "Enjoyed the company. If you are still interested, and if the weather relents a little, I can show you around a little tomorrow."

"I, for one, would like that," John said as he and David started heading toward the doorway and the stairs.

"And you can try explaining what it is, or was, that you are tired of," David added. "Good night, Bill."

Bill smiled. "I can try, David, although I am not sure if it will make sense—sometimes I wonder myself. Sleep well, both of you."

"And you," John replied.

John and David climbed the stairs to the second floor and said their good-nights before heading their separate ways down the hallway.

Downstairs they could hear Bill talking to the dogs while checking that everything was closed up and safe before retiring. On the way to their rooms, both were thoughtful after the conversation with Bill. David was a little unsettled because he didn't really understand what Bill had been trying to express. John was equally uneasy, but in his case, it was because he thought he did understand.

CHAPTER 4

An Inn for Yesterday

THE MORNING BROKE WITH A solid gray cover of cloud. The wind was still blowing and gusting strongly, but although there was still some precipitation in the wind, the heavy, continuous rain had eased off. Even the horses were poking their noses out of the stables opposite the back of the inn.

After showering and shaving, a well-refreshed John came downstairs shortly after seven thirty. Rip and Riley jumped down from where they had been sitting, on the cushioned shelf of the bay window in the entrance hall, and trotted over to greet him. The three made their way across to the dining room, but the two dogs stopped at the doorway, apparently aware there were times that they should not wander in. Several tables, along the wall by the windows, had been set for breakfast, and one older gentleman sat with coffee, reading, apparently waiting for his breakfast.

"Good morning," Bill said, entering from the kitchen. "Sleep well?"

"Very well thanks. Combination of exhaustion and a very comfortable bed."

"Seat yourself wherever you want," Bill said, taking a plate across to the older man.

"I think I'll wait for David—he shouldn't be too long."

"No problem. Take some coffee and a newspaper if you want," Bill said, gesturing to a percolator and a full pot set up on the bar.

"Don't mind if I do," John replied, heading over to help himself.

"You can sit at the bar if you like—or, if you prefer, go across to the library on the opposite side of the entrance way. Probably more comfortable."

John grabbed his coffee and a newspaper—wondering why a delivery person had braved the elements to bring the paper so early—and headed over to the solid wooden door across from the dining room. The door creaked a little as John eased it open, and he was greeted by a slightly musty odor—not an unpleasant smell but more the scent of calm and relaxation. John left the door open so that he would hopefully hear David come down and placed the newspaper and the coffee on a small table next to a well-worn leather Chesterfield chair. Before sitting, John took a look around the library and the small adjacent room. As the name of the room suggested, both the wall surrounding the door through which he had entered and the wall to its left were lined with book-filled shelving. The shelves extended from the floor up to about head height and were inundated with hardback and paperback novels of every description, many from decades past, along with a variety of non-fiction works and a good collection of coffee-table volumes. The shelving was topped off by a wider mantle, on which sat an array of artifacts, photographs, and some sporting memorabilia. The remaining wall space above the bookshelves was occupied by a number of watercolor paintings. The wall to the right of the room's entrance doorway was dominated by a large stone-built fireplace complete with all the accoutrements necessary for building and lighting a wood fire on days colder than today. To each side of the fireplace were large bay windows, again with seats built into the recesses, looking out onto a lawn area on the east side of the main house. The remaining wall was occupied by some low open cabinets, two wooden cupboards, and a door leading to the adjacent room. John was intrigued by the contents of the cabinets and cupboards. In one cabinet, he could see an audio system, complete with turntable and cassette player, which John guessed must have been from the 1970s, and in a cupboard to the side, there were three shelves full of old albums and even some singles. In another cupboard there was an assortment of board games, some very worn and tattered, including an old Monopoly and a Clue, which announced that it was "The intriguing new game from Parker Bros." Peering into the adjacent room, John observed two sofas and three comfortable armchairs, all facing a TV on top of a low cabinet set into the corner of the room.

Back in the library, John made himself comfortable in the leather chair, leisurely read the paper, and enjoyed his coffee for about half an hour before he heard footsteps coming down the stairs and David acknowledging the dogs.

"In here, David," John called out.

"Morning, Dad," David said, putting his head around the door. "Been up long?"

"Maybe forty minutes or so. Let's go and get some breakfast. I'm hungry just smelling the bacon."

Another couple of guests were descending the stairs as John and David crossed the entrance hall, and the four entered the dining room together—to be greeted by Bill's invitation to "Sit where you want."

Bill came across with the pot of coffee and filled their cups. "No menus for breakfast. Just tell me what you would like and within reason. I'm sure that Annie can fix it."

"A different approach," John commented.

"Well, in reality all the menu combinations would be varying permutations of the same basic elements—so my reasoning is, why not let folks just tell me what they want? Annie can accommodate most requests without a problem."

"OK, then. Straight scrambled eggs, bacon, and toast for me," David said.

"And a ham-and-cheese omelet, toast, and some orange juice for me, please," John added.

"Much simpler than poring over a menu," Bill commented before heading over to the other guests.

Breakfast was a very relaxing and satisfying affair and, with a few coffee refills, stretched on until after nine thirty.

"So what's the game plan?" David asked as they were finishing off their last coffees.

"There is still some rain blowing in the wind out there, so I don't really feel like going anywhere at the moment. Besides, it will be pretty sodden out there for the next day or so," John said. "And if truth be told, I do find this place very comfortable."

"Tend to agree. I wouldn't really relish going back to a tent tonight. So stay at least another night?" David asked.

"And see what tomorrow brings," John agreed.

When Bill came back from the kitchen, John informed him of their plan, as far as it went, and Bill confirmed that he had plenty of rooms for the next few nights.

"It has almost stopped raining," Bill added. "So maybe around eleven I will take the dogs for a long walk around the property—make sure everything is OK after the winds. If you want to come along, I can show you around a little."

"Sounds good to me," David agreed.

John nodded. "I think that I will go back to the library, maybe pick out a book, and relax for a while."

"Do you have wireless, Bill?" David asked. "Wanted to check e-mail and catch up with the world—and as you said, I am not getting any phone coverage."

Bill smiled. "Sorry—no wireless, no Internet coverage at all, really. One of the things that I try to avoid, although I do have an older computer in my office and can connect via the phone line if I really need to."

"No Internet?" David sounded incredulous. "How do you survive?"

"On the whole, just fine. I didn't want to be beholden to a screen every waking minute—I am sure that the world carries on whether or not I am aware of it."

"How about a TV? I know that there isn't one in the room, but is there one where we can catch up on the news at least?" David continued his inquiry.

"Don't worry; we are not completely cut off from the outside world." Bill laughed "There is a TV room for guests."

"I can show you—it's through the library," John said.

"Only the basic channels—but you can get news OK," Bill confirmed.

David was a little relieved and continued. "Now I am even more intrigued to find out what you were tired of—don't forget that you said you would try to explain, Bill."

"I will help Annie finish a few things in the kitchen and will come over to the library afterward to try to shed some light," Bill said, sounding amused again.

And with that, John and David crossed to the library. David went into the TV room and switched on the news, to try and catch up on the happenings with the storm, while John picked out *The Day of the Jackal*, by Frederick Forsyth, and settled down to just read.

Bill had finished with his chores by ten thirty and came across to the library, with Rip and Riley close behind—the dogs seemed more restless now, anxious for a run.

"Don't worry, boys. Give it half an hour and we can go out for some exercise, see if the storm has done any damage," Bill said to the dogs, taking a seat across from John.

David turned off the TV and came in to join them.

"All OK in the world?" John asked as David sat down.

"Yes—seems as though it is getting along even though we are out of touch. A lot of flooding down by the coast, but things are getting back to normal." And then changing the conversation, David looked at Bill. "So, Bill, you left us hanging last night—you promised to explain what you were unhappy with. What you were tired of?"

Bill grinned. "You won't let this one go, will you, young David?"

"It intrigues me as to what can create a strong enough feeling to uproot somebody and cause them to reassess his life as you did."

"OK, OK, I will try to explain, but it isn't one thing or a simple statement. It is a culmination of feelings—a realization in a way," Bill started.

"At the heart of it was simply being tired that the modest joys of living had been taken away and been increasingly replaced by an insidious world instructing me how I should live and telling me what I will enjoy—as if I was wrong to enjoy what I had been doing. I was wearied by a greedy corporate world trying to persuade me that all the progress and innovations that I was seeing were truly making my life easier, more enjoyable, and enabling me to do more and more—when, in fact, the opposite was true. I became increasingly frustrated by the fact that 'they' were insulting my intelligence by expecting me to blindly buy into everything that they forced on me—expecting me to sit back and not only accept it but actually think it was improving my life. And no, it wasn't just age tainting my perspective, David—it wasn't an older man wishing he was young again. No. I was tired of the fact that we had what I believe was a very good way of life and had it taken away—seemingly with no say whatsoever on whether or not that was what we wanted. Of course, I knew that I couldn't realistically have a say in what 'they' did or how the world progressed—but I rationalized that I could at least have a say in whether or not it affected me. I could sit and complain for the rest of my life—or I could try to change my world."

"What examples of progress were annoying you?" David asked.

"Well, bear in mind that I am not being absolute in saying that all progress is bad—I am not that foolish," Bill said. "And I am not saying that holes cannot be found in any example that I may offer. I am speaking in general terms and trying to explain how life, or at least my life, has been changed for the worse. Individually, they are small examples that can be considered irrelevant and petty, but they combine to exasperate. And I should also point out up front that I concede many things—medical progress as a good example—have clearly improved life and the quality of life."

David nodded in acknowledgment.

"Specific examples? Let me see. One thing was the feeling that I had to own a mobile device just in order to survive, and that I had to update the device almost from day one and replace it after a very modest period of time. Without such a device, I wasn't part of everyday life. Or, purely as an example, one of many I should add, I would find myself seething when I called a business, I don't know, the bank, or to file an insurance claim, even the doctor, and had to listen to endless computerized messages and menus for maybe ten minutes and then eventually be put on hold for another twenty minutes before finally hanging up without ever speaking to a human being. A computer-generated voice—why, oh why, should we have to listen to a bunch of microchips or whatever they are? An extremely frustrating experience—and to not even be able to ask, let alone get an answer to, my question. Just sheer frustration, coming from what should be customer service—a help to a customer. Sometimes the arrogance in thinking that 'they' know all the questions before we even ask—and therefore have all the pre-recorded answers for us simple beings. And the reason for having to endure this insulting process? Supposedly it makes my life easier—but in reality, it is simply a corporation that wants to save costs by dispensing with humans and placing a computerized system in their place. Who benefits from the cost savings? The corporation would claim that their customers reap the rewards. Garbage! The corporation saves the money, earns higher profit—while good people lose their decent jobs, and the customer is left to live with miserable service and no answers. The corporation gets richer—at the complete expense of their customers and employees. And you can do nothing—except complain to others suffering the same fate and passively accept the infuriation. Repeated time after time, year after year. In the end, you avoid making calls because the outcome is so predictable. Just let me talk to somebody. Do you remember the concept of making a phone call and somebody simply picking up the phone at the other end?"

"But how do you avoid dealing with such a process? I agree, it frustrates—but how can you avoid it?"

"Now I simply go into the bank once a month. I go in and see a cashier or talk to the manager if I need something. I don't want online banking and don't use online banking. If I want the bank, I just go in and talk to them."

John smiled and nodded before Bill continued, enjoying an audience.

"But that was an example. There were many facets of life that troubled me, sometimes offended me. I was somewhat sickened by reality TV. I wanted TV to be the thrill that it used to be, to engross me in a story and let my imagination go for a ride. I wanted radio to have a live person talking to me, a real person who made me feel part of an audience. And to have music that I can buy and that I can understand—oh, and I wanted cars that are real and that I can love again. How is that for a start?" Bill paused.

"Surely TV has improved over the years. The choices that we have today?" David asked.

"I understand your thought process, David. There is some quality entertainment. I'll give you that. But then reality TV arrived. The first reality show—maybe entertaining, amusing, different. But the hundreds of reality shows out there now, depicting everyday life or tasks. Fictitious and enhanced everyday life that has to be glamorized for ratings—it's absolute drivel. I find it insulting that the industry expects people to tolerate what is put before them—and even make believe that it can be real. It isn't entertainment. It is the cheapest and quickest way to make money. And similar to many other areas, they could not rest with a good thing—quickly resorting to force-feeding an endless stream. If a concept works, then a hundred times the same idea must work. What could be simpler? I miss the purity of the entertainment."

"We might have to agree to disagree a little," David replied. "But I am not oblivious to some of the garbage out there."

"Putting the quality of TV aside for a minute, let me try to explain my irritation. I know that this can all sound as if I am unwilling to learn to move with the times—a dinosaur—and you can think that if I took the time to learn, to change, that I would appreciated such changes. But I don't think that it is an unwilling me; I think that I am in a majority, albeit maybe a silent majority, that does not recognize their frustrations. As a way of trying to explain, let me ask you a question, David. Do you have children?"

David shook his head. "No, not yet—not married and no children."

"Not to worry. You can still probably appreciate my thoughts. The question that I wanted to ask is, when was the last time that you heard young children shrieking with laughter? Where have all the shrieking, giggling, laughing children gone? Where has the innocence of childhood gone? Everybody, including young children, sadly, has become so cynical of life because the mystery has simply been stripped away—so the sheer, innocent, pure pleasure has gone. Everyone is so worldly, so knowing, that we cannot get the pleasure from life that we did in yesteryear."

Bill paused for a moment, looking out of the front window to see how the weather was doing.

"Our imaginations are not allowed to be used. As kids we loved a toy, a day out, a night in watching a special TV show, a bag of candy, a treat, a vacation—now we are so inundated with what is next, what we need, that we cannot enjoy the now. The corporate world will not permit us to be happy, contented, because being contented is bad for business—we have to want more, need more—so we are not allowed to be satisfied, to be happy with modest things. Children are not allowed to have the naïve childhood that I had—because there is no profit in that. Corporations set out to direct children's enjoyment—to anesthetize it. John will remember as a child playing outside, playing ball, playing with an imagination—enjoying the fun of childhood and laughing with our friends on a warm spring day. He can remember when children were allowed to learn about life and fun—they were not shown how to play. It is bad enough that children today are steered toward screens that tell us what to do, how to have fun. But worse is that the children are playing online with their friends in the same game—not meeting their friends and enjoying the real game of life, but a digital meeting on a screen. You can understand children getting absorbed by a video game, but when have you seen kids actually giggling with enjoyment over a screen—laughing together?"

John had been listening with interest. "I take it that is why you have purposely discouraged the conveniences of modern communications?"

"When I stepped back and thought about it, I realized how addicted the world is to what the small screens say," Bill answered. "People have to know what everybody else is doing. They no longer have the confidence to live their own lives. There is a constant fear that they will miss out—will miss somebody else doing something, and that fear of missing something, something that somebody else is doing, prevents them from living their own life. You pick up your 'smart' phone, and you are paralyzed—addicted to knowing everything about everybody and not bothering to just live and enjoy. You are so afraid of missing something. Let the world go on—just enjoy your world. You are so afraid of missing out that, in fact, all you do is miss out. You should stop trying to live life through others' lives. Don't be so obsessed in snapping pictures of the moment—actually enjoy the moment. Believe me, it will be there in your memory; nobody can take it away. You don't need digital proof. Where has all the joy gone—the joy of your life, not somebody else's?"

Bill took a pause and smiled, realizing that he had become passionate. "Apologies. I started to lecture a little there—not my objective and definitely not my intention to imply that I have not been drawn into exactly the same traps as everybody else."

David had to question the concept. "But surely you have to admit that all these instant communications—whether it be e-mail, texting, Internet, even social media—are invaluable? Keep us so informed. What we would have been ignorant about in the past is now exposed for all to see."

"Oh, I agree that the Internet and e-mail are very beneficial, have transformed the world. And I know that we can never consider putting that genie back in the bottle. Texting I can take or leave because I see it as removing the human interaction of phone conversations and, for the large part, used for things that can easily wait—like they used to wait."

"So, overall, you agree these are improvements we should embrace?" David asked.

"It is the price we have to pay that disheartens me. They just won't rest. They could not rest with a useful Internet and e-mail. They had to take the useful initiatives and infect them with so much junk that the real purpose is all but lost. And by then we had sacrificed so much, David."

"What do mean by "sacrificed," Bill?"

"We had to sacrifice a way of life to accept this way of life. It strikes me that these instantaneous communications are invasive in so much as they cannot coexist with the way of life we had."

David nodded, not necessarily agreeing but at least seeing the argument.

"A lot to think about," David said, after Bill had paused for a few seconds. "But are you happier up here at the inn? Have you managed to find some of that contentment?"

Bill looked across at John and David, thinking back to younger days. "That is a question that I think about often. I can best answer it this way: A long time ago, my father told me that if it was at all possible, I should try very hard to live a life of my choosing, and if I could achieve that, then it would have been a good life. I confess that I did not really understand what he was trying to tell me when he passed on this advice. But over the decades, I have come to realize that very few people actually manage to live such lives. Well, I have chosen this life, and I can tell you that my father was right—he was very right."

Bill paused for a moment while John and David reflected on his contemplations.

"Do you want to come for a walk with the dogs?" Bill asked, sensing that the mood needed lightening a little. "I can show you around—work up an appetite for lunch."

John and David accepted eagerly, wanting some fresh air and exercise, and the three set out to take a look around the inn from yesterday—preceded by two energetic terriers.

CHAPTER 5

The Barn

WHEN THE THREE CAME OUT of the inn, they initially turned left, setting off on the dirt road that passed in front of the inn, and headed toward the cottages up the hill. The road was covered in white stones, so, despite being wet after the heavy overnight rain, it was not at all muddy, and the three crunched along, with the dogs running well ahead. The rain had completely stopped, and patches of blue sky could be seen through the slowly thinning and dispersing clouds. All the foliage remained dripping wet, and steam could be seen beginning to rise over the pastures as the sun started to break through. Rip's and Riley's coats were already soggy after foraging through undergrowth and the long wild grasses bordering the road. To the right of the road, as they walked, sloping upward, was the large, open green field the driveway had crossed through as they had entered the property yesterday. The driveway itself was obscured, but there was a stone wall, away in the distance, which presumably marked its path down the hillside.

"Where does the property end?" John asked.

"Roughly at the tree line along the top of the rise all round the open fields," Bill said, turning slowly to point out the rim of the naturally formed bowl within which the inn nestled.

"What lies past the tree line?" David asked.

"To the west there," Bill said, pointing out past the horse stables and pastures, "is fairly open farmland; whereas to the north, ahead of us, and the south, back there, it is mainly forest. And then you know that the road to town runs past the eastern side."

After walking for about five minutes, the three came to the row of cottages on the right-hand side. The cottages consisted of one white-washed building that John and David could now see was divided into three attached dwellings, each with its own chimney, front door, and gravel path running from the roadway through a neat little garden.

"Is this where Annie lives?" John asked.

Bill nodded. "Yes, she lives in this first end cottage with the green door, and Eddie, the inn's handyman-cum–Jack-of-all-trades, lives in the far end one—with the red door."

"And the middle one?" David inquired.

"Nobody lives there full-time. Annie and Eddie sort of use it as their guesthouse. They both keep it clean and in good shape, so that it's ready when either has occasional visitors—normally Eddie's mother, when she was alive, or Annie's grown-up son and family."

"Very nice gardens," David commented. "Annie and Eddie seem to take a lot of pride."

"Well, the gardens, front and back, are all down to Annie," Bill said. "She is out there most afternoons from spring through to fall. She grew up in city apartments and always regretted never having a yard. Eddie and Annie have a very good arrangement actually; she looks after all the gardening, and he looks after the maintenance of all three cottages—much more his forte."

The two terriers came trotting back up Annie's path after checking out around the cottages but being unsuccessful in their search for any friendly inhabitants. The three walked on, up the gentle incline of the crunchy gravel road, past a parking area and a large garden shed at the far end of the cottage row. The road started to curve slowly to the left, following the contour of the hillside and making the climb more gradual than if it had traversed straight up the slope. Hedgerows started to form on both sides of the road as they progressed, growing to a height sufficient to obscure their view of the inn and surrounding pastures to their left and creating the sensation of strolling through a green-walled tunnel open to only the now-blue sky above. Rip and Riley had pulled well ahead and were out of sight around the gentle bend of the road.

"Do you have family, Bill?" John asked as they continued up the gentle incline.

"Yes, the two children are my immediate family. I was married, for just over twenty-nine years, but my wife, Brenda, died back in early 1999. She was almost eleven years older than me, but she was still only sixty-five when she died of cancer. Lung cancer, even though she had never smoked in her life," Bill replied, "and we had the two children— my daughter, Jill, who is thirty-six, and Stephen, who has just turned thirty-eight."

"Do they live near here?" David asked.

"No, I'm afraid not. They went away to college and never really came back home, at least not to live. Jill lives down in Florida, where she went to college, and Stephen is married and lives out in San Francisco, where his wife is originally from, although he actually went to college down by DC."

"But they come and visit?" John asked.

"Oh yes. Jill probably comes up three or four times a year, while Stephen comes over once or maybe twice but usually stays for a week or so."

"Do the children enjoy the inn?" John inquired.

"Yes. On the whole they enjoy it," Bill replied, "but of the two, Jill probably enjoys it more. Stephen is in the tech industry out there in California, and he isn't thrilled by the relative isolation and lack of immediate communication here at the inn. But what about you, John? Doesn't your wife like to come hiking with you and David?"

"Married for twenty-three years, Bill, but divorced six years ago, I'm afraid," John replied. "My wife, Melinda, is actually five years younger than me. David here was born back in 1988, but he is our only child. We agreed to an amicable divorce when he was fifteen. Not the best situation, but as I said, we parted on friendly terms so, although David stayed in the house with his mom, he was free to spend as much time with me as he liked, particularly during the school holidays. Melinda remarried about four years ago, but she and her husband, Keith, still live in our old house, which is only about five miles away from my town house."

"Do you have siblings, Bill?" David asked.

"Yes, two brothers, David. My elder brother, Peter, who was two years older than me, unfortunately died of complications after a heart attack just over three years ago. He was only sixty-four," Bill answered, pausing for a moment. "And then there was young Brian, who was my little brother, born when I was three months short of my second birthday. He was just four months old when he passed away in his crib one afternoon in July. Today they call it 'sudden infant death syndrome,' but back then I don't think that they had yet identified the cause of death with a name or an acronym. I am sorry to say that I cannot really remember meeting Brian, but my mother would tell me that he and I giggled together out on the lawn that one summer. I sometimes imagine that I can recall Brian—but it might just be my mother's reminiscences and my wishful thinking. I don't know."

"Your parents didn't have any more children after Brian passed away?" John asked.

"No, they never did. My mother told me many years later that she was too afraid of losing another baby. She told me that losing Brian was too devastating, but having me and Peter there helped her get through it. But she knew that she would never have been able to live through that again, and so she never wanted to take the risk—to risk the family that she had. My father only ever asked that I never forget Brian after my mother, and he had passed away. I have tried to remember."

They walked on quietly for a few minutes. Approximately three hundred yards from the row of cottages, the hedgerow on the left side fell away, revealing the inn, now well below them, and a similar panoramic view of the surrounding fields and pastures that they had seen from the driveway on the previous afternoon. Just ahead of them, built on a large flat area of land, was the isolated cottage that they had observed.

This dwelling was quite a bit larger than each of the individual row cottages and consisted of a rough stone-built first floor, topped with natural wood shingles on the second floor.

"Beautiful views," John observed.

"I think the original owner of the big house built this one a couple of years later," Bill responded. "My guess is that he wanted both the views and the cooling breezes on the hot summer nights—long before air conditioning was dreamed of."

"Who lives here now?" David asked, surveying the view below.

"Nobody really lives here. It is Eddie's pet project, so to speak. Whenever he isn't busy at the inn or in their own cottages, he often tackles projects here. The place is in decent condition, but Eddie likes to renovate areas such as the bathrooms, kitchen, and some of the old flooring. We have thoughts of renting the place out, as part of the inn, to larger families or groups, but it has not been a priority."

"It would be a very restful place," John said. "Talk about peace and quiet."

"Oh, the boys and myself have spent a couple nights up here on a camping cot in the summer," Bill replied, nodding toward Rip and Riley, who had appeared from behind the cottage. "It is a very nice spot. Come and take a look around the back."

Bill led them around the side of the cottage to a large stone patio that faced in the direction of the inn and the red barn beyond. There were a couple of old wrought iron chairs on the patio, and on the far side was a brick-built barbecue pit that still looked to be in good condition. The patio facing into the valley was surrounded by a flat lawn area that extended for a short distance, and then the natural pasture started, and the terrain inclined downward to the buildings way below. The patio extended for the length of the cottage, after which there was a lawn for about a hundred feet and then the ground started to rise again, at first pasture but with an increasing number of conifers, which merged into the tree line at the top of the basin maybe a hundred yards away.

When Bill invited the dogs to "go fetch," each trotted over to recover an old tennis ball apiece from the barbecue pit. David then spent the next ten minutes launching the balls down the slope of the pasture, watching the two terriers eagerly chasing the escaping prey, retrieving and barking for a repeat. Bill and John sat in the old chairs, surveying the scene and enjoying the sun on their faces. The dogs knew when they had had enough—they started walking slowly back up the hill rather than dashing back. Eventually they no longer asked for a repeat and simply lay panting on the patio, basking in the sun, content in the knowledge that they had won again.

The three didn't talk for a while but just sat—David perched on the edge of the barbecue pit—and enjoyed the tranquility of the scene.

"Would you like to take a stroll back and take a look in the barn?" Bill asked, after the dogs had recovered for around ten minutes. "I need to make sure it has weathered the storm OK."

"Sounds good to me," John said, raising himself reluctantly from the chair. "What do you keep in there?"

"My cars," Bill answered. "I just want to check that everything is dry in there."

With that they set off back down the gravel road, the three men finding the going easier but the two dogs lagging behind now as a result of being a little tired but also because they were not nearly as keen to get to their destination this time. As they approached the row of cottages, John broke the silence.

"I can understand the idea of looking for a place to find contentment, but why up here, though? Instinctively I would have thought of warmer places," John voiced.

"Oh, believe me, I know, John. I did spend a long time contemplating—if truth be told, I probably still think about it on occasion," Bill responded. "When I thought about it seriously, I would spend hours imagining, often spend all night lying awake thinking—living in various locations and trying to see how it felt. Not worrying thoughts, just thoughts of how life could be. In the end, I could realistically see myself living in a couple of very different places, very different lifestyles. Obviously one place was up here in New England, where I had spent many, many happy days in my life; the other place was at a relatively off-the-beaten-path location down on a Caribbean island. I was thinking not of a mainstream island but more like one of the Windward Islands, where the ocean breezes blow in warm and steady off the vast Atlantic. I have always loved the oceans, loved being by the oceans, truly loved their serenity, and I could imagine that a small house looking out over the ocean would be nice. I could go back in time there; I could live life at a pace I wanted to live—I could appreciate those same breezes and look out at the same view that people have done for many decades past. I could be happy there."

Bill paused—still seeing the shore, the ocean beyond, and feeling the breeze.

"I haven't heard any downside yet," John observed.

"Probably because I never really thought of downsides as such," Bill continued. "Living in such a place would be good—but I never could quite answer how long it would be good for. Because I had an uncertainty about what would happen in my later years, assuming that I did not have the good fortune to die in my sleep while lying in a shaded hammock one fine afternoon. But my uncertainty about later life did not really affect my thinking. In the end, I knew that I had to be true to myself, sort of true to what I really wanted. You see, what I really wanted was to try to go back to my happy times, the happiest times of my life, and in order to do that, I had to be in an environment where I had spent those times. It wasn't just peaceful times that I was looking for; it was my past times. And when I stopped to think deeply, I knew that whereas all the days in the Caribbean would be very appealing, the good days up here in New England would be better—and I did so want to live those good days again."

Bill paused, but neither John nor David interrupted.

"I know that in many ways a Caribbean island would be a sort of paradise, but to my eyes at least, there are periods, there are times up here that are so beautiful, so wonderful, and that evoke such strong memories that I would eventually yearn for such times even as I looked out over my endless ocean."

"Do you mean times of the year or times in your life?" John asked.

"Times of the year, really," Bill confirmed. "It is not practical to identify them categorically—nor would everyone have the same appreciation, I suppose. Some such times that come to mind would be long, late-summer evenings when it is warm but not hot, sitting outside and watching the twilight go on forever and listening to the calm of the crickets. Or looking out on the magnificent vista of hills on a crisp fall afternoon, the leaves turning every splendid color, and watching those leaves twirl in the blowing wind and smelling cooler days approaching. For myself even looking up into a jet-black December night and seeing the first snow of winter drifting down out of the blackness and starting to cover the frosty earth below—and then waking the following morning to a bright white blanket covering an unspoiled landscape—people and wildlife looking out in wonder as if they had somehow forgotten that the world could look so beautiful. You do not know the times are coming—sometimes you just look around and appreciate what a fine place the world can be. Those are the times that I did not want to miss, John, times that I wanted to experience as often as possible while I am still around."

John nodded as if understanding Bill's reasoning.

By now they were passing the inn and heading over toward the barn, about two hundred feet ahead to the right and elevated on a flat area of the pasture. The inn's car park had a few more vehicles than had been there on the previous afternoon, and two teenage girls, dressed in jeans and faded shirts, were busy unloading some gear from the back of an old-looking SUV.

"Hi, Jenny, Sarah," Bill called across. "Are you going up to see the boys first? They probably got a little nervous last night."

"Yes—we are going to see to them for a few minutes and then get on with the rooms," the blonder of the two girls answered back. "We will exercise them later."

"A few of the local girls keep their horses in the stables there," Bill explained to John and David, nodding toward the pasture behind the inn. "And in return, they housekeep the guest rooms for me, school permitting. They seem to work out a rotation among themselves—both for the rooms and keeping the stables clean and organized. Eddie helps them whenever anything needs repairing."

The three men started up the narrower gravel roadway leading up to the large red barn, which looked splendid in the August afternoon sun. As they approached the building, Bill headed over to the large main double doors as opposed to the smaller single door set off to the right.

"Might as well let some nice fresh air in," Bill said as he released the large clasp securing the two barn doors together and started to slide the right-hand one open. David helped to heave on a second handle attached to the outboard side, and the heavy, solid wooden door slid creakily along its runner.

"Welcome to my pride and joy," Bill announced as John and David peered into the shadows of the barn at a small collection of older cars. "Welcome to my haven from the modern world."

John smiled at the sight of the half dozen or so polished cars resting in the barn. "I'm very impressed, Bill," he said quietly. "Actually, if the truth be told, I am envious. I really do miss the cars of my youth—and the memories of those cars."

"Take a good look around," Bill told them. "Not intended to be a museum—they are all open, so feel free to sit in them. I am just going to work on the VW for a few minutes."

CHAPTER 6

The Cars

A FEW SHAFTS OF BRIGHT sunlight penetrated the shade of the barn through small gaps in the old wooden walls, making it easy to look around. John knew most of the car models, but there were a couple that he had to go around to the back to refresh his memory on the names—spelled out in chrome script on the trunk. David was not nearly as familiar with the cars, so he accompanied his dad, in part to listen to the reminiscences of his father's younger days.

There were seven cars in the barn, a mixture of American and European models that had been on the roads in the sixties and early seventies, all in very good condition and obviously well taken care of. From the right side of the barn, as they had entered, John observed a four-door Chevrolet Bel Air that he guessed was built in the late fifties, a shining MGB sports car from England, a small and simple French Citroen 2CV, a Plymouth Fury, an "original" Ford Thunderbird, and set back a little on the left was a bright red, soft-top, E-Type Jaguar. Toward the rear of the barn, there was a wooden ramp leading to a slightly elevated area, and up there Bill was tinkering inside the passenger cabin of the seventh vehicle, a dark-green-and-beige VW camper van.

John eased himself into the tight driver's seat of the British racing green MGB sports car, and David walked around and managed to maneuver into the passenger side.

"You never had one of these, did you, Dad?"

"Sadly no. But my college roommate had a bright yellow one that he would let me use on the weekends sometimes. I do remember some memorable trips, overnight up to Cape Cod with my then-girlfriend and a few Sundays seeing the New England fall colors or the ocean at Rhode Island. Driving just for the fun of it with the top down. Or maybe *motoring* would be a better word. I cannot say that it was the most comfortable car, David, but oh, was it exhilarating zipping along some of those New England roads, low to the ground and using the stick shift and small engine for all it was worth! Never seemed to get cold, even on those golden fall days."

"Have you owned any of these cars?"

"Let me show you the Chevy," John said, extricating himself from the MGB and heading over to the maroon-and-off-white-colored Bel Air. "I didn't actually own one, but my father had a virtually identical model in the late fifties—the only difference was that it was pale blue instead of the maroon. We had that car from when I was probably seven until around eleven or twelve. Often when I remember my father, he is driving the Bel Air with the window down, arm resting on the ledge, and telling me about life and the world. There might have been others in the car, but to seven-year-old me, it was just me and my father."

John had climbed into the driver's side, and David opened the relatively huge passenger door and slid onto the shiny front bench seat. The Chevy felt cavernous after the tightness of the MG.

"It's like sitting on a sofa," David commented.

"I don't suppose that you've ever been on a front seat like that." John smiled. "By the time you came along, everything was bucket seats and fabric or leather—gone was the slippery hard vinyl. When I grew older, I would sit farther across on the seat, but as a young boy, I would sit right over by my dad, intrigued at the dials and switches, and marvel at the ease with which he could swing the car around turns with the large glossy steering wheel. I can remember watching the indicator climb along the large rectangular speedometer, never quite understanding how the red line was sometimes long and then squashed short as it came to the center of the dial. We were foolish but ignorant—no seat belts in those days. Just cruised along, my father steering with one arm resting on the window and one around my shoulder. Often going nowhere in particular, either an evening drive after he got home from work or taking the long way home after our Saturday errands."

David was intrigued by the ashtray in the front dashboard. "Essential for all cars in those days, David. No seat belts or the cup holders that you hold so dear today, but ashtrays, yes. Even for the back seat passengers, if I remember correctly," John said, turning and nodding as he could feel an ashtray set into the back of the front bench seat.

They slid out of the Chevy, with much less strain than had been the case with the MG, and while John walked around the old car, lovingly stroking his hand along the shining bodywork and then opening the spacious trunk, David strolled up to Bill, who was climbing out of the cabin of the camper.

"Very impressive collection, Bill," David said admiringly. "Is it a reflection of your love for these classic cars or your dislike of the modern ones?"

"I suppose the two feelings go hand in hand. I really do despair at the sameness of nearly all the cars and all the car manufacturers today—and, in turn, that has led me to yearn for these beauties from yesteryear. All you have to do is look around a mall parking lot today, or even worse, a car rental center, and see the lines upon lines of virtually the same design with different badges on. Nobody had to look at the badge to know that it was a Triumph sports car or a Gremlin. Today you can have a sedan or an SUV, end of choice. And worse still, just look at the limited colors on display—there will be white, beige, silver, gray, black, and a lot more white. What happened to colors? And what happened to chrome that, as a teenager, you could polish daily? They were not all great cars, so to speak," Bill said, looking around the models in the barn and nodding his head a little. "There were flaws and mistakes with probably all of them. But, to me at least, they were all trying to create an object to be desired, to be coveted and treasured. Many might have failed, but they all tried, and that is what made cars such an attraction then. Now the attempt is not to create a car to love—it is to create a profit, and that saddens me. I wanted to experience cars that were fun again—cars that were individual, had character, were exciting to drive. They don't have to be perfectly reliable, don't have to be aerodynamic, don't even have to be ultrasafe in crash tests—but they should be a statement, beautiful, exciting to look at. All those classic cars didn't work, weren't successful—but they were fun, were a thrill, and you could remember them. They were beautiful—and they are all gone."

John had come up to join them. "But I doubt that the car corporations could get their bean counters to approve many of these beauties in today's financially driven search for market share and profits."

Bill concurred. "There is no way that a production car company could even consider producing the E-Type today," he said, looking admiringly at the sleek, red, powerful-looking machine. "Can you imagine all that engine, all that hood, to uncomfortably carry a maximum of two people, with a trunk that would probably be filled by a large briefcase and with road handling that was reasonable, providing the roads stayed nice and dry? Can you imagine proposing that concept today? So much time and money spent creating something so beautiful but so impractical."

"What do you use them for, Bill? Do you take them out regularly?" John asked.

"Oh yes—take one of them out probably three or four days a week, except in the winter; the salt is terrible for them. And the camper I take on longer trips."

Bill considered for a few moments. "They are my time machines, so to speak. When I take one out early on a morning, particularly on a Sunday morning, if I stick to back roads where there is little traffic, then I can sort of go back in time. Those roads, the scenery, the weather haven't changed; the world hasn't really changed, just the people in it. So I can motor along and go back to my younger years, for a few minutes at least. Don't have any radios on, just occasionally slip a cassette tape in, if the cars even have a player, and it could be 1970 again. And life is so much more straightforward. They were beautiful—and they are all gone."

David had opened up the driver door to the camper and was looking in at the spartan interior of the cab.

"How simple and straightforward can you get?" Bill asked. "A seat, a steering wheel, which looks as if its shaft connects straight down to the axle, with one simple indicator stalk, a long gear lever, one single speedometer dial, and a couple of switches. And that's it. No dashboard, no nothing. Simplicity at its best."

"You said that you take this on trips?" John asked.

"Once or twice a year, I go camping for a few days. Maybe across to New Hampshire or down in Massachusetts—normally just myself and the two dogs, although Eddie has been with me once. Set up camp by a lake and spend the days fishing and enjoying."

John had been looking at the rear engine, tiny and simple by modern standards. "How do you maintain the mechanical parts, Bill? Are you handy with engines and the like?"

"Not really, John," Bill said. "There is a guy, Ken, who owns the filling station and repair shop in the small town a couple of miles up the road. He and his son love the cars almost as much as I do, and whenever one of the cars has a problem, which is fairly frequently, one of them will come over and tinker with it when he gets the time. I pay them for the parts, but I don't think that they charge for most of the actual time they spend. Likewise, Steve, the son, provides cars for weddings and other events, as a side business, and I happily let him use the bigger cars—if that appeals to the customers."

After a few more minutes, Bill announced that he had better get back to the inn to help Eddie and Annie with lunch but offered for John to take one of the cars for a short drive if he wanted. "Take one up to the town and back. It is actually good for them to run."

"Is it OK to take the Bel Air, for old times?" John asked.

"Perfectly OK, John. The keys are all in the wooden box by the side of the camper," Bill replied, smiling as he turned and headed out of the barn, sliding the second door wide open on his way out.

And so it was that John eased a Bel Air out of the old barn and crunched along the gravel roadway on a bright, sunny August day. The windows were down, the breeze wafted through, and John rested his left arm on the frame as he smiled across to his own son. Maybe it is a time machine, he thought idly as the powerful car started up the incline of the driveway.

CHAPTER 7

A Summer Evening

BY THE TIME THE MOTORISTS had returned, lunch was almost over. A few guests still sat chatting in the dining room, and a couple of people were at the bar enjoying a lunchtime beer.

"How was it?" Bill asked as he emerged from the kitchen with a stack of clean plates.

"Really enjoyed it. Thanks, Bill," John replied. "It definitely took me back a few years—really appreciate you letting us take it out. We parked her back in the same spot and closed the barn doors."

"Any time, John. Let me introduce you to Eddie," Bill said, gesturing to the man polishing glasses behind the bar. "Eddie, these are John and David, the two campers who thought better of braving the storm."

The three men shook hands. Eddie looked a little older than Bill, slim build, around five-seven with shaved gray hair, and though he looked as if he had had a tough life, his face lit up with a nice grin and eyes full of life.

"What are your plans now?" Eddie asked. "Going back to camping?"

"We were just discussing that as we came back down the drive, Eddie," John answered. "To be honest, we think that we would find it a little difficult to switch back into the roughing-it frame of mind, but we don't want to cut our vacation short. So if it is OK with you, Bill, we were thinking of staying a couple more nights before heading home."

"Like I said earlier, I don't need the rooms until the weekend—so happy to have you stay until then," Bill responded. "You can take a look around the area tomorrow if you like—nothing exciting but some pretty spots."

"Are there any trails to hike, assuming the weather is good?" David asked, adding and smiling, "I can't check the weather on my phone."

"Yes, if you want a good two-to-three-hour walk, your dad can drive you to the far side of the village, down to the bridge by the river, and from there you can take a really good walk, first along the river, and then there will be a trail heading roughly east up over the farmed hills. It will eventually bring you out at the top of the pasture beyond the stables. As for the weather forecast—just take a look out of the window in the morning," Bill said, smiling back broadly. "By all means take the dogs with you if you like; they always enjoy a long walk, and they will show you the way if you are uncertain."

"Sounds perfect—if you can drop me, Dad?"

"Is it OK to take the MG out, Bill? Will the dogs fit in?" John asked.

"Be my guest. The dogs are fine in the space behind the seats—just leave the roof up until you drop them off."

"Would you gents like any lunch?" Eddie asked. "Annie is still pottering in the kitchen."

"I think that I will just take a beer and go back to my book on the deck for the afternoon," John replied.

"Breakfast was big enough to tide me over until dinner. Thanks, Eddie," David said. "I am going to take a walk around some more of the property and work up a good appetite."

"No problem," Eddie replied, starting to pull John a glass of draft beer.

Once he had his glass in hand, John excused himself, retrieved *The Day of the Jackal* from the library, and proceeded out onto the deck for an afternoon of reading, which he suspected would be interspersed with an occasional doze. David meanwhile grabbed an apple out of the fruit bowl in the front lobby and made his way outside to explore the grounds some more.

Both had an enjoyable afternoon. At one point John's reading was interrupted when David approached the deck on horseback, accompanied by one of the two girls that they had seen earlier in the car park.

"I didn't know that you could even ride, David," John said, somewhat surprised.

"Haven't attempted it for many years, Dad—but yes, I rode during a couple of summers at the sleepaway camp when I was maybe thirteen or fourteen. I was taking a look around the stables and talking to the girls, and Jenny here asked if I wanted to take a ride," David said, nodding to the blond-haired girl on the other horse. "She promised me that Rascal here is, in fact, friendly."

John nodded hello to Jenny and said with a smile, "It is Rascal that I am worried for. Don't let him pretend that he knows what he's doing."

Jenny laughed back, and with that, the horses and riders headed off toward the larger distant cottage up the hillside, albeit at a walking pace.

The remainder of the afternoon passed without incident for John. Seventy degrees, a breeze from the south, an engrossing book, and nobody needing him, all contributed to a relaxing few hours as the world carried on.

John and David met up again at around seven in the bar and had another relaxing home-cooked dinner. The restaurant was definitely busier, and more chatter filled, than the previous evening. Bill later explained that there were always a few customers who came from the local town and the nearby farms, some to eat and some, particularly the farmworkers, just to have a beer at the end of the day.

Later, after the hearty dinner, John and David retreated to the bar, where Eddie was organizing a trivia quiz for those of the twenty or so patrons who wanted to play, which turned out to be almost everybody.

There was a lot of healthy, good-natured competition among the two-person teams, and the quiz quickly extended to a second game. John and David did not play together but were paired, by Eddie, with a middle-aged couple from Canada. Eventually the quiz concluded, and some guests started to drift off. David and the lady who had been his playing partner went over to the library to try a game of chess, which David had played a lot back in high school.

John wasn't quite ready for bed, so he took the last part of his wine out onto the deck to appreciate a quiet night in contrast to the noisy wind and rain from the evening before. Bill, Rip, and Riley joined him about forty minutes later, Bill with his evening whisky.

John asked about the daily routines of innkeeping, and Bill proceeded to explain that it was very similar to running any house, just on a bigger scale, except that if things needed doing, they had to be attended to promptly rather than being added to the to-do list.

"Is it a lot of work, Bill? Hard work?"

"Not really. I never look on it as proper work, and having Eddie, Annie, and help from the local folks makes it a good team where we all do our fair share. We have the luxury of when things require fixing, Eddie jumps on that, enjoys keeping the inn running, so I don't have to worry about that side of it."

After a few moments of thought, Bill continued. "I suppose you have to keep in mind that when we set out, we envisaged an inn that would be a haven for ourselves and our guests, and an assumption would be that any inn entails work. So we cannot then grumble about the amount of work involved. It is what we chose, John."

"So have you accomplished what you set out to achieve here at the inn? Have you managed to create what you envisaged when you started?" John asked and then added, "And managed to keep the things you didn't want from the outside world out of Yesterday's Inn?"

"What I tried to achieve, John, is contentment, pure and simple. Contentment for myself and contentment from knowing that I was attempting to create an oasis where others could maybe sample a little of the life I remembered and missed. I was so tired of my memories being better than my now, better than my present. Memories shouldn't always be a reflection of happier times. But they were, you see, so I set out to go back to my memories."

"With you so far—but which elements of modern-day living have you decided are not welcome?"

Bill smiled. "If I really distill it down to one issue, it is simply computerization. But you need to understand that I am not referring to physical computers, as such, but more computer technology or these computer chips that are capable of accomplishing so much. Computer technology that can revolutionize our lives beyond imagination make our lives so much 'easier' and enable us to do so much more. But I now recognize that by being tempted and encouraged and forced to do more and more and more and keep abreast of every aspect of everything, we appreciate and enjoy less and less. You see, the one thing that this technology cannot achieve is to give us more time. It cannot yet make the forty-hour day. Nevertheless, there is constant persuasion to accomplish more—an incessant drive for us to cram more and more into the time available, and inevitably the result is that we cannot achieve anything, or appreciate anything properly. As a glaring example, how often do you see people supposedly watching TV but with a laptop in front of them and a smartphone alongside? They are convinced that they can multitask. That they can pay bills on the computer, maintain several social media communications on the cell phone, and still watch a TV program at the same time. But they cannot. Multitasking is just a fallacy. Inevitably the result is that nothing is accomplished properly. The same is true throughout our daily lives. People believing that they can eat and hold numerous electronic conversations simultaneously. People proud that they are always contactable on vacation—and then convinced in their own minds that they have unwound and relaxed. Working and relaxing simultaneously—fantastic but not possible. You have to do one thing and do it properly. If relaxing is the task, then relax. Sit on a sunbed and relax. One task. You cannot cheat time by trying to sneak in something extra. I hope that people do relax here."

Bill paused and took a sip from his whisky.

"From that comes the insatiable desire to know everything about everybody—just because they can. People are so addicted to knowing what everybody else is doing, seeing how everybody else lives, what everybody else thinks, that they do not live their own lives anymore. It is rare these days for people to simply express their own thoughts on an issue without first seeking validation from social media, seeing how the thoughts are 'trending.' All too often people offer a regurgitation of views from social media as definitive proof that a certain argument is true or correct. It is increasingly difficult for some folks to form an independent opinion. For some reason, they feel a need to understand how their lives compare to the lives of others. They come to need validation. And they get mired in a life not lived. Maybe I should advertise the inn as 'Yesterday's Inn—come and live *your* life.'"

"But wouldn't most people consider these to be conveniences—keeping us accessible?"

"No, I don't know if they are really conveniences—for the large part they are devices, mechanisms that inconvenience you—that actually hinder you from doing what you want to do. You are hypnotized into following your screens for every waking minute. The convenience, as you put it, is being able to use your smartphone to transfer money from your bank account to fund your coffee-shop app so that when you go to buy your next coffee, you can simply log on and wave your phone at a scanning device. This avoids the complicated alternative of just taking cash out of your pocket and giving it to the cashier. The real objective of your coffee-shop app has nothing to do with your convenience—it is simply for the vendor to have early access to your funds and ensure you visit that particular franchise as opposed to choosing a competitor's coffee shop. Millions of dollars lent free to the vendor, for your convenience. The perceived convenience is, in many cases, simply a strategy of more and more being imposed on the consumer—not for the consumer's convenience but for the convenience of the corporations. Surreptitiously, the model is developing whereby individuals are increasingly compelled to participate in a tidal wave of 'You just take care of it yourself,' 'It is very easy,' 'It is very quick,' 'It takes no time at all,' until all the 'no time at all' adds up to all your free time. Who benefits from self-checkout at the supermarket? Who does it really help? Who saves time? Who saves money? I can tell you that the only winner is the store—because now you are doing the work of the checkout cashier and not asking for a salary. Thank heavens for bar codes."

Bill paused again, contemplating his one-sided debate.

"I used to think that they should have stopped time in 1967—it was just a date that I picked. But I do think that they should have stopped progress before we were infected and infatuated by computerization—before computer technology started to dictate our existence. I don't know, take your pick, sometime in the seventies? Certainly before I had to listen to a computer-generated voice excitedly report that 'he' was able to understand complete sentences. Only to fail miserably at the only six sentences I attempted. But please give him a minute while he 'thinks.'"

Twilight had disappeared into a warm, dark night. The flitting bats had given way to the chirp of crickets, and a light breeze, which had grown out of the west, was blowing down from the pine trees beyond the stables and the pastures, sufficient to cause Rip and Riley to rouse themselves from their prone positions to sample the new scents on the air.

"If not conveniences, would you see the developments as progress?" John inquired.

"They say it is all progress. In the name of progress. But I don't want progress. I want my life back," Bill responded before pausing for a few moments.

"I know what I set out to achieve, John, and from that perspective, I think that I have given it a good shot," Bill concluded. "You have to keep in mind that I did not set out to change the world. I just wanted to change my world."

"Have you actually managed to slow the pace a little and enabled your guests to relax, to enjoy the inn and its surroundings?"

"I suppose that the guests are probably better able to answer—and you are a guest. I think that it takes a while for people to wean themselves off the yearning for constant and instant communication. It definitely takes people days before they can leave their rooms without their phones. But in time I think that they do resist their cravings and then they get into the enjoyment of living life—their life. The summertime is generally more of a laid-back time—but I find guests very much appreciate the holidays here. The holidays have become such hectic, chaotic, stressful periods, which drain finances and patience beyond belief, that guests seem to welcome turning back the clock to holidays from yesteryear."

"The Christmas holiday?" John asked.

"Really from mid-November through Thanksgiving, Christmas, New Year, into early January. It is a nice setting up here, and we try to create a genuinely peaceful and festive time. You and David are more than welcome to come and stay with us—just bring yourselves."

"I might just take you up on that. Will see how the family plans play out," John replied as David came out and joined them on the deck.

"Good game, David?" Bill asked.

"Yes, finished about fifteen minutes ago. Soundly beaten but enjoyed the company and the conversation afterward. Her husband doesn't play, or maybe doesn't like losing," David replied. "Take Bill up on what, Dad?"

"Oh, he was saying that we should come back up during the winter holidays to experience the real atmosphere of the inn."

The three sat quietly for maybe five minutes, watching the stillness of the night sky with only the occasional stomp or snort coming from the stables as accompanying sounds. John and Bill took the last sips of their drinks.

"So have you managed to create a *now* that matches the memories of your younger days, Bill?" John asked as they stretched their legs.

"I have found contentment again, John. And I have found an inner happiness that I had not known for many years, although I sometimes wish that those I have lost could be here to share it. As for memories, what I have come to understand is that I am creating the memories for other people now. I am creating good memories, and maybe I am part of those memories. I feel very fulfilled." And then as an afterthought, Bill added, "But making those memories comes with a responsibility that is real and permanent, John, because you feel the obligation to keep the remembrances alive for people so that they will remain as pleasing recollections after many years, and maybe companions, have passed."

With that thought, Bill rose and stretched slowly, allowing full circulation to be restored. John did likewise, taking his time, while David collected their two glasses. Rip and Riley jumped up, apparently not feeling the need to stretch in any way.

"I will bid you a good-night, gentlemen," Bill said. "If you could pop those glasses on the bar, David, I will get them in a few minutes when I get back—I am just going to take the dogs for their last walk."

"Thanks for a really pleasant day, Bill. Very glad we came across your inn," John said, holding the French doors open for David. "Have a good night."

"Come on, you two," Bill called and headed down the rear steps off the deck.

CHAPTER 8

Preserving Memories

BILL STEPPED OFF THE DECK onto the soft lawn and into the darkness and solitude of the August night. There were no moon and no clouds, so the stars twinkled brightly against the black canvas. As he started to stroll across the inn's back lawn, Bill retrieved and lit the small cigar from his shirt pocket. He had never smoked seriously in his life, but since moving up to the inn, he had gravitated toward an occasional cigar late at night while he walked around the property. His father had sometimes smoked cigars when he had taken Bill to ball games fifty-odd years ago. Just regular ball games that stayed with him over the decades. Today he wouldn't be allowed to smoke, Bill reflected.

As long as the weather was decent, Bill usually ended his day by taking a walk. The strolls had a few purposes. Besides allowing the dogs to explore the scents and sounds of the nighttime and occasionally chase their nocturnal adversaries, Bill liked to check on the outbuildings, make sure that the horses seemed happy, the barn doors were closed up, and that nothing seemed amiss up at the cottages. But he also enjoyed the seclusion of the night. It gave him the opportunity to reflect on a day well spent and to contemplate life in general. Nobody disagreed with him on his strolls.

Tonight he was contemplating what he had been trying to say to John before they called it a night, about creating memories for people and the responsibility that Bill somehow felt with respect to the inn and those memories.

In a way, establishing a place like this does come with a price, Bill reflected. Having attempted to create a place that people appreciate, that people return to because they enjoy the experience, you realize that you have some sort of obligation to make sure the place survives. Because you sense that allowing the place to ever be abandoned will dash all those memories.

Bill had always been distressed by the sight of deserted properties, regardless of whether or not he had known them when they were "alive." Over the years he had come across some places that had saddened him deeply and saddened him in a way that stayed with him, in the back of his memory, surfacing in the quiet times. The common theme among most of those places was that they had been abandoned, left to just decay as if they never were. He could remember driving through Arizona a number of years back, along what had once been a section of the major interstate route that weaved its way through small townships. But the old highway had been replaced many years previously by a modern multilane highway, a few miles to the north, a highway that bypassed all the towns and businesses—a fast, impersonal piece of asphalt that posed no impediments for the drivers; it just sped toward the distant horizon that never got any closer. The old route he was on shimmered in the heat of the Arizona sun as it passed through old communities that he guessed had been much more vibrant when all the traffic, and the business that the traffic would bring, had been traveling the route. Now the businesses seemed lonely—lonely and dusty. He would stop at a diner and be the only customer, served by an owner who no doubt couldn't make ends meet but had nothing left to sell and nowhere to go. On a section of this route, a few miles outside one of the townships, he came across an abandoned gas station and then, about two miles farther on, a deserted motel. The gas station still had three older-looking gas pumps on the forecourt, with the faded winged-horse logo adorning their tops. In the rear of the property was one long building, housing the old restrooms, the station's store, and what must have been a sizable repair shop. The door to the store was open so he could wander through the building into the adjoining repair facilities and out through the open bays. He didn't know how long the place had been abandoned, but there hadn't really been any vandalism, just some of the lighter storage racks and other objects lying on the floor—presumably blown over by the wind, which could pass through the open door and out of the broken windows at the back. The thing that stuck in his memory was that on one of the shelves in the repair shop, there was a new air filter, still in its box with a cellophane window, unopened and untouched, stocked long ago to repair a car that never came. When the memory surfaced, he would sometimes wonder why that one filter had been left. Farther along the road was the Desert Oasis motel, boasting "forty-eight deluxe rooms, TV, breakfast, and pool." The rooms were arranged on two levels in an L shape, all looking out into the bleached pale-blue crater, complete with the remnants of a rotted diving board, which had been the pool. Tacked onto the end of the L closest to the old road were the motel offices, which were empty except for the reception desk behind which a carved wooden sign read "We hope you enjoy your stay—and hope you come back real soon" and a row of old mechanical vending machines, which he gazed at for a few moments. What had happened to vending machines that could dispense hot coffee, with or without milk and sugar, or even soup and hot chocolate? How could a world so modern and innovative no longer be able to provide those cardboard cups of comfort any time of the day or night? Any flavor of soda or any amount of cold bottled water, yes, but a hot beverage was a thing of the past. He went into a couple of the rooms, still with stripped-down beds, basic furniture, and white bathrooms complete with plastic shower curtains. Bill couldn't help but reflect that when the motel had been opened, it would have been so modern for its day. He wondered how many families had stopped here to break up their cross-country drives to enjoy some relaxation and let the kids expend their pent-up energy in the pool. A happy place for happy families was now deserted, as if those times had never been. The flip board below the motel sign still said "vacancy," and as he drove away, he supposed that it would always swing to and fro in the desert breeze and always say "vacancy."

He remembered looking around a derelict house while traveling through upstate New York on a delightful day in the late spring. The rural settings were beautiful, and the small communities very friendly, but he sensed that the economy had seen better times and that, if anything, the population was decreasing rather than on the rise. He had seen many dilapidated barns, no longer the majestic red symbols of American rural life, and that saddened him a lot. And he had passed a number of isolated houses that must have simply been abandoned over time, and he wondered what turns life could take that would cause people just to walk away from their dreams. So when he came to a large neglected house set back from a quiet stretch of road, he plucked up the courage to at least take a look. The neglect was indicated by ivy-type foliage growing up some of the outside walls, screen doors hanging off, some broken windows, gravel driveway overgrown with weeds, and little differentiation between what had once been a garden and the encroaching wild vegetation. The house itself had probably been built in the early twentieth century, all wood with a large deep porch along the front. If it had been painted with a color, it wasn't anymore, just flaking pale paint and darker shutters. The front screen door was off its hinges, but the door itself was locked, or at least jammed closed. The top half of one of the kitchen's sash windows, which looked out onto the porch, was fully open so, although he didn't really feel that he should go inside, he could easily lean into the ground floor and see some of the rooms. The large kitchen, which to Bill resembled a farmhouse kitchen, stretched across the house from the front through to a back door, which he assumed led out to the backyard. On the left side of the kitchen was a large brick fireplace; a big wooden table still remained in the center of the room with some wooden spindle-backed chairs around it. There was a coating of dust on everything and some windblown leaves and other debris strewn across the bare floorboards. Immediately to the right of the kitchen, facing the front door, was the stairway, leading to the upstairs, which looked a little shaky with a number of broken supports on the stair rail. And farther to the right, Bill could see part of the living room, which seemed devoid of any furniture, just another fireplace empty except for a couple of charred, half-burnt logs. And as Bill's gaze swept back to the left, it stopped on the wide doorframe between the kitchen and the entrance hall. Although he could not decipher the numbers and letters, he could make out the pencil marks on the painted frame recording the growth of at least two children through their years in the old house. That was too much for Bill; he turned away and sat precariously in the one rickety rocking chair that remained on the porch and looked away into the distance, past the quiet road, as the occupants of that house must have done on countless summer evenings over many decades. How could a place that had been the safe, happy haven for many families, had seen children grow and laugh and be safe in their home—how could such a place be left to die, be abandoned to the elements? If the children were to return and see their house now, see what their parents had worked so hard for and been so proud of, been proud of them, their children, would it not taint those memories forever?

But the most forlorn places that he had ever seen were not buildings; they were abandoned drive-in movie theaters. He had actually come across two in his travels. The first, during a rainy afternoon on a quiet road in Pennsylvania, was surrounded by fields and had presumably been carved out of the farmland but never returned to farming after it had been vacated. There was a gate across the property, so Bill could only observe the large once-blacktopped area now broken up by strong weeds pushing up from below. The movie screen itself was no longer there, just a wide frame to indicate the direction that all the cars would have faced on those evenings of long ago. Bill stood peering through the gate at the drizzle sweeping across the spoiled asphalt and couldn't help but feel dejected. But the second theater that he came across, by chance, on the outskirts of a small town in northwest Texas in the late afternoon a couple of years later, made him even more despondent. This time the gate across the property was wide open so that he could drive in past the small dilapidated wooden structure that had once been the ticket booth. The drive-in area was a large expanse of white concrete slabs. There were some weeds growing between them but only small specimens this time, presumably because of a lack of water in the heat and dust of west Texas. Bill drove across the expanse, past rows and rows of speaker poles that were mainly still standing and stopped toward the middle, looking across at the mostly intact screen. One corner of the screen was flapping in the light breeze, but otherwise this must have been what the occupants of the cars looked out at, on those summer evenings, waiting for the projector to come to life. He walked across the still-hot concrete to what had been the concession stand. Painted on the front wall was a washed-out Coca-Cola insignia—no longer close to red, more of a pale brown. And there was some reference to hot dogs, but Bill could not make out exactly what was being offered. He walked back to the car and sat on the hood, watching the red sun melting into the shimmering horizon to the west. He stayed there for a long time, somehow feeling that it would be disrespectful for him to abandon the place as well, and imagining that the old theater might appreciate a customer being there again. As he sat and the light turned to gloom, the breeze increased a little, and, as if on cue, a small tumbleweed rolled across the now-cooling concrete—not stopping as though it too knew there was nothing to see. Bill sat and looked at a screen that had made memorable evenings for so many families, for a community, now left to bake through the days and remain lifeless through the nights. That was a forlorn place that saddened him greatly. Deep down he felt that places that created good memories for people should not be allowed to die, because surely the memories die as well.

When he tried to picture days gone by, he knew that so many people must have been very proud on the day that those businesses had opened—the gas station, the first day that a brand-new motel opened for guests, or the first evening that the drive-in movies lit up the night skies. And how many couples or families had been so proud of their new home, been so happy on their first night tucked up in their beds? How could such proud accomplishments be abandoned?

Bill did not want anybody to ever come back to a deserted, neglected inn, to stables not having horses peering out over the split doors, or to a vacant barn with the wind blowing away his cherished memories.

They say that change is a good thing—but Bill knew that not to be true. Bill acknowledged that improvement was probably a good thing, but not change. In fact, change took away what Bill liked the most in his life—and that was continuity.

CHAPTER 9

The Hay Field

THE FOLLOWING DAY DAWNED TO a cloudless sky, with or without a forecast.

Breakfast was the same pleasant, informal affair. David's order didn't change, but John opted for poached eggs on toast with some ham on the side.

"So are you off for a walk today?" Bill asked as he poured their coffee.

"That is the plan," David confirmed, "and I promise to leave my phone switched off and in my room."

Bill laughed. "I believe that you do get a signal in the town, but you just try walking and enjoying the scenery, without worrying what the rest of the human race is doing and without the fear of somebody disturbing your mood with a vitally important call or a picture of their dog performing a new skill."

John and David browsed the morning paper enthusiastically, both before and after their breakfast arrived at the table, ignoring the commonly held etiquette that it was rude to read at the table. There had been a time when reading the newspaper had been an everyday ritual for John, but the practice was a distant memory now. David had never really known the pleasure of the breakfast paper routine.

By the time they had finished enjoying their breakfast and catching up with the world, an hour and a half had passed, and it was almost nine thirty. While David popped back up to his room to change shoes, John double-checked with Bill that it was OK to take the MG.

"More than welcome, John—enjoy yourself," Bill assured him as he headed back into the kitchen.

And with that, John went out into the entrance hall, where Rip and Riley were sitting patiently in the front window. David returned a few minutes later, and the dogs didn't need a second invitation when John motioned for them to follow. The four ventured out into the pleasant sixty-five-degree morning and set off for the barn.

After opening up the large double doors with David, John went into the shady interior, opened the driver's door of the MG, and gestured for the dogs to hop in. Again, they didn't need to be asked twice. It had been a long time since John had driven a stick shift car, so he consciously took his time starting the engine, putting it into first, and then easing out the clutch. It was still a little jumpy getting the car over the barn threshold and out into the sunny morning.

David had been standing by the doors to pull them both closed after John and the MG emerged.

"I didn't know you could drive stick," David commented as he slipped into the passenger seat.

"You would be surprised at the secrets of my younger days," John replied and then promptly stalled the car, as he came off the clutch too quickly, much to David's amusement. But after that first misstep, John quickly mastered the manual gear changing and deftly maneuvered the car down the gravel roadway, across the inn's parking lot, and up the driveway on the far side, heading for the road to town. The two dogs peered eagerly through the gap between the two seats and out of the somewhat restricted windshield.

The small township was just over three miles away. Among other businesses and stores, there was an older-style food market, not anywhere near the size of a supermarket; a bank; post office; a pleasant-looking tavern that also served pizza; a general store; and an old silver-style sixties diner at one end of town and a filling station at the other. There was angled parking along the main street in front of all the stores, with about half of the spaces being occupied.

"I would think that is the service station where the father and son help with tinkering and maintaining Bill's cars," John said as they were heading out of the town.

About a mile and a half farther on, they approached the river crossing, which, from Bill's description, was where David should start his walk. John pulled over onto the grass verge and the four of them extricated themselves from the car, the dogs giving themselves a brisk shake after their confinement.

"Thanks, Dad," David said. "Are you going straight back or taking the car for a drive first?"

"Probably going to explore a little and appreciate the driving. You enjoy your walk—and I'll see you back at the inn. Better not delay—the dogs are not waiting for you," John replied, looking over David's shoulder, where he could see Rip and Riley trotting off down the path leading to the river, confident in where they were going this morning.

David smiled at the eager dogs. "See you this afternoon—thanks again for the ride."

"The ride is perfect. Enjoy yourself," John called to David's back as he followed the dogs.

John watched David stride off along the riverbank, Rip and Riley running well ahead but glancing around occasionally to make sure that they had not been abandoned. Before reaching a small copse of trees, David half-turned, waved back toward his father, and then the three quickly disappeared from view.

John directed his attention to the MG's soft top, which he carefully unclipped and gingerly pulled back, conscious of the fact that the material was not as supple as it had once been. Having successfully folded and covered the top, John jumped back into the snug driver's seat, started the engine, which sounded excitingly louder with the top down, and looked at the road ahead. Where to go? The main road, which John had followed down from the town, crossed the river via an old stone bridge and then seemed to follow the course of the river, going north, over on the far side. Alternatively, there was a smaller road, branching off ahead, immediately before the bridge, which appeared to turn away from the river and head up into the hills to his right. John chose the smaller side road, thinking that he might get to an elevated vantage point where he could admire some views of the valley. He eased out the clutch, and a smile started as he remembered the breeze that began to blow though his hair—blowing away the years.

The road narrowed as it started to climb though the wooded landscape, still room enough for two cars to pass but only if they slowed down. The MG felt at home on the smaller road, which climbed through cool, shaded woods for about two miles until the car emerged triumphantly into the bright sunlight again. The incline continued, but the trees had given way to farmed fields, initially only on the right, but very soon there were hay fields on both sides of the secluded road. In the fields to the left, sloping downward away from the road, the hay had mainly been cut and baled into giant cylinders dotting expanses of stubble; whereas the fields rising up on the right still had the golden yellow grasses thick and swaying in the summer breeze.

The road leveled off about a mile farther on. John slowed down, eased the car off the road surface to the right, and parked on a gravel patch in front of an old wooden bar gate at the base of one of the hay fields that hadn't yet been cut. He swung the door wide and, after maneuvering himself out of the car, stood to admire the views down and across the valley. Propping himself against the closed driver's door, he surveyed the cut fields and woods beyond, inhaling the earthy scent of cut grass blowing off the fields.

After appreciating the landscape for a few minutes, John decided to see if he could actually reach the top of the hill if he trekked up through the uncut fields behind. Walking around the front of the car, he cautiously climbed the wooden gate and jumped down into the field. The hay reached up above his knees as he started to walk across to the left, heading for the stone wall that marked the side of the plot and that, John reasoned, would provide an easier path. There was a huge lone tree a long way up the field on the left side. John headed toward the tree, thinking that this would probably mark the crest of the rise. After a good ten-minute ascent through the field, he reached the tree, but, although it did represent the top of the field, indicated by another stone wall, he was wrong in his assumption, because the rise continued through at least one more hay field beyond. He decided to take a rest after his exertions.

John sat with his back against the lumpy bark of the tree, cushioning hands behind his head, legs outstretched and the warm sun on his face. He closed his eyes and listened to the quiet. He didn't actually fall asleep but rested his eyes for a good fifteen minutes until the sense of guilt over doing nothing made him slowly open them again. He looked down across the field of yellowing hay and at a lone sparrow hawk hovering high up, silhouetted against the pale-blue sky. The hawk was apparently motionless way up there in the August sky but no doubt paying rapt attention, from its vantage point for any movement within the grasses of the meadow. After about three minutes of perfect stillness, the hawk dropped like a stone, disappearing below the level of the hay only to reappear after a few seconds to resume its station in the sky. Presumably the prey had been the quicker on this occasion. The panorama was somewhat hypnotic to John, and he didn't want to break the spell. Maybe life's pleasures are supposed to be this simple, he thought as he looked down at the little green MG parked down below. Life used to seem this simple before; maybe it still was.

Sitting against the tree felt very real to John. It could be that nothing would ever change in this setting. He would not be there, of course, but this tree and the field of golden swaying grasses would be there each August and would be just as true for others to appreciate if they took the time. He stretched out and enjoyed the day for a while longer.

There are days when the world can seem so straightforward, John thought, so uncomplicated. He mulled over some of Bill's philosophies and wondered why the days past were more carefree. His mind wandered back to a conversation he had had with David while hiking earlier in the week, after dinner on their first night of camping, as they sat and listened to the evening. David had been second-guessing his course elections and even career path. "Does age bring wisdom, Dad?" David had asked. "Will I look back and wonder at the decisions I make now?" John had responded, "There will always be decisions you will come to regret, David, but you can never know the outcome. If you could have the knowledge of old age in your youth, it might be easy." But as he lay there, with half-closed lids, in that field, John knew that he had been wrong when he had implied that. It is the knowing that takes away the love of life. He thought to himself, I wish that I only knew now what I knew in my young days. Wish I could still believe now what I believed then. That is the truth, thought John drowsily. That is why the days were more carefree.

Eventually, John reluctantly decided that he had better head back to the inn before David returned from his walk, and they started to wonder where he had got to. He rose slowly, patted the old tree as if it had feelings, and made his way back down through the hay field toward the road below, his walking through the grasses leaving a slightly trampled path in his wake. He paused astride the five-bar gate as he was departing the field and looked back to remember the peaceful setting. The waving hay provided the only movement, and the stationary hawk the only other sign of life. John hoped that the patient bird would catch its meal soon.

Easing himself back into the car, he started the eager engine. Before turning the car to head back down the narrow road, he pushed the play button on the small cassette player attached to the underside of the dashboard, uncertain whether or not there was actually a tape in. Bob Seger drifted out of the single speaker, remembering the night moves of his youth…"When you just don't seem to have as much to lose…With Autumn closing in." John drove back and appreciated the day.

CHAPTER 10

Leaving Yesterday

JOHN DROPPED DOWN THE WINDING driveway to the inn a little faster than he had done the previous day when driving the Bel Air. It wasn't the sportiness of the MG that induced him to drive quicker; it was just that he felt a lot more confident in the smaller car compared to the much larger, and admittedly much more comfortable, Chevrolet. The car crunched up the gravel road to the barn, and John did a three-point turn, partly on the gravel and partly on the grass alongside. He hopped out and opened up the doors before slowly backing into the gloom of the barn.

Once the car was safely back in its allocated spot among its colleagues, John carefully pulled the soft top up and secured it back into place. The barn had a hushed, almost reverential, feel to it—a little like a museum where people quietly gazed in admiration and respect at the exhibits. It would have seemed disrespectful to have shouted in the presence of the cars. Having finished closing up the MG, he stopped by the little Citroen 2CV, opened the driver's door, and peered inside. John found himself smiling at the simplicity of the interior and the instrumentation. He mentally compared these seats to the size and complexity of modern car seats, with all their electronic adjustments—moving lumbar components, head rests that tipped and tilted every which way—and of course, the essential heating possibilities. In the Citroen it was just a thin-backed seat, maybe as comfortable as an old school desk chair. He smiled again when he went over to the E-Type Jaguar and sat in the driver's seat for a moment. It wasn't the simplicity that caused him to smile this time; it was the sheer flamboyance of the machine. He had seen a number of the Jaguars over the years but had never actually sat in one. It was so low, and the hood seemed to extend forever, dipping away so that you couldn't see the end. The interior was not complex by modern standards, but to John at least, it was designed and built to please the driver. John peered over at the Thunderbird and wondered about a time that could produce such flashy cars and such simple cars at the same time. He smiled again.

Before closing up the barn, he looked back at the exhibits. "Who would have thought? In a barn in Vermont of all places," he reflected as he strolled across to the inn.

Lunch was in full flow as John entered the bar. When prompted by Eddie, he asked for a roast-beef sandwich, which he then took out onto the deck to enjoy at leisure while awaiting the return of the hikers. About half an hour later, the two light-brown terriers came trotting down the pasture, seemingly unfazed by their three-plus hours of exercise, heading for their large bowl of water at the far end of the deck. David followed about ten minutes later, not moving as fast as the dogs had, but, John had to admit, didn't seem any the worse for his exertions.

David came and sat up on the deck with his father.

"Good walk?" John asked.

"Very enjoyable," David confirmed, "surprisingly relaxing walking through the countryside on my own—not forgetting my two guide dogs."

"Easy enough to find your way?"

"To be honest, I would probably have missed the place to turn when I was leaving the river. But the dogs stopped and rested in the sun, waiting until I caught up to them. Once I was close enough, they jumped up and continued up the fields, assuming I had the sense to follow."

"They got back about ten minutes ago," John said. "How about a beer?"

"Love one, thanks."

With that, John took his empty plate back inside and reappeared a couple of minutes later with two glasses of ale.

"I think that I will take advantage of the peace and quiet and go lie down this afternoon," David said as he sipped his beer. "I feel as if I have earned it—and Bill did encourage us to relax."

"Don't blame you, son. I think that I will finish my book before we leave. Maybe take a walk later on."

The two sat and enjoyed their drinks.

John's afternoon went as planned. He finished the book by around three thirty, at which point he decided to take a walk and get some fresh air. Heading out through the bar's doorway, John passed through the reception area, where, much to his surprise, Rip and Riley jumped down from their perch at the bay window and accompanied him out the door.

"Have you two ever had enough?" John asked, but they had trotted on ahead.

John had initially thought about walking back up the entrance driveway to see what lay within the trees along the higher eastern edge of the property. But as he was crossing the parking area, heading for the stone-walled drive, he noticed Bill standing over by the paddock, behind the stables, one foot resting on the lowest rung of the fencing while folded arms, positioned on the top rail, supported his chin. John decided to stroll across, and when more of the pasture came into view, as he rounded the side of the stables, he could see that Bill was idly watching Eddie, who was making repairs to some of the ranch-style fencing on the far side of the paddock area.

"Penny for your thoughts," John offered as he approached Bill, whose attention seemed to be far away.

"I was remembering the simple things of life, John," Bill responded. "Remembering them and wondering if they went away with age or just went away. Recognizing that you lose sight of many, many things along the way. And if they resurface by chance decades later, it makes the era rush back to you in a wave and makes you wonder where it all went—all those experiences."

John rested himself against the railing, and the two gazed out at the grazing, tail-swishing horses. The sun was still relatively high but declining slowly toward the western tree line. John reasoned that Bill would continue with his thoughts in his own time.

"I was thinking of the summer afternoons and especially evenings I knew as a child—running free in the fields of the countryside in days that seemed to go on forever. When my parents would have to come outside as night fell and call for us to come in for bed, we never wanted sleep. But as soon as our weary, unshowered heads hit the pillow, we would be out for the count until we arose, seemingly with the sun, to join our friends outside again for another day of adventure. Where have those days gone, John? Is there a video game or an app to substitute for those days?"

John nodded but remained quiet.

"And I had wondered whatever happened to the ice-cream man. Whatever happened to the excitement of children on a summer afternoon when they heard those magical notes from the approaching van? How can something so relatively simple as an ice cream have been so wonderful—and have disappeared without anybody noticing? Maybe I should buy an old truck for my collection and go around the town in the dog days of summer."

"But at least here at the inn you have tried to recapture some of the things that have been lost along the way. It is a good place, Bill, a relaxing place where life can be enjoyed. That must mean something when you think back."

"I hope so. I mean I hope some aspects have been recaptured." Bill paused before continuing with his original line of thought. "I believe that many experiences are lost along the way, but if you can remember times, then maybe you haven't really lost them—it is the things that you cannot recall that are lost and you will not get back. So I do try to remember."

They watched Eddie toiling away with the fencing for a while.

After a minute Bill continued with his musings. "It's strange, really. As I look back and try to remember times, I understand very much how

I value the simple things that I was allowed to repeat over and over. Some people have a constant desire for new experiences, to not repeat what they have already seen or done. But if the truth be told, John—I have such fond memories of going to the same places or running the same errands with somebody I truly loved. At the time I thought nothing of those repetitions, but now I recognize the great comfort I get from repeating the same thing with people I love and don't want to let go of—because, you see, if I can keep doing that thing, then I don't have to let go. And there are times that I have never wanted to let go of, John. Times that I wanted to last forever. When I do eventually have to stop, when I recognize I have done something for the last time, then it leaves an ache that saddens me immensely. I look back, and the times have gone, and they cannot be re-created."

Again they were quiet before John spoke. "What sort of things, Bill?"

"The most mundane things, John. Repeating the same everyday tasks or visiting the same unexciting places. Breakfast at the same diner or carrying out the same errands week after week. The repetition creates familiarity and a lasting connection—a connection that you know is in your loved ones' memory just the same. Like camping with David, John. You know you cannot do it forever, but treasure it while you can. How do I know? Because Brenda bemoaned having to drive the kids here, there, and everywhere, for years and years, couldn't wait until she didn't have to anymore. And cried the day Jill got her driver's license and cried again the day she left for college because she had nobody left who depended on her. Brenda didn't know how much she would miss those little interactions."

"How about you? Did you cry?" John asked.

"I didn't cry then—I cried alone many years earlier, when I understood that inevitably they would grow up and go to college."

John nodded an understanding.

"I recognize what you are saying about appreciating the people you have around you through your life and appreciating the time you get to spend with them. I know it will never be long enough. There are too many people I didn't keep in touch with over the years and have no idea how their lives turned out."

After a pause, John asked, "Are there specific things that you regret not having done or seen?"

"I have never really subscribed to any sort of bucket list, if that is what you are asking. I have never been somebody who thought they should be doing more. Have never debated whether or not my life should be more exciting," Bill replied, before adding, "I know when I am contented, and that is enough for me. Sometimes I have heard comments that the inn is very pleasant but 'there is nothing to do.' And sometimes I have reflected that 'nothing to do' can be a good thing."

"I don't believe that it is how much you do in your life that is important, Bill—it is how much you enjoy what you are doing," John replied.

Eddie had finished his repairs and came around to join his audience.

"Was it damaged by the storm, Eddie?" John asked.

"I don't think so. Just a couple of cracked rails, maybe the horses got boisterous, but all fixed. And how was the MG, John? Take you back?"

John smiled broadly. "It was great. Noisy and bumpy and exhilarating—and refreshing with the roof down. I could take today every day."

"But you are heading south tomorrow?" Eddie asked.

"Have to really, Eddie. Have to get ready for some work next week."

"Bill tells me that you are a sportswriter. Sounds like a good way to earn a living. Are you off to some event?"

"Getting ready for the start of the football season in a couple of weeks—doing a historical piece about the ninetieth season—going back through the decades."

"You sound like Bill now, looking back to earlier days," Eddie commented.

"I suppose sports are a barometer to other aspects of life," John said thoughtfully, "inasmuch as I wish that sports were as unspoiled as they used to be. I know it is one trend that cannot be reversed, but sports were something to behold when they were pure."

"Many things were," Eddie agreed.

"Money spoils many things," Bill lamented, "and I have never really seen the reverse happen. Money and greed spoil things—but if the money goes away, if the money deserts, then the old 'unspoiled' times do not return—instead, the endeavor fades into ruin."

"But we have it good, and heaven knows, money won't spoil us," Eddie joked. "I am off to get the evening ready before Annie gets upset."

"Thanks, Eddie," Bill replied, easing himself off the fence rails. "You are right. Let's grab a beer before dinner, John, and you can tell me where you went in the MG."

Three older men strolled back to the inn after an afternoon's toil in the fields.

When he took the dogs out late that evening, when he was alone with his thoughts below the vast sky, Bill recalled what John had said about trying not to lose sight of the people of your life. During the last few years, Bill had often thought back to all the people he had met at various times in his life, both people he had befriended or simply casual acquaintances. There must have been thousands during the many years, and he would sometimes wonder what had ever become of all those people. How had their intertwined lives turned out, if life had gone the way of their hopes? There was no way to ever know, but Bill worried that many of those people had not lived the lives they had envisaged in their youth, when their lives were all before them—that life had not lived up to the dreams of youth. Life was always so promising during the formative years, everything within reach, but thirty-plus arrived, and the future evolved into existence and the handing over of their hopes to the children. He lamented that more people could not chose a course for their lives rather than realize too late that the dream had gone.

There was an unwillingness on the parts of both John and David to motivate themselves the following morning. Neither acknowledged the fact, but both were a little reluctant to leave a place they had happened on by pure chance and where they had remained for fewer than three days. But eventually, after a full and drawn-out breakfast, David packed up their Jeep, and the two were ready to head out.

David fussed over Rip and Riley while John said his good-byes.

"All being well, I think that both of us will be back over Christmas, Bill," John said, shaking Bill's hand firmly. "You have a good place here. I don't want to analyze why, but it is a good place."

"Anytime you want to drop in—both of you—you are very welcome. I think you know that it's good to know that people understand the inn and enjoy a little of what Yesterday is trying to create."

"Thanks, Bill," David added as he shook hands. "Appreciate the genuine hospitality. Take care of these two."

"And don't forget to switch your phone back on," Bill called as they headed down the flagstones of the front pathway to the small parking lot.

Part 2: Winter Peace

CHAPTER 11

Fall Returns

ABOUT A MONTH AFTER JOHN and David had left the inn, fall came back. This was the time of year that Bill looked forward to. During the hot days of summer, it was sometimes difficult to believe that the perfect, crisp days of autumn would return. But invariably the temperature dropped into the sixties, the forties at night, and the panorama of green around the inn started to transform daily, into a spectacle of every shade of yellow, red, orange, and brown. Bill loved to sit out on the deck when the light winds blew and watch the leaves swirl across and eventually fall to carpet the pasture and the roofs of the stables and barn. The falling leaves were delightful, but Bill recognized that they were also nature's timer, indicating that this perfect period of the year would not last forever. Eventually the trees would be bare, signposting that winter was allowed to start.

The near-unchanging days of summer had given way to the always varying days of fall. Bill enjoyed opening the windows throughout the inn and letting the fresh air blow through without the discomfort of humidity. He was well aware that the period between too humid and too chilly would not last for many weeks, but while it did, he appreciated the fall fragrances drifting through the inn. Lying awake in bed listening to the sounds of the nights was another pleasure that the open windows of autumn brought, even if it did mean needing an extra blanket against the dawn chill. The wide polished-with-wear floorboards of his bedroom, which had seen well over a century of falls arrive, were getting cold to his feet as he rose on the now-darkening mornings.

A flock of passing Canadian geese called in for a few days, as they had during the last few Octobers. Bill never knew exactly what they were eating, but they spent some six days pecking around in the pasture. The geese were mildly interesting to the horses, which didn't seem to mind sharing their pasture with the visitors, but provided a great deal of enjoyment for Rip and Riley. The two dogs would watch the geese for long periods, either from the inn deck or the distant cottage patio, and then simultaneously decide that it was time to give chase. The dogs never grew tired of the long sprint across the pasture, the geese reluctantly taking flight in plenty of time, and then the weary trot back to the inn or cottage to collapse, satisfied that they had done their job of protecting the property—as the geese landed to return to their pecking.

The other birds that were a barometer to Bill were the crows. Bill assumed that they must be around throughout the year, but it was only after the trees had completed their majestic display of colors that he noticed them again. The trees on the rim, surrounding the basin in which the inn nestled, appeared as pencil etchings against the pale-gray skyline now, and it was primarily around these trees that the crows circled and cawed through the late fall days. The crows' cries seemed to Bill to be a clear sign that bleak days were on their way while the newly visible crows' nests in the tree silhouettes, which Bill supposed were now abandoned, made it apparent that another summer had passed.

The pale autumn sun returned and always caused Bill to reflect, often with a sense of sadness. The weak October sun cast increasingly long afternoon shadows as the horses and riders crossed the pasture. The sun was low and orange now, with no real heat anymore, and it invariably created remembrances of autumns past for Bill: remembrances of sporting events, including his own son's soccer and football games, taking place on fields no longer lush green but more khaki colored and lashed with those same long afternoon shadows as the athletes ran around. They were pleasant afternoons to be savored before the cold winters blew in. Games were recalled not for the result or the intensity, but remembered for the pleasure of being outside on such a fall day, for cherishing the crisp fresh air and recalling all those young people… but young no more!

And then there was Halloween. This year Annie's son, Alan; his wife, Sam; and daughter, Tess, came to stay for ten days, and they took it upon themselves to head up the decorating efforts. Annie's granddaughter Tess, at seven years old, was just the right age to appreciate the fun and imagination of the Halloween festivities. Together they decorated both the outside and inside of the inn and then created an old graveyard up toward the barn. Sam and Tess carved out a lot of pumpkins and placed the jack-o'-lanterns around the inn and the various outbuildings. Eddie helped transform the isolated, unoccupied cottage into a haunted house while the girls who kept their horses at the stables prepared a hay ride using Eddie's small tractor, a wagon that one of the local farmers lent them with bales of straw, destined for the horses' winter feed, as seats. During the last two weeks of October, especially during the now-dark early evenings, Eddie would conduct rides around the property, both for families from the local community and the inn's guests, culminating in a visit to the derelict haunted house. The flames of the jack-o'-lanterns danced eerily on those dark, earthy, chilly evenings. Bill and Annie contributed with hot apple cider and donuts served out on the deck when the rides were over.

When Alan and Sam visited, they usually offered to help with the inn's breakfast on a couple of mornings during their stay, which allowed Bill to partake in one of his great pleasures—breakfast at the local diner. Bill could remember breakfast at the diner with his mother and father, as a boy, and the feeling of enjoyment and comfort had never left him. So whenever Alan and Sam offered to help Annie at the inn, Bill and Eddie drove into town at around seven thirty and spent a good hour and a half appreciating the simplicity of a diner breakfast, including the endless coffee, as they sat either in one of the diner's booths or sometimes up at the counter. They spoke very little during these outings—both being content to read the newspaper, take their time over the meal, and enjoy the ambiance. Bill would have to take some abuse from Molly, the owner of the diner, regarding the fact that he had to get away from the inn to get a decent breakfast.

After the festivities of Halloween, the local area, like the rest of Vermont, was making the final preparations for the imminent ski season. Although the inn was not next to any of the ski mountains and was not advertised as any sort of ski lodge, Bill did recognize that many of his guests came to the area to ski, and he tried to accommodate their needs. A few years ago, Eddie had incorporated a large, sturdy shed onto the exterior wall on the far side of the barn. The lean-to shed was painted the same dark red to blend into the barn, and guests were welcome to store their skis and other paraphernalia in the shed, not heated but safe from the elements. The other requirement that Bill had quickly been made aware of was the need for a warm area to dry the never-ending layers of clothing in readiness for the next day on the slopes. To solve that dilemma, Eddie had constructed wooden drying racks down in the basement, close to the always-running boiler. Guests simply laid all their damp clothing, especially gloves it seemed, on the racks, and by the next morning, everything had dried a little stiffer but ready to go through the same ordeal again. Bill liked the skiers. After energetic days on the slopes, the children would generally fall into well-deserved sleep soon after dinner, and the adults would enjoy drinks and good conversations well into the evening around the blazing log fireplace in the bar.

Thanksgiving marked the end of Bill's favorite season and ushered in the beginning of winter and the six weeks of holidays. Bill did like Thanksgiving. In his eyes, it remained a peaceful time and the holiday least spoiled by commercial interests. But as much as he appreciated Thanksgiving, he did lament the passing of another fall. It would be nine months before the leaves would blow across the pastures again.

CHAPTER 12

The Holidays at the Inn

BY THE TIME THANKSGIVING ARRIVED, Bill's guests comprised a mixture of some skiers but also many people who liked observing the wintry landscape from within the warm confines of the inn. From mid-November until early January, the menu at the inn changed to more of a holiday fare, and an increasing number of the guests seemed to return year after year to experience a holiday devoid of the incessant clamor that they simply could not avoid had they stayed at home. Thanksgiving Day and the weekend were marked by a lot of overeating, afternoons and evenings relaxing and drinking around the log fire in the bar, football on the library TV for those who wanted, and walks around the property in an attempt to work up an appetite for the next meal. In addition to some guests returning each year, Bill was pleased to see that some families were arranging mini reunions at the inn over the holidays. Older parents seemed to especially appreciate their busy grown-up children taking the time to spend Thanksgiving together. Bill's own two children came to stay for the long Thanksgiving weekend. Jill drove all the way up from Florida with her boyfriend, while Stephen and his wife made the long trek across from California.

There was intentionally no sign of Christmas or any Christmas decorations until at least a week after Thanksgiving had passed. John arrived back at the inn a week after Eddie hung the first twinkling Christmas lights.

John had completed and submitted the articles that he had been working on and let the various publications that he worked with know that he would be away, and out of touch, until early January. He had booked a room for almost three weeks, arriving on a cold Saturday afternoon in December before the inn had seen its first real snow. He paused as he reached the top of the driveway and got out of the car, as he and David had on their first visit, as if to reacquaint himself with the surroundings. The inn looked somehow cozier now. In the quickly fading winter daylight, the yellowish lights, showing through many of the inn's windows, glowed warm and invitingly. There was smoke curling away from three of the chimneys, and a light breeze bore the comforting smell of wood fires up the hill toward John. Further back at the stables, John could make out a couple of horses' heads poking out above the half doors, with periodic streams of warm breath blowing out into the chilly air. The most noticeable difference to John, compared to his first view of the property, was the bareness of the trees standing out charcoal black against the wintry gray skyline. John jumped back into the car and headed down.

As he approached the front door with his bags, John could see two familiar faces peering out from the bay window of the reception hall.

"Good to have you back," Bill greeted from the doorway into the bar as John was closing the front door behind him. Rip and Riley had jumped down, wagging their tails in recognition.

John patted the dogs and shook hands with Bill. "Glad to be here. Looking forward to a couple of restful weeks."

"And how is young David?" Bill asked as he went behind the reception desk.

"Fit and well, thanks. He is working for another full week, then going to stay with his mother over Christmas before coming up here to join me for four nights over the New Year."

John filled in the registration book while Bill picked out the room key.

"I have you in room seven—has a nice view out of the back," Bill said, handing the key to John. "Otherwise nothing much has changed. Dinner any time after about five thirty—hopefully the menu is a little more festive than in the summer."

"Looking forward to it, Bill. I'll unpack, relax a little, and see you later for a beer."

"Enjoy," Bill called back as he and the dogs headed toward the kitchen to offer help if Annie needed it.

The menu was very seasonal now. Besides turkey there was goose, roast pork, duck, and baked ham on the menu, with other daily specials written on a chalkboard. The vegetables had also adapted to the season, including sweet potatoes with cranberries and brussel sprouts, but John was happy to see that the peas remained.

The restaurant was noticeably busier than had been the case on their unexpected visit in August. The majority of the diners seemed to be inn guests, but there were also a number of couples and a larger party that arrived just for dinner. John reasoned that in the summer, many of the inn guests would venture farther afield for dinner, but now that the early nights of winter had arrived, there would be a tendency to stay close for the evening. Likewise the bar had more customers and was louder with much conversation. After a dinner that included the pork and some bread pudding, John sat up at the bar and joined in a conversation with Eddie and various other guests who were winding down their day.

It was almost eleven o'clock before Annie and Bill, accompanied by another woman, emerged from the kitchen for the last time.

"I'll wrap up here, Eddie, if you want to see Helen to her car and then walk up with Annie," Bill said, settling on one of the bar stools.

"Suits me, Bill. Most folks have finished, just John here and those guests finishing off their wine," Eddie said, nodding to a couple sat over by the fire. "Would you like a drink before I wrap up?"

"I'll take a glass of Malbec, please, Eddie. Do you want a top off, John?"

"Just a touch more of the Pinot Grigio, please," John replied, sliding his glass across the bar.

Once Eddie and the two women had ventured out into the near-freezing December night, Bill and John sat and caught up a little. Bill explained that during the two-month holiday period, things got a little too busy for Annie, Eddie, and him to handle, so there were a few women from the town who came out to help on an alternating schedule, normally two each day. There had been two ladies earlier, but Helen had stayed on late to help Annie finish off in the kitchen and get a few things ready for breakfast, which would arrive all too quickly.

"So what do you have planned for two full weeks up here, John?"

"If it's OK with you, I plan to spend time really getting to grips with writing a book that I have been dabbling with for over three years now."

"Why do you say if it is OK with me?" Bill asked.

"Because it means sitting and working on my laptop for hours at a time—not quite your preference," John replied, smiling.

Bill laughed. "You know that I have no problem with computers as such, only what they are used for. Writing and similar activities are what computers should be used for, in my mind, and I wouldn't ever suggest that people shouldn't use them to make their lives easier or more productive. It is the addiction to the Internet, social media, and endless games that computerization has created that I try to discourage. The addiction and isolation. But I don't live under the illusion that I can prohibit people from using the Internet and everything that goes along with the 'net'—I just don't actively encourage it."

"I know. I was only joking with you," John replied, grinning back at Bill.

"So what is this book about, John? If you have been working on it for three years, you must be well along by now."

"Well, you can probably guess that the central theme of the book is sports," John replied, "but my vision for the book, the intent really, has changed a lot since I started the project."

"In what way?"

"When I started out, my thinking was that I would write a book recounting episodes from my thirty-odd years writing about the world of sports and sports figures. But my thinking started to transform more into what I think sports represents, should represent, and the lessons that can be learned from sports."

"What changed, John?"

"In a nutshell, golf's British Open earlier this year happened, and I have not been able to shake the impression that it left on me. Writing about sports has always been a pleasure. I saw the trials and tribulations of life through sports and could see that hard work, dedication, skill, and playing the game 'the right way' often resulted in just and deserved outcomes. There seemed to be a fairness, and life seemed to be reflected in sports—and the story eventually had the correct outcome. But that changed for me in the Open this year. 'They' got the story line wrong, for the first time that I can remember, at the British Open—and 'they' were not fair to Tom Watson. So the latter part of my book is trying to portray how close we came to seeing the most unlikely result in the history of sports, in my opinion. It was a convergence of circumstances that I really doubt we will ever come close to seeing again—in my lifetime or anybody else's lifetime, for that matter. Maybe I just want to bring people's attention to that week in history—for people to know how close we came to seeing the impossible. Do you remember it?"

"I remember well. Even though I am not normally glued to the television, I can remember watching the closing holes early on that Sunday afternoon."

"After we visited the inn last summer, I got to thinking that deep down, the reason I was rooting for Tom on that day was maybe, just maybe, it was a last glance back at the halcyon days of the seventies and eighties. Yes, I am biased, but I do have fond recollections, especially of tennis and golf from those decades, memories of the characters and the rivalries. But I do wish we could have seen it—what Tom almost achieved would never have been bettered, or equaled, in any sporting field."

"It sounds like a book worth reading, when you get it finished."

"If I could write my feelings, it would be easy," John reflected.

"Isn't that the truth?" Bill replied.

By now the wine drinkers who had been sitting by the fireplace had finished their drinks and bade Bill and John a good-night as they headed upstairs.

"What else do you have planned, besides progress on the book?" Bill asked as he went over to the coffee table by the fire to collect their glasses.

"Looking forward to an enjoyable Christmas at the inn, a calm Christmas, I suppose. And I am hoping to see the inn after a nice snow-fall. I imagine it to be a very picturesque setting," John replied.

Bill was behind the bar putting the glasses in the small dishwasher and wiping down the bar and other surfaces. "It will be a good time, John, peaceful and, yes, calm. You should go with Eddie in a couple of days to get the tree for the entrance hall. He would appreciate the help."

"Sounds good. But what about the snow? Any signs of that in the forecast?"

"We have had some light snow showers, maybe an inch or so, but nothing that has stayed for more than a day or two," Bill responded as he sat back on the bar stool to finish his wine. "But, according to the forecast in the paper at least, colder temperatures are definitely on their way."

"It feels cold out there tonight. It was hovering around freezing when I arrived."

Bill looked out of the restaurant windows into the blackness of the December night. "Yes, I would say that it is cold enough for snow—if the precipitation comes."

After a few moments staring out into the darkness, Bill continued as if thinking aloud. "It was a December night like this that finally steered me toward the inn, John."

"In what way?" John asked.

CHAPTER 13

Lonely People

"It was eight years ago," Bill said thoughtfully. "A bitterly cold night in early December, and I had been working late at our office in the city. I used to alternate between taking the train and driving into work, depending on the weather and how late I thought that I might work—I didn't always like being dictated to by a train schedule.

"On this particular day, I had the car with me, and at around seven in the evening, I eased out of the parking garage into the dark night streets. There were a good number of people around, but they were all well wrapped up and walking briskly with heads bowed, trying to avoid the chilling wind blowing through the canyons. There were no people out strolling on that evening. My intention was to make my way across town to the West Side Highway and then take my route north to the suburbs and the sanctuary of my house in Connecticut. I had been commuting into the city for years, and up until that evening, I had been fortunate enough never to have any car problems. But on this occasion, while nipping through a poorly lit, narrow cross street, I didn't see a bad pothole and managed to damage my front passenger-side tire—blew it out.

"I had no alternative but to pull over and, having surveyed the damaged tire and weighed my alternatives, proceeded to change the wheel. The cold was biting, making the exercise all the more miserable and exacerbating every element of an operation that did not go smoothly. I had managed to position the jack, slacken the nuts on the wheel, and was about to take the car's weight on the jack when a man crossed the poorly lit street and asked if I needed any help. He looked a little unkempt, and although he did have a grubby-looking lightweight jacket, he was clearly underdressed and feeling the bitter cold. I confess that I was a little nervous of the man, because of his appearance, and skeptical of his motives, but I did need help, so I thanked him and accepted his offer.

"Between the two of us, we managed to change the wheel reasonably efficiently—the man appeared to be more familiar with tools than I was, which isn't saying too much. And when it came time to lift the wheels off and back on again, the stranger insisted on doing that part so as not to ruin my clean clothing. I remember him remarking, 'Mine cannot get any dirtier than they already are—no point in you getting yourself messed up.' When I thought about it later that night, it saddened me that a person should view himself in that way.

"Anyway, once we had changed the wheel, and thrown the damaged one in the trunk, I thanked him sincerely. I remember feeling very uncomfortable, not wanting to offend the man by assuming that he didn't have any means, but in the end asked him if I could buy him a coffee or something to eat. He turned to me and nodded acknowledgment, his eyes smiling, replying that something warm to eat and drink would 'mean the world to me.' I knew that there was a small diner at the end of the block, so I took the chance of leaving the car parked there on the street. I could never understand the street parking rules, but it wasn't apparently blocking any traffic, so we left it there and walked briskly down to the corner."

Bill paused to take a sip of Malbec. "That stranger, who helped me so willingly on a cold December night, was Eddie, and it was that night that caused a number of vague plans to start to germinate in the following weeks. Having reached the diner, we took a table by the window and gladly accepted the coffee offered by the waitress, to help thaw us out, while looking through the menu. Eddie settled on a cup of soup and a Philly cheesesteak, if I remember correctly. But what I remember very well was the very enlightening conversation over the next hour or so. Eddie explained that yes, he was technically homeless but had a small room at the back of a homeless shelter on the west side of the city. He helped out at the shelter, performing various repairs and chores in exchange for a regular bed in what was technically a storage room at the shelter.

"The initial discomfort and uncertainty that I felt talking to a homeless person was quickly eased as I spoke to Eddie. After only a few minutes, I recognized that he was a regular guy who had fallen on hard times as opposed to my subconscious fear of somebody suffering from various forms of substance abuse. He spoke well and intelligently and, despite his appearance, kept himself as clean and presentable as his circumstances permitted."

"How had he come to be down on his luck?" John asked.

"What I learned that night, and what has remained with me over the years, is just how quickly somebody's fortunes can change and how difficult it can be to reverse life's direction once it is heading in a downward spiral. Eddie had been raised in Brooklyn, did well in school, and went to college, studying architecture, among other things. He worked for several small construction companies before getting married in his late twenties and moving up to a small town in southern Connecticut, where he started his own general contracting company. Things were going well with Eddie's company and his life in general until he maybe tried to take a step too early or too fast. The housing market was booming, and Eddie took the opportunity to buy a plot of vacant land in the adjacent town, intending for his construction company to build a house and cash in on the housing boom.

"As you might have guessed, a number of events combined to cause his entrepreneurial project to run into problems. From what Eddie told me, there were problems with the initial permitting, the plot preparation was more extensive than expected, the cost of borrowing proved more expensive than Eddie had anticipated, but the most damaging by far was that the housing market dipped significantly about six months before Eddie's company was ready to complete the house. When all was said and done, Eddie emerged from the project with substantial debt, as opposed to the hoped-for profit, and the ensuing money troubles accelerated problems in Eddie's marriage. Six months later, Eddie was divorced, and part of the settlement entailed selling his own house. Somehow he ended up with a fraction of their assets but all the construction company's debt. The downward spiral had started and was difficult to arrest.

"By now Eddie's parents had retired down to the Carolinas, but nevertheless he gravitated back to Brooklyn, where he could live more modestly than up in Connecticut. For the next ten years or so, Eddie lived in a small apartment and made a living working as a subcontractor for various building and contracting firms in the Brooklyn area. He managed to make ends meet, but a combination of the opportunities in Brooklyn not being as lucrative as in the more prosperous Fairfield County area of Connecticut, coupled with the debt that persisted from the collapse of his own company, resulted in Eddie never being able to get ahead. He was in his late forties now, his life had stalled, and he was becoming resigned to never getting his own company and independence back again.

"And then Eddie was dealt another blow, this time not of his making whatsoever. While working on the job site of a small apartment complex, Eddie was badly injured in an accident involving a partial collapse of scaffolding. He ended up with severe internal bleeding and a collapsed lung in addition to a broken leg and badly twisted knee. When all was said and done, Eddie was unable to work for almost eight months, by which time he had lost his apartment and had substantial unpaid medical bills. Yes, the construction company did have insurance but not sufficient to make up for his inability to work or his long-term recuperation. He did manage to rent a single room for a while, but he struggled to find regular work after he was fit and well again, and the debt that had accrued was becoming crippling. Eventually he had to give up the rented room, and without any fixed address, his prospects for any work, and his life in general, deteriorated very quickly."

When Bill paused, John asked, "Were Eddie's parents still alive? Could they help?"

"His father had died about six years previously, after Eddie's divorce but while he was still making ends meet in his apartment in Brooklyn. His mother had stayed down in the Carolinas; he went down to see her fairly regularly when he was doing all right. But after the accident, he didn't want to burden her with his problems, didn't want to admit to her how bad things had become—a long way around saying that he was too proud to tell her the truth. Eddie told me that he did tell her that he had been hurt, but not the severity or that he had been unable to work for such a long time and had lost his apartment. As things got worse for Eddie, his calls to his mother became infrequent and his visits nonexistent."

"So he ended up in a homeless shelter in the city," John observed.

"When he could no longer afford the rented room, he did live on the streets for a few weeks. It was early summer, so although he still couldn't believe how far he had fallen, or comprehend how he had been unable to stop it, at least the temperatures were bearable on the street. Eddie said that he learned his way around the vagrant existence remarkably quickly, and over the course of the next few weeks, he went to a number of homeless shelters, initially for something to eat but occasionally for a place to sleep as well, on nights when it looked like rain. Eventually he gravitated toward the shelter where he was now staying and, after a few weeks, found that, with his skill set, he could help out the people running the shelter and, in return, could get just a little stability to his existence."

"You said that vague plans started to germinate after your chance encounter with Eddie?"

"I knew that I was increasingly yearning for the life that I used to know, wanted to find some peace of mind, as I tried to describe to you last summer. And in the days after my encounter with Eddie, the idea of doing something about it started to really take root, and the notion of selling up and buying an inn, or something along those lines, somewhere off the beaten track, grew. The more I thought about it, the more real-istic and possible it seemed, and the more excited I became. Maybe sub-consciously my meeting with Eddie, even though I didn't really know him from Adam, got me to thinking that if I ventured out, I wouldn't necessarily have to do it on my own, that there could be other people who would want to start afresh."

"How did you keep in touch with Eddie—guessing he didn't have a cell phone?" John asked.

"After we had finished eating in the diner that night, I thanked Eddie for his unsolicited help and wrote down my cell number if I could ever be of help to him. I also asked him the name of the shel-ter where he was living; in case something came to mind later that I thought could help him out in some way. At that stage, I had made up my mind that I wanted to make a change to my life, to try to create a lifestyle that would bring me contentment, but had not crystallized my thinking as to exactly what direction to choose. During the next six weeks or so, I put a lot of thought into which path I wanted to take, and the idea of an inn, somewhere in New England at that stage, ger-minated and grew.

"By the end of January, my mind made up, I got to thinking through the more detailed aspects of my plan. Obviously, I knew a lot about build-ings and how they can be renovated and modified, but actually doing the work is more of a mystery to me. And my mind turned to Eddie, his skill set, and how I would need to have people to depend on in this venture. So in early February, I went down to the west side, found the shelter, and, after an hour or so, located Eddie—not having a surname made it a little difficult at first because there seemed to be a few Eddies. After I had reconnected with him on that first visit, we sat and talked for quite a while. I explained my general idea of trying to establish an inn, the thoughts of creating a haven from the complexities that everyday life had become, and asked him if he was interested in working on the project once I had found a property."

"He was excited?" John asked.

"At our first meeting, the ideas were maybe a little overwhelming for him. After all, I had been mulling over these things for a long time by that stage, so to spring it on Eddie was probably somewhat confusing. But by the time I met with him again the following week, he was definitely interested, and by the time the meeting was over, he was visibly excited—maybe he saw that I was serious, and he was allowing himself to hope a little. And by the time spring had arrived, we were traveling up to New Hampshire and here in Vermont to look at the three properties that I had narrowed it down to. We had made a decision by the end of May, and Eddie moved himself into a couple of rooms here at the inn in June—although in reality the move consisted of one small duffel bag. The house here had been unoccupied for about eight months, but Eddie got to work, quickly networked with various contractors in the immediate area, and by the fall the project was starting to take shape."

"And Eddie never went back?"

"He did actually go back with me one time in the late summer, just for a day. He had left the few papers that he had with a friend in Brooklyn, for safekeeping. We visited the shelter together—it was a little tough for both of us."

"Tough in what way, Bill?"

"Even though Eddie had been away from the shelter for only about three months, I could see that he didn't enjoy seeing where he had been living. Maybe he was a little embarrassed at seeing the surroundings that he had had to accept. But I did admire the fact that he took time to sit and talk with all the people whom he had come to know at the shelter. He showed a great deal of compassion that day—and was saddened and moved by their circumstances. And as for me, I got to spend a few more hours with some of the people whom I had met on and off during that spring. Only I sensed that they saw Eddie through different eyes now and were maybe just a little envious of him—wishing that they too could find a way out of their solitude and desperation. I wouldn't say they were resentful, but somewhat saddened. And I suppose that I also wished I could help more—there were a lot of good people in a sad place. But I knew that I couldn't realistically offer refuge to the homeless population of the city."

"When you say that they were good people, Bill, surely there were a fair number of 'not so good'?" John asked.

"Oh, without a doubt. I am very sure that they were not all angels and that many were directly responsible for the plight that they found themselves in. Some had got themselves straightened out, but many could not. However, the majority of those Eddie befriended in his time at the shelter had similar stories to his own downfall. I suppose it is only natural that, despite where you find yourself in this life, you tend to gravitate toward folks that you can relate to. I suppose they are the good people whom I was referring to, John. They definitely caused me to pause and reflect on a number of things I had never contemplated."

"About how fortunes change or about the reality of living a homeless life?"

"I don't claim to understand a lot about being homeless or a great deal about the obvious hardships that the people suffer. But I did gain some insights into a life that I had previously been very ignorant of. I am embarrassed knowing how little thought I had given to homeless people prior to my chance encounter with Eddie, and it did cause me to do some soul-searching."

"Insights about anything specific?"

"I suppose that my eyes were opened to the absolute despair that the homeless must feel every single day. Despair caused by being unwanted and unheard. Think about how much reassurance and comfort it brings to you knowing that somebody likes you, not necessarily loves you, but just likes you for the person you are—it gives you purpose and makes you feel warm inside. Being liked buoys your self-esteem. But these lonely people not only have nobody to like them—they could probably live with that—but what must it feel like to actually be disliked by the majority of people you meet, in reality be feared by almost everybody and, if truth be told, to know that to a large extent society wishes that you didn't exist, that you would somehow go away. And besides these souls being unwanted, I also recognized the dejection felt by decent people at not being able to express themselves. We all like to voice an opinion, to have our opinion considered, maybe not agreed with but at least considered. Well, try to imagine what it feels like to not only be unable to voice your opinion but not to even have somebody that you can just talk to, to confide in. You must feel so irrelevant. You have no opinion, no voice, no worth in a society that you were once a part of. Think how much that must hurt, John. Your mind and feelings haven't gone—only your prosperity."

"I admit that I have never seriously considered the plight of homeless people—ashamed to say. But you are right—I would agree the word that best describes my feeling is *fear*—I wouldn't say *dislike* but definitely *fear* because of my ignorance, I suppose."

Bill continued his thoughts. "In truth, people really don't want that much. They are told that they want a lot—need a lot. But what most people want in this life is to be happy, John, and although I believe people can be happy with very little, they cannot be happy without the respect of somebody and the thought that they will be missed when they pass. They want to be a memory to someone—even if only fleetingly. Nobody wants to die unremembered, John."

"Visualizing that last thought strikes a chord, thinking of how the dreams of a child can evolve into dying penniless, unremembered, and forgotten."

"The people I met were all proud people—people who, when they were young, had dreams, had hopes, had aspirations for their lives. None of those people would ever have thought that they would be living in poverty, maybe homeless, would be looking out at a world that was passing them by and that they were no longer a part of. But above everything else, John, I was looking at people whose parents had brought them into this world, had nurtured them as helpless infants, had had such hopes for their children, and never in those parents' wildest dreams would they have imagined that those little children would become forgotten by life—would be considered worthless to this world. How can it end that way? And the strange thing is, John, I came to realize that nearly all those poor and homeless people maybe felt sorry for themselves on occasion—but the sadness that overwhelmed them throughout their miserable days and nights was that they hadn't been able to make their parents proud. One man told me that when he dreamed, he would meet his mother again, as he remembered her from his youth. His mother would be watching him, and she would be proud of her baby boy—smiling and acknowledging, 'I am proud that you made it, son—thank you.' All he wanted in his lonely life was to make that dream a reality."

After pausing for a moment Bill added "If you only remember one thing John—just recall that they were all children once. And they were carefree."

"Was that why you brought Eddie up to the inn, Bill?"

"No, that wasn't the reason as such—but maybe one of the end results. At the time I needed trusted help, needed somebody who could move lock, stock, and barrel up to the wilds of Vermont, and Eddie and his expertise were a perfect fit. It was only in the ensuing years that I have come to realize how much the opportunity meant to Eddie and the profound effect it had on his life."

"Have any of Eddie's family or acquaintances from his previous life come up here to the inn?" John asked.

"Only Eddie's mother, John. About a year after we opened the inn, Eddie asked his mother if she would come up. She was elderly at that stage but still able to live on her own in the Carolinas. Eddie drove all the way down to collect her and bring her up to the inn. By that time, he hadn't seen his mother for over three years, and she spent ten memorable days with us in early May. A lovely lady. Although Eddie was happy to spend the time with his mother, again his pleasure was nothing compared to the joy and admiration that you could see in his mother's eyes. She had waited a long time. She came back again twice more, each time in May, for two-week stays, until she got too old to make the long trip. I never met a more contented person—just contented being with her son."

"You mentioned the effect that it had on Eddie's life—I assume you mean more than the obvious and tangible changes," John said.

"It has been a very fulfilling relationship for both Eddie and me, John, but maybe the best insight into what it has truly meant to Eddie was revealed when his mother passed away. Eddie's mother died about two years ago now. I sat with him late into the evening after he had been given the news. He wept like a young child. Wept without inhibition. But not sobbing, just letting tears roll down his face. When I tried to console him, he explained that he wasn't saddened because his elderly mother had passed away but because he realized how close he had been to not letting her die proud of her only son. I sat and thought it through and recognized how devastating it must be for somebody to have to live with the knowledge that a parent who loved them so dearly had died not being proud of their child. The parent deserves to be proud—we all deserve to be proud of our children and not to have to worry that they will not fare well in this world. Pride is a very strong emotion, one of the strongest. A child, no matter how old, wants to make his only mother proud because that is the only way that child can truly thank their mother. No, Eddie wept because he had made his mother proud at the end there—and he was eternally grateful to me for enabling it. It made my life, John, made me thankful for what I had unknowingly brought to good people."

CHAPTER 14

Silent Night

THE HOLIDAY PREPARATIONS WERE AN enjoyable time.

John and Eddie, along with Rip and Riley, went to get the Christmas tree for the front hall a couple of days later. It turned out that Eddie was a strong proponent of cutting down his own tree, so the two went over to a tree farm about five miles away and spent an hour tramping across a large, desolate field and through the forest of conifers, chain saw in hand, before Eddie found his perfect tree. Once they had felled their prey, the two hunters threaded the sturdy rope, which Eddie had had the foresight to bring along, through the lower branches, and together they dragged it back toward their old SUV truck, the dogs leading the way. The ground was frozen hard, making the crossing of the deeply furrowed field a lot easier than it would otherwise have been, and by the time they reached the truck, the light snow, which had been covering the tree's branches and making it look very seasonal, had all been shaken off. One of the farmhands helped them tie their catch on to the roof of the truck, estimated the height of the tree, and charged Eddie accordingly.

Once they arrived back at the inn, Bill and Annie came outside to check the tree and gave their nodded approval. The three men proceeded to manhandle their prize through the inn's front door and position it in the waiting stand right in front of Rip and Riley's bay window. Everybody seemed to have his or her designated roles in the tree's decoration through the afternoon. First Eddie trimmed the lower branches and splayed out the limbs where necessary after they had been tied down on the truck. Next Bill spent over two hours putting the many hundreds of lights throughout the tree, and finally it was Annie's job to carefully arrange ornaments on the branch tips, including some chocolate treats on the lower limbs for the younger guests. Eddie returned with the stepladder, as it was getting dark outside, to put a very simple angel atop, after which Bill performed a mini lighting ceremony. The tree provided all the illumination necessary for the entrance hall, with the exception of a small lamp on the reception desk for guests checking in. The glow from the tree and smell of freshly cut pine added to the warm and festive feel pervading the ground floor of the inn while the twinkling lights, shining through the bay window into the darkening December afternoons and evenings, invited those in the cold outside to come into the cozy comfort of the inn.

When the tree was all set, Bill placed a few wrapped presents underneath and explained to John that the guests were welcome, in fact encouraged, to place their gifts to friends and loved ones under the tree until Christmas day. "Most of the guests just put one or two gifts under the tree, and it makes for an enjoyable Christmas morning. The guests seem to respect the idea, and those with children include one or two packages under the tree, but doubtless the youngsters get additional gifts either in their rooms or even when they get back home. The growing number of wrapped mysteries of every shape and size, in the days leading up to Christmas, seems to bring joy to young and old alike. I have always believed that the pleasure derived from the anticipation is at least as great as that experienced by the occasion itself—probably greater. And the increasing pile is guarded faithfully by Rip and Riley, especially the small wrapped spherical ones that Eddie places under the tree."

John noticed a different daily routine than had been the case during the summertime, when the guests seemed to want to rise early and get on with their days. Now that daylight didn't creep in until around eight o'clock, the inn's days started later and at a noticeably slower pace.

Whenever John arose, sometimes as early as seven o'clock, there were already fires blazing away in the bar and library fireplaces, and the smells of baking bread and freshly brewed coffee permeated out of the kitchen area. Whereas in the summer, breakfast was generally a relatively quick meal as a means of getting to the main event, which was the day, now breakfast time was an occasion unto itself, including the browsing of the newspapers in the bar or library, accompanied by coffee, for an hour or so before even addressing the bacon, eggs, and other hot favorites.

After breakfast there did seem to be some midmorning efforts made to get at least a little exercise and fresh air. A number of guests took walks in the bracing cold, maybe as a means of working up an appetite for lunch. The younger guests liked to visit the stables to watch and help a little with the horses as they were fed, brushed, and ridden during the morning. By late morning the children remained outside with the horses, playing with Rip and Riley or generally enjoying the fact that they could roam free and unrestricted in what was a relatively safe environment, while the parents returned to the inn after their exertions.

Lunch was a relatively informal affair, more often spent in the bar area by the fire, frequently accompanied by eggnog laced with a little rum, whiskey, or sherry to ward off the cold. Then there were the board games that seemed to materialize in the library during the afternoons and evenings. John occasionally saw games of Monopoly, involving up to six players, stretch into a second day—with an audience at least as big as the number of players at times. The setting of the inn seemed conducive to Clue, and spirited games were often organized in the early evenings after dinner, involving old and young alike.

Bill put on a Christmas-themed movie in the TV room each evening and sometimes earlier in the afternoons if the darkening December days warranted staying in the warm confines of the inn. There was a mixture of the older classics such as *Miracle on 34th Street* and *A Christmas Carol*, combined with more modern films like *The Polar Express*, which Bill admitted to having a great liking for, and even the comedy favorite *A Christmas Vacation*. People didn't necessarily stay riveted to an entire movie but often came in and watched part of something that they had seen on countless occasions. The soundtrack of the movies, the background noise of chatter and laughter that accompanied the board games, and the well-fed conversation from the fireside of the bar combined to create a friendly and seasonal spirit, even for somebody on his own at Christmas. Bill, Eddie, Annie, and John all remembered and appreciated the atmosphere.

John's intention of dedicating his days to his writing came only partly to fruition. Yes, there was peace and quiet to focus on the task at hand, especially in his room, but John found that the temptation to simply relax, particularly during the afternoons, was difficult to resist. Bill put it down to John appreciating the ambiance of the inn and company of others there to relax. John put it down more to the eggnog that he found hard to resist at lunchtime.

"I must admit that I have not been as relaxed, and certainly not felt as guilt-free while relaxing, in a long while," John expressed to Bill as they were taking the dogs for a walk on a bright, crisp day three days before Christmas. "I am not sure if it is what you purposely set out to foster, but you have managed to achieve a little of the Christmas from yesteryear, Bill."

Bill smiled and nodded. "Thanks. To some extent, it is purposeful, but I feel that it is also what people want it to be." They walked on in silence for a minute or so.

"I have tried to create a peaceful and meaningful Christmas time," Bill said, "as opposed to a holiday preoccupied with how much we can give, receive, and spend. I have always liked the sentiment of peace and goodwill to all—it seems to me that is something to strive for. I understand that Christmas is a religious occasion, and really do appreciate the significance, but for myself I simply try to enable and promote an environment where people can reflect, relax, and appreciate life with family and friends—a celebration of the ending year. Relaxation is not laziness; it is something that we earn and should encourage."

Both were thoughtful for a short while.

"The commercialization and enticement that is the chaos of Christmas today is a good insight into what dismays me about life and the pace of living today," Bill continued. "I can remember the delight of Christmastime on those cold December days, when I was young enough to still believe, strolling through the lights of Main Street and looking mesmerized at the display windows of the shops. I can recall the pleasure I got as a child peering through those store windows with my mother. Peering at the treasures and dreaming of what might be. In my memories at least there would be snow on the ground. I know that I didn't have a care in the world then—but those times surely were magical, John. And later, when I grew up, one of the great satisfactions at Christmastime was to actually go Christmas shopping. I would go out, on a darkening, chilly afternoon, to find a specific gift for a loved one—whether it be a girlfriend, wife, mother, or children. There was a piece of jewelry or a special toy that you wanted to buy, and there was meaning in going out to buy something that pleased you and you knew would please those you cared for. Don't let your thinking get tainted by images of crowded malls and trying to buy an endless number of gifts to meet an unspoken obligation. Instead, remember when there were significant gifts for each of the people in your life, and saving up and buying those presents had meaning for you.

"Now Christmas shopping is to some extent considered to be a chore that has to be endured. In days gone by, you knew the gift that you wanted to buy, and mercifully you didn't have to physically or electronically search dozens of outlets to try to find the lowest price or decipher sales literature involving every percentage off under the sun. You didn't have the fear that somebody else was buying the same thing cheaper. It was buying meaningful gifts rather than a competition of how much you can buy for how little money. Today it has become so much about spending that the magic has all but disappeared for everybody but the very young—and by very young I would guess up until maybe six or seven."

Bill paused before continuing with his reflections. "The sheer amount of the spending is tough enough to grasp. But today people have so forgotten the pleasure and meaning of shopping that increasing numbers abdicate, do not even try to capture the magic, by resorting to trolling the Internet and simply pressing the purchase button countless times to accomplish their obligations. Pressing purchase buttons rather than peering through store windows on a winter afternoon—how can the excitement have been abandoned so completely? How can they have taken that joy away from us?"

"I recognize that Christmas has evolved into how much and how quickly people can spend money," John agreed, "and I have long mourned the simplicity of the season and the captivating times that we used to know."

"There are some who do not recognize what has been taken away from them, there are some who unfortunately have never known such happiness, and then there are some who probably are not bothered. But they should be bothered, John. They should be bothered because those times really were wonderful, and they can never be re-created."

"The times of brightly lit Main Streets and storefronts at Christmastime?"

"The times of strolling those streets at Christmastime with your mother, John. Or with your children. Those times have been taken away."

On Christmas Eve, Bill approached John in the morning to ask if he would mind taking Annie into town that night so that she could go to the carol service at the little church up on the hill. Bill explained, "Every year, Eddie and Annie make a point of going to the carol service together. It is something that means a lot to them from their younger days. But Eddie is getting over his cold and doesn't really want to be stifling sniffles in the hushed environment of the church while trying to sing carols. And although Annie wouldn't say anything, she either wouldn't go or, if she did, would not like it on her own."

"Would enjoy it very much, Bill. I haven't been to a carol service in a long, long time," John replied as he thought about just how long it had been. "I used to go as a boy, used to love it. But I lost it somewhere along the way. Must be forty years ago—with my mother and father when I was home from college. Life always seemed too hectic, at Christmas, after that. Didn't recognize that would be my last carol service—or that it would be the last time that I would go to church with my parents."

It was a cold night, hovering around freezing, with a three-quarters moon and patches of high clouds drifting slowly across the sky—which was no doubt being scrutinized by countless hopeful children as bedtime approached. When Annie and John got out of the Cherokee, in the small car park of the old stone-built church, their plumes of breath were clearly visible in the moonlit air. It felt like Christmas. John took Annie's arm as they crunched across the gravel and up to the ancient wooden doors of the church, the sound of organ music clearly audible even before the doors creaked open.

The carol service lasted about ninety minutes, and John relished the service and the atmosphere of the church—which must have experienced over two hundred such evenings. John didn't intend to liken the service to a concert, but he felt pleasure when some of the carols that he remembered from his youth were listed on the song sheet. He sang heartily through "Oh Come All Ye Faithful," "The First Noel," and was pleased that the service ended with his personal favorite, "Silent Night."

Walking back to the car, Annie remarked, "I do love the carol service, John. I only had my family for a relatively short time, and we didn't get to have many traditions. In fact, the carol service is the only one I can really remember now. But those were nice evenings that we had—and tonight is a nice memory of a time that seems long ago now."

All was calm. All was bright.

Christmas day itself was a good time.

The day definitely started a little earlier than had been the case during the immediately preceding days. It seemed that, regardless how old people got, there was still that little anticipation surrounding Christmas morning that remained, although unlike at home, no doubt, the guests did get dressed before coming downstairs. The morning involved present opening but not the frenzied, and seemingly continuous, activity that had become common in a lot of households. In its place was a rather calmer atmosphere and more genuine appreciation of the gifts received.

The bitter cold outside encouraged nearly everybody to stay indoors by the firesides after lunch, some reading Christmas gifts, some engaged in an impromptu game of Trivial Pursuit, while a number watched the Christmas film offering. John should have guessed that Bill's choice for the movie during the afternoon would be *It's a Wonderful Life,* before the black-and-white original actually started. The temperatures continued to fall through the afternoon, and the skies got grayer until nightfall brought the blackness of a winter night.

CHAPTER 15

Christmas Snow

DURING THE NIGHT THE SNOW came. The beautiful, quiet white snow.

When John awoke he had to squint as he peered out of his window at the pristine white blanket covering the pastures. The expanse of ground and the fact that the surface was absolutely undisturbed gave the appearance of a blue-white coloring as the snow sparkled under the rising sun. Looking at the covering on the roof of the stables and the rounded mounds on the fence posts, he judged that over nine inches had fallen through the night.

The sight of the snow was somehow exciting to John. It had always been the case since he had been a child, although he couldn't identify exactly why that was. He seemed to move a little quicker when snow first arrived—maybe there was a fear that it would melt away. Today was no different. He descended to the entrance hall, greeted Rip and Riley, and looked out of the front window with the two dogs, admiring the picturesque snow-covered scene. He was surprised to see that Ken and Steve, from the service station in town, were already busy plowing the driveway down from the road above. He was surprised because John did not expect that many people would be arriving or leaving for a few hours at least, but by the time he had finished a relatively quick breakfast, he understood that there would be quite a few visitors that day.

He sat drinking his third cup of coffee, watching the girls by the stables, who had just arrived to take care of their horses, and chatting to Bill as he busied himself to and fro with dishes and coffee.

"Here come the children," Bill said as he looked out of the window while clearing the table next to John.

John looked out in the direction of Bill's attention and could see three teenage children and half-a-dozen younger friends talking with Eddie and the girls by the doors on the shorter side of the stable building. Eddie directed the teenagers to one of the stable doors, from which they emerged after a few moments carrying a bale of straw between them. The children lifted the bale into a small pull cart that Eddie had returned with, and together they transported it through the snow, across the lower end of the pasture, to the far side of the paddock, well clear of the split-rail fencing. Once Eddie had shown them what to do, the children spent the next fifteen minutes bringing another six bales to the same location and lining them up, leaving gaps of about two feet between bales, so as to create a temporary wall at the base of the pasture.

The growing collection of assorted sleds in the area by the stables had revealed to John what the children's plan was. By the time sufficient hay bales were in place, the number of children of all ages had increased to around twenty, some being guests at the inn who were busy retrieving sleds, under Eddie's direction, from the ski shed at the side of the barn.

"Seems to be a well-rehearsed plan," John said to Bill, who had paused to watch the children make their first climb to the top of the pasture.

"Yes, the kids never seem to have enough of it—and Eddie enjoys organizing it for them. When all is said and done, they get plenty of exercise and fresh air."

John grabbed a jacket and gloves from his room before going out onto the deck to watch the fun. He was fascinated by the fact that no matter where along the top of the pasture the children started their descent, the contours of the snowy field funneled them down to the flatter area at the bottom, where they gently ran into the wall of hay. Bill, Rip, and Riley came out to join him for a while, and they watched the endless procession of children trekking up the hillside and listened to the shrieks of laughter as they sped back down, sometimes in a well-disciplined fashion and sometimes spinning out of control and tumbling off the sled or tube into the snow halfway down.

As they stood enjoying the spectacle, a few of the children's mothers came out onto the deck to set up a table along with mugs, plates, and all the trappings for hot chocolate. Ten minutes later two mothers brought out a large urn of the hot chocolate while Annie accompanied them with plates of hot cinnamon rolls and what smelled like freshly baked cookies. Bill helped himself to a cinnamon roll while one of the younger children, who had come down to seek help from her mother to thaw out her quickly numbing fingers, scampered back across to the base of the sled run to let her friends know that refreshments were on hand.

"Plenty of sugar here to keep their energy up," Bill joked.

"Do you provide the food and drink?" John asked.

"Not really. The parents all chip in and the mothers, and some fathers, more than help out in the kitchen getting these treats and then lunch ready for the famished children. And to be honest, quite a number of the families hang around for an early dinner as well, so the inn definitely doesn't lose out on these snow holidays. I actually love the simplicity of it all and watching the pleasure and excitement that they get from hurtling down a hill."

The routine of the morning continued for the next three hours. The children would sled for maybe forty-five minutes, take twenty minutes to rest and refuel, and then scamper back up the hill for more runs. The two dogs enjoyed the activities immensely. They would occasionally venture across to the area around the hay bales, although the depth of snow and their short legs meant that they had to hop rather than run. But for the majority of the time, they were happy greeting the children as they came back for hot chocolate and never tired of chasing the elusive snowballs the children threw for them, which inevitably disappeared into the snow.

After a lunch consisting mainly of grilled-cheese sandwiches, the crowd diminished a little, although there were a good dozen children who either remained on the slope or helped the girls in and around the stables. Some of the older children assisted Eddie with clearing up some of the assorted gear from the morning, although he left the hay out in the pasture. The remaining parents either helped out in the kitchen, clearing up from the morning's offerings and preparing for dinner, or gathered around the fireplace in the bar, relaxing with Bill, Eddie, and some of the inn's guests. The additional help in the kitchen allowed Annie to walk back up to her cottage for a couple of hours to take a break. It had been an enjoyable but long morning.

After the group in the bar had thinned out a little, Eddie busied himself restocking the woodpiles for both fireplaces and the large kitchen stove, all of which devoured large quantities on these busy cold days. He also kept an occasional eye on the remaining children to make sure they were not needing his help. Bill and John were left on their own seated by the crackling fire, which Bill was keeping well fed with logs.

"I meant to ask you, Bill, after I went to the carol service two nights ago, what did Annie mean when she said that she only had her family for a brief time?" John asked. "You told me a lot about how Eddie came to be up here to the inn, but you didn't really mention Annie."

"It was actually Eddie who knew Annie," Bill answered, "and to some extent, his and Annie's lives had a similar path. I'll explain how Annie joined us at the inn, but I will try to keep it a little shorter than when I recounted Eddie's story."

"I enjoy hearing about people's lives—people I have come to know."

"Well, Eddie knew Annie and her husband, Tim, from the time he went back to Brooklyn after his divorce. Annie and Tim owned a small diner-cum-luncheonette in the neighborhood where Eddie got his apartment, and he often went in there for meals, especially breakfast, when he was working. They had bought the diner three years earlier; she did most of the cooking while Tim took the orders, ran the counter, and generally dealt with the customers. They had a son, Alan, who must have been seven or eight at that time. About a year after Eddie first met them, Tim was involved in a terrible car accident early one Saturday morning. He was on his way home from the produce market, at around five thirty, and another guy was on his way home after a long night of partying. Tim died in the hospital, without ever regaining consciousness, which left Annie struggling to keep the diner and raise Alan on her own. You can probably guess some of the story from that point. Annie just couldn't manage to run the business by herself; she had to sell up and take different jobs over the years, cooking and waitressing, often working two jobs and late hours just to make ends meet. She did manage to keep their apartment and make a reasonably comfortable life for herself and Alan. But she couldn't really save anything, living from paycheck to paycheck. Eddie stayed in touch, regularly calling in to eat wherever Annie was working. Alan finished high school, and Annie, with the help of loans, even managed to put him through a decent college. By this time, Annie was in her midforties, Alan had his first job, albeit saddled with student loans, and Eddie had been injured in his accident. Annie could still find work without any real problem, but it seemed that the older she got, the class of the restaurants where the jobs could be found seemed to diminish year by year, and subsequently the take-home pay would shrink just a little. She was working longer hours and getting paid less. By the time Eddie found himself homeless, Annie was working as a cook at an Irish pub in Brooklyn and still living in her same apartment. Alan was working and living in Philadelphia, and although he always tried to support his mother, his resources were stretched because he was just starting out. Eddie feared that Annie's story could go the way of his own, at least to some degree, so when we started talking about needing to get a permanent cook and somebody to manage the kitchen, he immediately suggested Annie. And the rest is really history, so to speak."

"Annie was happy to move away from the city?" John asked.

"At the end of the day, the city had not been too kind to her. She was very happy to get a fresh start and another chance to build her life."

"She always seems to be happy."

"I think that she has found a home again. Somewhere where she feels appreciated and can look after people. I know that the occasional thank-you from a guest or an acknowledgment that a dish she has cre-ated is enjoyed means a lot to her."

"You mentioned that Alan and his family come to stay with her."

"Yes, they came up for Halloween," Bill replied. "He still lives in the Philadelphia area and has a good job with one of the large account-ing firms. Obviously Annie loves him and adores her granddaughter—they are trying to have another. But sometimes Alan visiting inevitably reminds Annie of her previous life and what might have been with Tim. Sometimes she is content with her cottage and her life at the inn—happy to grow old now maybe."

Outside the sky was beginning to streak with orange, as the daylight was fading fast. The last of the sledders were helping Eddie to put the gear away in the shed and close up the barn against the approaching winter night, and the horses, who had been stretching their legs in the paddock and watching the activity on the hill, were happy to be led back to their warm stalls. It was always surprising how quickly daylight turned into night in the winter, how quickly the curtain was drawn across such an enjoyable day.

"Those kids will sleep well tonight," Bill said, smiling. "I should go and help out in the kitchen. I'm sure there will be a few early diners before the families head home for the night."

John retired to the TV room to catch up on the news, reflecting to himself that anything could have happened in the world that day, and he would not have been any the wiser. As it turned out, the world had survived just fine without him.

David arrived at the inn in the afternoon, four days after Christmas. The temperature had not managed to get above freezing since the snowfall, so the fields and roofs were still blanketed in white. There was barely a difference in color between the snowy earth and the bleak sky, where they met on the distant horizon, making the bare trees at the top of the rise around the property stand out even more starkly as David made his way down the long driveway. The local schools were still out on their Christmas holiday, so there were still a good number of children enjoying the sledding, but nowhere near the attendance of that first day.

Rip and Riley greeted him like a long-lost friend as he closed the front door against the cold.

"Hello, boys. Do you think I'm back just to take you on another long hike?"

David found Bill in the bar tending the fire. "The inn looked nice in the lush greens of summer, but now in the snow it looks like the front of a Christmas card. All you need is an old horse-drawn carriage outside to complete the picture."

"Might give it a try, David—we have the horse part," Bill replied, rising and shaking David's hand. "I think your dad is in the library, working on his book, I believe—or taking a nap."

Bill made his way through the bar and out to the reception desk. After consulting the large registration book, he turned and took a key off the board, handing it to David, who had started to fill out the book without being asked. "Room twelve at the far end, looking out up the hill toward the cottage. Go, relax, and catch up with John. I will see you later."

John was in the library and still awake, although if David had arrived half an hour earlier, that would not have been the case.

"How is your mom?" John greeted David.

"She's fine. We had a good Christmas, but the weather was not as wintry as it is up here. How have you been doing? Relaxing Christmas?"

"I'm actually glad you're here. I must admit that I have been relaxing a little too much, and I want to get out and do some walking," John answered.

"Is there any more snow coming?" David asked.

"According to the weather on the news, we might get another dusting tonight but nothing significant."

"We can go out in the morning, then. You can tell me what you have been doing for two weeks," David concluded.

"Best to do any activity in the mornings, David. Believe me, after lunch you will not feel like doing much of anything."

"I'll go and unpack then and see you at dinner," David said as he started to head out.

"Glad you could make it back, David. I have enjoyed myself—a sort of home away from home."

CHAPTER 16

There Might Come a Day

THE NEXT DAY WAS MUCH brighter, blue skies replacing the pale, overcast appearance of the previous day. The sunnier outlook seemed to enliven Rip and Riley, so, after a leisurely breakfast and checking in with Bill, John and David ventured out for a long walk around the property with the two dogs leading the way.

There was a light covering of newly fallen snow from the previous night, but underneath the ground crunched under their feet as they made their way over any untrodden terrain. Initially, they headed toward the barn, intending to climb the hill on the far side and then circumnavigate the property, hopefully coming out at the solitary cottage before making their way down the gravel roadway back to the inn. John started chatting by recounting his two weeks at the inn and tried to describe the relaxing routine that he had found. He told David about getting the tree, the carol service, and the first day of snow and watching the sledding.

"When I describe it, it sounds quiet and mundane, but I have really relaxed. There is a small part of me that has wondered what friends and family might be doing over the holidays, but only a small part."

As they climbed up the undisturbed field leading away from the barn, their breathing heavier from the exertion and very visible in the chilled air, John also recounted an abbreviated version of how Eddie and Annie had come to be at the inn. As he told the story, he and David commented more than once about their lack of insight into the plight of the homeless. David also described Christmas with his mother and Keith and other news from the family front. As they continued to climb, their efforts increased, and they fell into silence—silence except for their labored breathing—and thought.

"David," John announced after a few minutes of contemplation as they neared the crest of the long rise from the barn.

"Yes, Dad?"

"There's something that I wanted to talk to you about—actually have long wanted to talk about. But I really need you to let me say it—to not interrupt, although you might not want me to finish." John looked over at David, seeking his understanding.

David hesitated—a little uncertain. "Is everything OK?"

"Yes, everything is fine, but I need to be able to say what I want to say."

"OK, Dad. I can try to stay quiet."

"Thank you." John nodded. "It isn't easy—but it is just something that I would like to say—something that I would like to know that I have said."

John paused, collecting his thoughts.

"There might come a day, David, when I can no longer express myself as I would want to express myself—and it frightens me."

David didn't say anything—but clearly looked puzzled.

"That wasn't a good start—sorry," John continued as if by way of explanation. "Let's try again. What I want to say, David, is that I don't know, nobody ever knows, how the world works out and what my later years will bring. I hope that I simply enjoy my time and have the good luck to die peacefully and quietly—and I honestly do not mind if that is a year from now or thirty years from now. But what I am frightened of is that I will start to suffer from some form of dementia—and that I will never be able to express my feelings, my thanks—or if I do, that you will no longer believe me, David."

David was good to his word—he remained quiet.

"David," John resumed after collecting himself, "what I want you to know—what I want you to know to be true and sincere—is that I have enjoyed all my life, have enjoyed the world that I have known. But above all else, I have loved you for every day of your life and have been so, so proud to have you as a son—and I want to thank you, David."

David could not remain quiet. "But I know that, Dad," he said quietly, placing an arm around John's shoulder.

"I know, David. I know. But I need you to remember, if ever I am not what I am this day, if ever I am different—what I am expressing to you today is the truth. I need you to remember the man whom you know today, no matter what you might see, or what I might say, in my later years. You see, I am afraid that you might see me deteriorate, so to speak, and you might struggle to remember the truth. But please, David, please know that today is the truth, and in those future days, remember me today—not what you might see. Remember a man who loved life and loved you—never anything less. And if I look at you out of apparently unrecognizing eyes in those distant years, please do not see those eyes but remember my eyes today—the eyes of your father. The other eyes are not me—my eyes love you for being my son. Just remember that I told you that, David—do not believe anything else and remember back."

"I think I understand what you are trying to tell me, Dad," David said, after John had paused for a minute, "but I don't understand why you are telling me now. It just seems a strange time."

"But there is never a right time," John tried to explain. "You see, I do not know how these things work—I do not know if there are periods of clarity and understanding during which I would be able to express my feelings and you can still believe me, or do things deteriorate so quickly that I do not recognize what is important to me and as such never understand the need to say things or appreciate that time is running out? I just do not know, David, but I am happy that I have said things now while I know that my mind is good—thank you. I cannot avoid leaving you, but I can avoid leaving you with uncertainty."

After walking on for a minute, walking and watching their breath escape and dissipate into the cold morning air, John continued his thoughts. "Before Christmas, before you came up, I was in the restaurant early one evening enjoying one of Annie's dinners when I observed an older gentleman having dinner with his wife. They looked a very nice couple appreciating their later years, but it became apparent that the husband was suffering and the wife was desperately trying to maintain normalcy. Sometimes the husband would get irritated when his wife would make decisions for him, assuming she knew what he wanted or needed. I am in no way saying that I understand the difficulties and sadness that the wife suffers and her attempts to avoid letting her husband make a scene in the restaurant. But my heart went out to the husband, the pleading in his eyes, because he could not be, or was not allowed to be, understood. I imagined that maybe he wanted to express the feeling that things are no longer 'normal' for him, and why was it so wrong for others to know that?"

John paused before continuing. "I have never really told you a great deal about my father's death, David, or at least not discussed the specifics. I would think this is not uncommon among families, not to dwell on past sad events. I have explained to you that your grandfather had a stroke when he was only sixty-seven, but that is probably about as much detail as I have explained. Well, he did have what was termed a 'severe stroke' but survived for about four months before dying from a second stroke at home. During that four-month period, he wasn't the father that I had known; he could barely speak at all and really struggled to get us to understand what he wanted. But I am not bringing up your grandfather's passing to sadden you; there are no real happy endings. I wanted to explain that, before his stroke, my father had not taken an opportunity to tell me that he loved me or was proud of me. Yes, as a child he had always expressed his love, and I knew of his love, but in my adult life he had not really told me again as the years passed. I have always assumed that he would have done so, on his deathbed so to speak, but he was robbed of that opportunity. And whereas I was saddened by having to assume that he would have told me had he been able, I am also left to imagine, in reflective times usually late at night, that my father died wishing he had spoken with me while he was able. Maybe that was what he was struggling to say when I sat with him at home, but I will never know. To this day I wish that I had been able to say good-bye to him."

By now the two had walked all the way along the top of the horse pasture and could see the roof of the isolated cottage in the distance, ahead of them to the right and down the gentle slope of the snow-covered field.

"What I wanted for you to really understand is that I am happy now, and this happiness is what you should remember. When I do leave you, it will not mean that I never loved you—or love you any less by leaving. Know that today will always be the truth."

"Don't go anywhere, Dad."

John put his arm around David's shoulder as they walked on through the snow.

CHAPTER 17

We Had a Good Time

NEARLY ALL THE GUESTS, EVEN the younger ones, saw the New Year in around the fireplace in what was a very jovial bar. There didn't seem to be a need to watch the ball in Times Square or to be shown how to have a good time by a never-ending string of celebrities. But there was a close eye kept on the clock as midnight approached, and Bill provided champagne while Annie brought out Shirley Temples for the younger members of the gathering. There were several toasts, including Eddie's appreciation of seeing another year come in and reflecting on the people who were not lucky enough to have made it. Before one o'clock the revelers had dispersed, much to the relief of Rip and Riley, who seemed eager to get to bed. Bill gave Eddie and Annie a hug as they left for the bracing walk up to their cottages and then shut everything up for the night. Tomorrow would be a new year—but hopefully with no changes.

During a decidedly later breakfast the following morning, Bill mentioned that he was going to spend a couple of hours up in the barn, checking on the cars and helping Ken, who wanted to tinker with the VW bus on his day off, if they wanted to tag along.

"Just head on up there whenever you want," Bill said. "I will check out a few of the guests who are leaving this morning and then come on up. Take the dogs—they enjoy the barn."

So midmorning, wrapped up against the cold, John, David, and the dogs ventured up to the barn, where one of the big doors was partly opened, presumably to allow some light in. They introduced themselves to Ken, who was busy poring over the engine of the bus, and explained that Bill should be up shortly.

"Is there something wrong with the VW?" John asked.

"Nothing really wrong, but I need to give it a good service if Bill is going to take it on his trip in the spring. And I wanted to check on the spares that we have so that I can order anything we need in plenty of time. I like to send Bill off with an extra of anything the bus might need, because spares are so hard to come by for this old beauty. Luckily, it is a very simple little engine, by today's standards, so not nearly as much to go wrong."

John stayed with Ken, taking a look around the bus and admiring the uncomplicated design yet resourceful use of space. John did not claim to be a mechanic, by any means, but even to him the engine seemed to be very simple. The word that sprang to mind as he looked around was *quaint*—and it made him smile.

David went off to investigate what Rip and Riley were up to on the far side of the barn, where a lot of scratching and yapping, as opposed to their usual barks, could be heard. What he found was that Riley had dug himself far enough into one of the hay bales so that basically only his rear half and a rapidly wagging tail could be seen, while Rip was guarding the opposite side of the bale, eagerly awaiting the resident mice to make their bid for freedom. The mice, displaced from their winter retreat, had to literally attempt running for their lives past the delighted Rip, trying to find somewhere that the eager terriers couldn't access. Some made it past the enthusiastic guard, while others did an about-turn and retreated into the hay bale only to repeat the ordeal if Riley detected them again.

"They do catch one or two occasionally," Bill said as he joined David, "but I think they enjoy the chase more than actually catching something."

"Do the mice ever nest in the cars?"

"They don't seem to go in the cars at all. They probably have enough warm places to hide out in as long as we leave the hay bales in here," Bill replied, "at least until the dogs disturb them for a while."

Bill and David left the dogs to intimidate the mice and went back to the bus to see how Ken was getting on.

"How does she look?" Bill asked Ken, who had his head and shoulders under the hood of the rear engine compartment.

"Morning, Bill," Ken replied, emerging. "Looks pretty good. I will change the oil and check things over again in April, when it is a bit warmer. I've made a list of a few things we should stock up on before you leave in May, but we still have most of the spares from last year."

"Where do you go on your camping trips?" David asked.

"Over to New Hampshire, more on the eastern side. I normally set up camp by a favorite lake in the hills but relatively close to the Maine shoreline. I do like to spend some time looking at the ocean before the heat of summer really sets in. I like the Atlantic shore when a fresh wind is blowing and whipping up the seas."

They had gone around to the passenger side of the bus, where David opened up the double doors into the rear part of the bus while Bill leaned into the open window of the front door to talk to John, who sat in the driver's seat admiring the basic instrumentation.

"Have you ever driven a bus, John?"

"No—but it does look intriguing, sitting so far up at the front like this."

"It can be fun—not powerful by today's standards, but definitely fun," Bill replied and then asked, "Are you and David planning on coming up to go hiking and camping again next summer?"

"I expect that we will," John replied, turning toward David behind him, to get his thoughts. "We try to make it our annual event."

David nodded agreement. "I hope that we will be back, after our interrupted attempt this past year."

"If you are interested, and if you can make it earlier, you are welcome to come along on the VW excursion," Bill offered. "It is normally a good trip."

John and David looked at each other quizzically.

"Sounds appealing, Bill. What do you think, David?"

"It would be fun. I can still get my share of hiking in the New Hampshire hills," David replied. "How early in May do you leave, Bill? I probably cannot get away from school until around mid-May."

"I don't have a set time. If you let me know what dates are good for you, I can arrange around those."

"Let's check things when we get home, but it definitely sounds appealing," John said.

David nodded agreement. "Do you actually sleep in the bus, Bill?" he said, looking intrigued at the rear of the bus, where there were two bench seats facing each other across a small table.

"Not usually, no. The seats do fold down into beds if the weather is very bad, but normally I take my tent and use that. Although the seats and table are great for eating at—makes it very civilized."

John climbed out of the bus and walked around, patting the smooth, rounded, polished front, adorned by the large VW insignia and large headlights. He was smiling broadly.

"You like the idea, John?" Bill asked.

"Sounds like fun," John said and then added, laughing, "Can I drive sometimes?"

"No problem; we can take turns. She isn't fast but definitely fun."

Rip and Riley had made their way across the barn, presumably having displaced all the inhabitants from that hay bale at least. Ken was closing up the engine compartment and wiping his hands on the cloth poking out of his back pocket.

"You will be heading out tomorrow morning?" Bill asked John and David.

"I'm afraid I have to get back," David replied.

"I wish you hadn't reminded me, but yes, I have to do some work," John also confirmed.

"In a way, it is good to hear that you are reluctant to leave," Bill said as they headed toward the still-open barn door.

Ken said his good-byes, after which Bill headed back to the inn to prepare for lunchtime. David closed up the big door while John stood surveying the picturesque view of the inn in its winter setting. When he had finished, David came and stood by his father, watching him looking off into the distance—but what he was watching David did not know.

"This has a meaning to you, doesn't it, Dad?" David asked. "This makes some sense to you."

John continued to stare at the tree line, framed against the pale winter sky, running along the top of the long pasture. He stared at the trees but was not looking at them.

"No, I'm not saying that it makes sense as such," John reflected in a softer voice, "but I do know that I miss the enjoyment of my life as a boy and as a younger man. I have known for a long time that I miss that enjoyment. There are times when I miss it very deeply indeed."

John paused and blinked a few times before continuing with his thoughts. "Don't get me wrong. I'm not saying that I do not enjoy my life now, do not enjoy where my life has taken me—that is not what I am saying. But I have very often yearned after the sheer enjoyment of those times that I left behind many years ago. You always assume that it is getting older that dims the enjoyment, that complicates life, that makes life so very hard sometimes. But maybe, just maybe, David, it isn't me getting old. Maybe we have managed to take some of the joy out of living. Maybe there is an element of truth to Bill's remembrances."

"But if that is the case, what do you think happened?" David pursued, trying to not let any skepticism into his voice. "How did enjoyment get taken away?"

John thought for a minute. "I tend to agree that greed happened," he replied at length.

"What do you mean, exactly?" David pushed.

"Remember that you are just asking my opinion," explained John, "but I think that greed got in the way of people properly considering the consequences of their ambitions and actions—that greed drove progress."

David remained silent.

After a little more contemplation, John cleared his throat and continued. "I suppose that deep down, what really upsets me is that 'they' decided to change our lives, decided that 'they' knew what was best for us, decided that 'they' knew what we wanted—but never actually asked us what we wanted. They changed our lives without asking."

"Isn't that always the case—throughout history?" David responded, more intrigued now.

"Without a doubt—yes," John agreed, "but in my admittedly biased opinion, unlike other times in history, we actually had a good time, not a perfect time but a good time. We had a good time, and 'they' decided to change it—because 'they' were greedy. 'They' knew that times would get even better—but they were wrong. Times didn't get better, David. They didn't get better. I cannot prove it to you but would ask you not to believe that times are better now. There are things that are better—many, many things—but don't believe that times are better."

The two were quiet for a minute or so.

"You know, David, we thought that those days would never end," John lamented as if in conclusion. "But they did end, and I miss them ever so much."

"But don't they have to end?" David asked.

"They have to end because you get old," agreed John, "but these days ended because 'they' took them away—that is what saddens me."

The two walked down to the inn, with two weary dogs trailing behind.

As they walked John added a final reflection "I can identify with many of Bill's observations and frustrations. I'm not saying that we should go back, I'm simply lamenting that we ever came."

The following morning, John and David were ready to depart at the same time, after a breakfast slightly heartier than usual, rationalizing that they each had a long drive ahead. Eddie was setting up his long stepladder in the entrance hall, surrounded by a number of storage containers, when the two came down to see Bill and check out.

"Time to start taking our tree down, Eddie?" John asked.

"I'm afraid so," Eddie replied as he started to remove the ornaments. "Annie enjoys decorating the tree, but her heart is not into packing the ornaments away again. I don't blame her."

Bill walked them to the front door.

"Keep in touch, and let me know when you can get away in May," Bill said, shaking hands.

"Will do, Bill. I for one would like to tag along, all being well," John replied.

"And I will let you know my timetable, but hopefully I can make it work," David assured Bill.

The three stood by the open door, watching Eddie and taking a last look at the twinkling tree lights Eddie had switched on for the last time—until next year and a new tree.

"It's funny," Bill said reflectively but loud enough that the other three could hear. "I don't often contemplate whether or not I will experience certain things again, but for several years now, I stop and wonder when I will see my last Christmas. I always hope that I will get to see another tree and another Christmas, and I am sort of relieved when Eddie goes out the following year and the lighted tree appears again. But I know that one time my wishes cannot come true."

The four shook hands, and John and David started to head out of the front door.

John turned and said, "We will be back for sure, Bill—and I know there will be more Christmases."

Part 3:
Bygone Times

CHAPTER 18

On the Road

THE BUS, GLEAMING IN THE morning sun, climbed up the driveway away from the inn on a warm morning in the third week of May.

Spring had arrived a couple of weeks later than in some years, but now the landscape was lush green again with flowers in the gardens, the snow-covered fields a fading memory. The lonely crows had given way to the songbirds, who were either busy building their nests or feeding their young. Wild bluebells scattered throughout the pastures gave the fields a purple hue, when viewed from the right angle, early on those May mornings.

Bill was driving as they set off, but he assured John and David that they could have their fair share of time at the wheel. John was in the front passenger seat while David sat on one of the bench seats in the back, facing forward, poring over maps laid out on the table. Eddie and Annie were happy to run the inn on their own for a few days, but Jenny and Sarah were coming in whenever they were not busy with school-work, and their mothers would both come in during the evenings to help in the restaurant.

Traveling from west to east across Vermont and New Hampshire, the bus tended to stay on more of the back roads mainly because the major highways generally went in a north-south direction in the states. They didn't travel fast, but the views were superb. They stopped regularly to stretch their legs, let the dogs get some exercise, and change drivers. After about three hours, they took a longer break for lunch at a rest stop atop one of the higher hills, admiring the majestic undulating carpet of tree-covered hills that stretched as far as the eye could see in every direction.

"How far to go, Bill?" David asked, looking toward the eastern horizon.

"Probably only another hour to an hour and a half."

After their lunch break, David took his first stint at driving. It was a few years since he had learned to drive a stick shift, so he took the opportunity, while the bus was at the rest stop, to acquaint himself with the long gear stick and the very awkward, stiff gear changes. After a few minutes, he felt reasonably confident and so, after stalling only once, they stuttered and jumped back onto the road, heading downward into another valley.

As he became familiar with the controls, David started to beam with pleasure as he piloted the bus along the cambered blacktop roads of New Hampshire, keeping clear, where practical, of the small cracks in the asphalt that seemed to be ever present toward the edge of the road. While maneuvering in the parking lot, David had noticed the lack of power steering, but once out on the road, the bus was fun and responsive to drive. The driving position was probably better described as perching, as opposed to sitting, in front of the large, practically horizontal steering wheel. The steering column went almost vertically downward from the wheel into the floor of the cab as opposed to a short column angled into a dashboard, which was all David had ever known. The rationale for the upright steering column was both because of the bus-like angle of the wheel but also because there was no real dashboard to speak of. There was a rudimentary instrument panel combined with a shelf stretching across the entire front of the bus, set just below the split windshield. The lower part was an open shelf for the necessary driving oddments, with a solid overhang above the shelf into which were set the large dial speedometer, a couple of small gauges, a wide slotted grill, the mandatory little ashtray on top, and a clock, not in front of the driver but on the extreme right-hand side in front of Bill, the passenger, who also had a handle to grab on to. Set into the grill, which David assumed was housing a speaker, was a small radio, with two knobs, and attached to the underside of the overhang, in the shelf space, a simple cassette player had been mounted. The instrument panel, shelf, vents, steering wheel, and column were all finished in a beautiful lacquered off-white paint, which seemed to be in immaculate condition despite the many decades of service. The other control of interest, and challenge, to David was the long vertical gear shift, which emerged from the floor and came up to the height of the shelf, topped off with a small black spherical knob, contrasting the shiny white coloring of the rest of the interior and seats.

As they motored along, Bill leaned forward, unclipped his half of the split windshield, and pushed the bottom open, allowing a nice through flow of fresh air without a strong wind in the face. This made David smile all over again, because it seemed simple and logical but so against all the design concepts he was used to.

"Sorry for smiling so much. It just seems so strange compared to what I have grown up with. It seems as though it shouldn't work—but it does. No array of rocker switches, push buttons, and lights to tell you what to do; no electronic zone climate control; no touch screen to control media and everything else in the car; no fingertip controls on the steering wheel, and where are the essential three or four multifunction instrument arms coming out of the steering column? Just one little stick that only clicks up or down to control the indicators and a couple of measly pull knobs. We need controls, Bill. Most cars have more controls just for their driver's seat than there are in the entire bus." David laughed.

"It's an interesting observation," Bill said as he sat alongside David. "This van compared to one of today's SUVs. There is no comparison when it comes to complexity of instrumentation, automation, and comfort for the occupants—but they both get from A to B in roughly the same time and carry about the same number of people. In my mind, the advances do not accomplish a great deal, but I know that I am being simplistic."

Cat Stevens's *Tea for the Tillerman* had finished playing in the tape player, so, again to David's bemusement, Bill ejected the cassette and slipped in Jackson Browne's *Greatest Hits*.

"You like the older music as well, Bill?" David asked. "Music and cars from the same era?"

"I am not sure when they stopped manufacturing cassettes," Bill replied. "From memory, it seemed to be all CDs after the early nineties—which made all the cassette tapes sort of redundant, so they were sent to accompany all their brothers, the vinyl records that were gathering dust, having also been put out to pasture. So in reality the cassettes have to be older music. But to be honest, that is the music that I prefer listening to—still resonates with me as meaningful music."

"Implying that more modern music isn't meaningful?" David asked, still smiling.

"You should appreciate these singers and their music while you can, David. I am sorry to say that they might not be around for too much longer, and they will be missed very much."

"You don't think there are similar or good songwriters around today?"

John interrupted the musical discussion from his seat in the back, where he had been studying the maps of New Hampshire that David had left out, by asking if they could pull over at the approaching coffee shop as they passed through a small town.

"I need a bathroom break, and happy to get coffee for everybody," John announced.

Bill and David placed their coffee orders, and Bill added, "Appreciate you getting the coffee, John. It will give me the opportunity to try to educate your son about the music we had back in the seventies."

"Good luck. I have tried," John called in through the open windshield as he headed toward the Coffee and Tea Shop.

David had turned off the engine, unbuckled his seat belt, and stretched in his seat.

"I do admit that there must have been a lot of great music in those past decades," David said. "I didn't live the history of the groups and songwriters and the defining albums, but much of the music stands the test of time for me and many of my friends. I enjoy listening to a lot of it but do really not appreciate what it must have been like to have been around when the material was released new to a waiting public."

"You should know this, David—that music and songs will track the path of your life like nothing else ever will. Music can evoke memories and feelings and will take you back to a time and place that you have all but forgotten, to relive the thoughts and feelings from the moment in time when you heard that song. You can liken it to being hypnotized inasmuch as every time you hear the opening chords or verse of a particular song, you will be mentally transported back to that moment in your life, and you will sing along, albeit in your head maybe, like you did way back when, and you will have that time and friends from your youth—at least once more."

Bill paused his thoughts as he listened to Jackson Browne singing about "Everyman."

"There were a number of singer-songwriters in the later sixties, seventies, and into the eighties who wrote for a generation—actually more than one generation. They enjoyed what they wrote, and they believed in what they wrote—they had a message for those generations. Do you ever go to see any of those older artists, who have survived the decades, in concert?"

"One or two when I was relatively young, with my mother and father," David answered, "but not on my own. Quite a few of the newer performers, with friends, but not the older singers, no."

"I know it is hard to always believe older people when they try to persuade you about something, no matter how well intentioned they might be. But if you ever get the chance, you should go and see some of those singer-songwriters from the seventies and eighties. While you still have chance, you should go and see them performing the compositions that they are so proud of because the opportunity will not be there much longer. They don't really perform for the money anymore—they are fairly comfortable from that perspective. They perform for the sheer pleasure that it brings to an audience who are remembering back to their youth and simpler times—and they perform because of the pride and satisfaction that they get from songs that they wrote all those years ago. If you see them, you will understand that those songwriters had something to say, often something with deep meaning, and for those songs to still resonate many decades later is very fulfilling for artists in their twilight years now. It means that their songs are true, that their feelings have truth, and that for a brief moment, they can take their audience back to the time when they were all young and had all their dreams before them. You should see them perform, while it is still possible, David, so that fifty years from now, when you are elderly yourself, you will be able to say that you saw these artists and they were real—their songs were real—their songs had meaning. Because, you see, by that time the world will be so jaded by computer-generated images and music that nobody will be able to recognize the expression of true feelings or observations anymore. So try to see Paul Simon or Bob Seger or Jackson Browne or Cat Stevens, if he performs again, and tell your children that these people were real and they had messages that they wanted to be heard— that they wrote from their hearts. They probably will not recognize the significance, David, but tell them all the same."

Jackson had moved onto singing about "The Pretender."

"I am sure there are such gifted songwriters and songs today," Bill continued, "but there is such a diverse array of media outlets nowadays, so many options in how people watch or listen to their entertainment, that people's tastes become fractured and diverse, making it very difficult for performers to be accepted by the wide audiences that were once possible. The intended audience spends so much time trying to interact with so many people via so many channels that they just skim the surface—listen briefly and move on; they cannot afford the time to focus. Can you imagine getting home with a newly released vinyl album and sitting and playing it repeatedly for hour after hour? We would do that until we knew the songs by heart. Now people listen to the music with one ear while paying attention to numerous other devices at the same time—before jumping to the latest You Tube fad or other important development. Fame has become so much more fleeting that I doubt whether singers can have the longevity anymore. I doubt whether many songs can reach a generation today, David, or get the validation of that generation—I am sorry for that, and I am sorry the music experience that I knew is fast disappearing."

"I suppose that deep down I am sorry too. Sorry and a little jealous that I never had that experience and closeness to the music."

John returned with their coffees, and after everybody was comfortable again, David pulled out of the angled parking spot on the main street and headed the bus off on the last stretch of their trip to the lake.

CHAPTER 19

Mountain Lake

THE SECLUDED MOUNTAIN LAKE WAS surrounded on all sides by higher tree-covered hills and was relatively quiet this early in the season. The bus pulled into the camping area shortly after three o'clock, and they could only see two other groups camping, both at the opposite end of the site to where Bill directed David. The area was grassland that sloped gently down to the large lake, which had a slight chop on the water in the afternoon breeze. There were a lot of very large pine trees spread through the camping area, and under the spreading branches of each tree, the green grass was in competition with a dense carpet of brown dried pine needles, which looked very cushioned.

"We can have the pick of the spots, gentlemen," Bill said as he guided David toward an area that had two large pines with a clear grassy slope down to the lake between the trees. There was also a large wooden picnic table, bleached to a light gray color by endless summers in the sun, set off to the left on the grassy slope.

"I would suggest parking the bus here in the open between the trees and then setting up the tents on the pine-needle carpets, one on each side, far enough away from the trees in case of lightning but still on the carpet of needles," Bill said. "I have set up my tent here before, and the bed of soft needles makes it very comfortable underneath the tent. As far as I know, there is no forecast of any thunderstorms, at least according to the paper this morning."

David parked the VW at the spot indicated by Bill, and the three spent the next hour pitching their tents and setting up the metal fire tub, which Bill had brought along so that they could safely burn logs in the evenings, and their chairs on the gently sloping grass in front of the bus facing the lake. Rip and Riley explored the area with a passion, including the edge of the lake, but didn't wander too far from the base they were establishing. Once their preparations had been completed, they took the dogs for a stroll around the site to get their bearings, not that there was too much to become acquainted with. Bill showed them the bathroom building complete with showers, although he warned them that there might be only cold water yet, explaining that the season didn't officially start until Memorial Day, so although the camp was open to visitors and had been dewinterized, the campground stewards might delay starting to heat the water for a few more days. They also went down to the lake edge, where there were half a dozen rowing boats and a few canoes pulled up onto the grass, complete with a pile of oars to the side.

"The campers are free to use them out on the lake," Bill explained. "It's nice to go out fishing sometimes."

They went along to the farther end of the campground to introduce themselves to the other visitors. There were two couples in their midsixties, sitting outside a good-sized RV, and a father with two sons, in their twenties, who were camping in what looked like an eight-person tent and explained to the new arrivals that they enjoyed going off for day hikes in the area while the weather was still relatively cool.

Having exchanged pleasantries for a few minutes, Bill, John, and David started back to their own camp, fanning out, at Bill's suggestion, in order to gather up branches for firewood that might have fallen during the long winter. Even Rip and Riley contributed with one apiece. The collection, along with a couple of bundles of split logs and a bag of charcoal that they had brought along, was more than enough fuel for the evening's fire.

"Annie put steaks in the cooler for the first night," Bill said as he set about twisting newspaper and arranging some small twigs in the bottom of the fire tub. "Once the fire gets going, we can grill them out here, if that is OK with you."

"Sounds good to me," John agreed as David nodded. "Do we have something to cook them on?"

"Yes, Eddie found an old grate that fits over the fire, a few years ago. Once the fire gets going, and the grate gets hot, the steaks cook slowly on there—plenty of flavor. You just have to pick one and periodically check how well cooked it is—because I do like mine to be well done. I'll put some potatoes up there to cook at the same time and a pan of baked beans on the small stove. We should be all set."

The steaks took a long time to grill, not being covered in any way, sizzling and spitting away in what was now twilight. But the waiting diners were not in any rush, had nowhere to be, and enjoyed sitting back in relative silence, watching darkness encroach on the lake and listening to their dinner cooking itself. The mood and quiet was enhanced by a couple of bottles of Malbec for Bill and John to enjoy and beers in the cooler for David.

Eventually they all had steaks done to their liking, so they interrupted their reverie, helped themselves to the other dishes, and then set about eating their long-awaited feast.

"Tastes very good," John said, "but there again, when you are this hungry, it is much easier to appreciate the food."

"The lake is a peaceful place, Bill. Thank you for inviting us along," David said, staring out onto a lake that they could no longer see because of the darkness and the backlight of the burning logs.

They sat, ate, drank, and chatted, not rushing the simple meal. Once they were all finished, David rinsed off the few dishes while Bill and John sat back and relaxed. Within fifteen minutes, the mix of food, wine, and quiet proved too relaxing for John, and he dozed off, leaning back in his chair.

"John's OK?" Bill asked. "Maybe just tired?"

David smiled. "Don't worry. My dad falling asleep means that he is happy. For as long as I can remember, if he is able to, he likes nothing more than to doze after a meal. I can remember distinctly when I was a young boy, he would sometimes feel tired while he was reading to me in bed—his eyelids starting to close a little and repeating the lines sometimes. I would ask him if he was all right, and he would smile back at my young, concerned face and say, 'David, I always feel sleepy when I am contented, and I feel very contented being with you at the end of the day—so I feel sleepy.' He has never changed—he is feeling contented now."

They looked across at John, his mouth wide open, at ease with the world.

"Isn't it strange, I cannot remember much about the hundreds of stories that he read to me, but I can remember him telling me that like it was yesterday?"

Bill refreshed his glass of wine and handed David another beer.

"I have noticed that for some reason being out here in the wilds tends to encourage me to drink, not to excess, but I do feel relaxed out here," Bill said. "And the wine makes me somewhat reflective, and sometimes a little sad."

"Reflective is good, Bill, as long as you don't get argumentative." David laughed. "What are you reflecting on?"

"Well, right now I am dwelling on what you were just telling me about your dad reading to you as a boy. I remember reading to Jill and Stephen, and can remember very well how the stories captivated their young minds and transported them to fictional places. They were entranced because of their innocence. They didn't look to find fault in the stories; they looked to believe without question. Basically, they were innocent."

"Does that sadden you?"

"Recalling reading to the kids brings happy memories," Bill said, "but what causes me to be reflective, and causes me some sadness, is when I think back to the children losing that innocence that I was describing, David."

"But children have to grow up, have to lose that naïvety."

"Oh, I know, David. But what saddens me very much is that I never recognized that my children's innocence was slipping away. I probably wanted to believe that it would be there forever, but one day came to the sad realization that their days of relishing the toy store, being thrilled by sledding or the annual traveling carnival, in awe at the candy store, and dreaming of Christmas and birthdays and lists had all disappeared. They had grown up, and the magic of wishing and dreaming had been lost. It really did sadden me tremendously—both that it had been lost but mainly that I had not appreciated those times as I should have, should have appreciated them when I had them."

"But wouldn't the same be true of losing your own innocence? Did that sadden you in the same way?"

"No, because it is not the same," Bill replied. "The thing is that when you are young, you cannot wait to grow up, to be independent, and you long to become worldly. So if you do recognize your innocence fading away, you embrace it because you are keen to get out into the great, big world. You do not look back and yearn for your loss and certainly do not realize how precious it actually was. But your children are different, because they are your second chance at seeing the innocence. You can see the world through their eyes and appreciate their enjoyment and know the enjoyment you once knew. When that window closes, you see it being lost for the second time, and you know that it will not return. That was your last opportunity, and it is no more."

"Not with grandchildren?"

"I wish it was, David, but in reality, it is the father they look to for guidance and to protect their innocence. In their eyes, the grandfather has always been too old to understand their world."

They both fell silent for a while, sipping their drinks, watching the darkness, and listening to an owl repeatedly call but not seem to get any response.

"He sounds lonely," David said. "Hope he finds a friend."

Bill nodded but stayed quiet for a while longer, eventually breaking his silence with the observation. "On nights like these, it is good to think. On nights like these, you can see your life very clearly. I used to think that a glass of wine dulled my thinking—but I have come to know that it lets me see truths on nights like these."

"What sort of truths?"

After mulling it over for a minute, Bill replied, "The truth of the sad part about getting older is that you know too much, too many of the bad things of life. That you can no longer view this world through the eyes of your childhood."

David drained his beer and flexed his legs, preparing to get up.

"Getting late, Bill. Do we have a plan for tomorrow?"

"The forecast on the radio was saying that it will be fine tomorrow but overcast with strong gusting winds," Bill said. "It might be the best day to go and see the ocean—I like seeing the ocean when it is angry."

"That would be good with me," David agreed. "I will check with Dad when I rouse him in a few minutes."

"We can make a final decision in the morning—we have no commitments," Bill said. "I think that I will call it a night as well—I enjoy the wine, but it definitely makes me sleepy."

Bill slowly arose from the low chair, sent the dogs off into the dark before bed, and set about making sure that the embers of the fire were safe.

As he was tending the fire, he had his back turned to David.

"David?"

"Yes, Bill?"

"When you were telling me about what your father said to you—when he would be reading to you as a boy. Know that in life you remember the important things —you don't always know that they are important, but they stay with you. The books and the stories—they were not important David. You have held on to the truly important thing." Bill was glad that he was turned away.

"Waken your dad gently."

CHAPTER 20

The Maine Ocean

THE DAY DAWNED GRAY AND overcast, the lake shrouded in light mist that seemed to be rising, like smoke, from the surface and then dissipating at a height of maybe twenty feet. The forecast wind had not arrived yet.

John was the first to waken, not surprising, after he had got a head start at sleep the previous evening. He made his way across to the bathrooms and had a shower, which was cold and invigorating but consequently very quick. It was still only six thirty when he got back to their camp area, so he let the revelers sleep while he set about making some breakfast on the two single-burner gas stoves that they had brought along. John filled the bottom of Bill's old coffee percolator with water, put ground coffee into the suspended basket, and then put the contraption onto one of the burners, up on the picnic table for some stability. He then searched in the cooler to see what Annie might have packed away for their breakfasts, finding half a dozen eggs and a pack of bacon. The percolator was starting to bubble and hiss, allowing the boiling water from the bottom to rise and drip down through the coffee. John didn't want to disturb that process, so he took the large frying pan from the small cupboard in the bus and started heating that on the second stove. He threw the bacon and uneaten cooked potatoes, from the previous evening's meal, into the frying pan and poured himself a small mug of black coffee to sample the strength. Once the bacon was approaching crispy, he squeezed the contents of the pan over to one side and then cracked the eggs, one at a time, into the pan. Bill had woken to the smell of brewing coffee and sizzling bacon, but David slept on until John gave him a shout as the eggs were frying. The results of John's cooking efforts were not too appealing visually but tasted just fine, and the three hungry campers sat down and enjoyed the meal by the misty lake.

"Thanks, Dad. A nice start to the day," David said as he was finishing up.

"Not up to Annie's standards, but I enjoyed it," John replied. "I think that was basically the end of the supplies that Annie packed for us."

"Things don't keep very long in the cooler, so I have stopped bringing too much along," Bill said. "We will stop and get some more while we are out today."

"Is the plan still to head to the ocean today?" John asked. "David was telling me last night, but I wasn't completely with it."

"Unless you prefer to do something different," Bill said, "I think it would be a good day."

Neither John nor David had a preferred plan, so after quickly clearing up from breakfast, Bill and David grabbed quick showers, and the three jumped into the bus, heading for Maine and the coast.

The leisurely drive took just over two hours, dropping them down out of the wooded hills and lakes of New Hampshire into the more open countryside approaching the rugged coastline of Maine to the south of Portland. The mist disappeared as soon as they departed the lake, and they were in high spirits as they drove the back roads accompanied by Paul Simon. The wind increased steadily the closer they got to the coast, so that by the time they reached the rocky cape of their destination, it was blowing strong, fresh, and salty in their faces as they emerged from the bus. Even though the temperature was in the low sixties, and they had opted for shorts over long pants, all three were thankful they had elected to bring their sweat shirts or light jackets. The sky was still overcast, but the clouds were high and visibility was clear as they stood on the craggy headland looking out at a gray ocean that stretched as far as the eye could see, subconsciously narrowing their eyes and blinking away the wind.

They were standing on an outcrop of granite, and from this vantage point, John and David surveyed the sizable cove into which they had emerged. They were situated at the southwest point of a large half-moon inlet that looked to be about half a mile across, as the crow flies, to the cape on the opposite side to the north. The coastline in between the promontories alternated between rocky bluffs, approximately forty feet above the frothing waves, descending down to stretches of sandy grass-land almost at sea level, from which one could scramble across large rocks to the occasional small shingle-and-pebble-filled coves and the ocean. From their rocky platform, they looked across to the focal point of the tableau, which was the black-and-white lighthouse perched on top of the lawn-covered cliff of the opposite headland. The layout of the lighthouse comprised of the traditional high white tower, the top quarter of which was contrasted in black, with a collection of assorted red-roofed white structures built in the area around its base. As they looked seaward, the ocean appeared gray under the overcast sky but flecked with continuous whitecaps whipped up by the gusting wind. They watched a lone gull bravely and silently doing battle with the elements only about twenty feet above their heads.

"I do love the ocean on days like this," Bill observed as he donned an old cloth baseball cap that he had brought from the bus. "I don't know anything as bracing."

"I am always in awe of the vastness of the sea," John said, looking seaward. "Always wonder what might be just over the horizon. It is a beautiful spot."

"Wouldn't you have liked to live at the ocean, Bill?" David asked. "I remember you saying that you had considered living in an ocean location that was more tropical, but what about a wild and spectacular setting such as this?"

"I would love to wake up to the sound of the ocean and to have views like this. To lie in bed at night listening to either the gentle waves washing ashore or, alternatively, the howling wind of a winter storm would be good. It has always appealed to me, and I must confess I would have

Robert Geoffrey

no complaints at all," Bill replied. "But you could wait a lifetime to find such a property on the market, and I also realized that if I wanted to create an oasis from modern communications and pressures, then I could not achieve that at the ocean, because there is no way to get a property with sufficient land or one that is somewhat isolated. It would be a good alternative but maybe not quite achieving a setting from yesteryear, if you follow my logic."

David nodded his understanding and added, "The lighthouse out there must have some spectacular views."

"I was going to suggest we take a hike around and have a look at it," Bill said. "I've walked it with Eddie a couple of years ago. It's probably about a two-mile walk but with plenty of ascending and descending along the way."

John and David gave their enthusiastic agreement, and Rip and Riley, who had been sitting patiently on the granite slab with their ears flapping in the gusting wind, jumped up as soon as there was an indication of making a move.

"There is a nice lobster café on the far side of the lighthouse headland, so we can get some lunch over there after working up an appetite," Bill added as they set off.

The terrain between the headlands was a combination of stretches of coarse grasses with a lot of low gorse bushes interspersed with expanses of flat granite plateaus. There were also a decent number of conifers dotted along the shoreline, a little on the stunted side but still seeming to defy the apparent lack of soil depth. Bill and John walked and clambered steadily, while David and the dogs took frequent detours to explore the pebble beaches and scramble across some of the natural rocky breakwaters that extended into the sea for a short distance.

After a good hour of walking, scrambling, and exertions in general, they reached the far headland and followed Bill down to the Lobster Shack, which was set on a flat area of grassland just down below the main buildings of the lighthouse. There they enjoyed large bowls of New England clam chowder, accompanied by a seemingly unlimited supply of fresh bread. They sat out on the deck overlooking the ocean but were sheltered from the brunt of the wind. Rip and Riley entertained themselves chasing away any of the seagulls who ventured too close to the tables.

It was just after one o'clock by the time that they had finished lunch. The overcast sky was trying to break up a little, as evidenced by shafts of sunlight penetrating through the blanket of cloud to reach down to the ocean, and the wind had decreased to a strong breeze. They spent the next hour looking around the buildings at the base of the lighthouse, including taking a self-guided tour of the small house that had accommodated the resident lighthouse keeper and his family for more than 150 years, until automation had finally made such a position unnecessary some twenty years prior. There was also a very interesting museum, well stocked with artifacts, detailing and explaining life on the peninsula in those bygone days and the history of the lighthouse and the mariners whose lives had depended on it.

"Would you like to take a climb up to the top?" Bill asked. "It wasn't actually open when I came out here with Eddie—they were still completing some renovations before the summer season."

"If you want, why don't you and David go up for a while, and I will stay and look after Rip and Riley," John offered. "I don't suppose they would particularly like being up there on a narrow ledge. When David comes down, I can come up and see the views."

"Thanks, John—I agree that they are probably better off staying on the ground," Bill said. "We won't be long."

And with that Bill and David headed over to the tower to start the long climb up the spiraling tight iron staircase. There were two floors within the lighthouse, as they ascended, each with more relics, from the lighthouse's history, a workshop, and also a living area, where the lighthouse keeper had stayed during nights of bad weather in order to tend to the original oil light. When they eventually emerged, through a small weathertight doorway, out onto the grating surrounding the light itself, the view was spectacular. Blue skies and the occasional small white cloud were now overhead and out to the east over the ocean, while the blanket of darker cloud was receding behind them to the west. They both stood, hands gripping the chest-high, salt-encrusted railing surrounding the platform, gazing out at the views and limitless expanse of ocean in front of them.

"Beautiful," Bill said, after a spell of just looking. "It can be hard to always remember how lovely nature can be."

After a few more minutes of quiet, Bill added, "Never take nature for granted, David. We don't always slow down to appreciate the beauty in front of us—maybe until it is too late."

"Too late?" David repeated.

"We always assume that it will be there later, that we will have time to pause later. But often finding that time can become harder. We had the time as children, maybe—but not as adults."

After a short while, Bill furthered his thoughts. "Let me ask you a question. Think back a little—when is the last time you can recall lying back in a green grassy field with the sun on your face and watching clouds drift across a summer blue sky? Have you ever lain there watching the clouds for a long time, making things up in their shapes, admiring the peace, tranquility, the beauty of white clouds drifting across a summer sky? Have you ever had nothing to worry about?"

David pondered for a few moments. "I cannot really remember lying back and watching, no. Obviously I have watched clouds, but I can only remember doing it as I walk along. Why?"

"I am not singling you out as such—I think that few people take the time particularly as they grow out of childhood, so you are probably in the great majority," Bill explained, "but I was trying to give an illustration of how people, society as such, do not have time anymore, time to enjoy life, time to appreciate life. People are so engrossed in having to be aware of everything about everyone that there is simply no time to know about life, about the world that we live in. If we take the time to be on our devices, we have to forgo the time to do something else. That is why I was asking."

After a pause Bill continued. "What would sadden you more, David—sadden you at the end of what I hope will be a long and happy life—the realization that you had failed to send texts or e-mails to dozens, hundreds of people, that you had failed to update your social media whatever the latest fad is, or that you had never paused to admire the beauty of nature, never paused to watch clouds drift across a summer sky when you had the chance? How sad would it be to miss the world that you had lived in?"

"Point taken," David said. "I suppose the easy retort is that it is a busy world—but I take your point that we maybe make it busier than it needs to be."

Looking down below, they could see John looking up to their vantage point and the dogs laid out on the lawn taking a rest. Dogs rarely seem to consider what could be above them.

"Do you both like lobster?" Bill asked, changing the topic.

After receiving David's affirmation, Bill continued with his thought. "How about we order three fresh boiled from the café down there and take them back in the cooler for dinner tonight?"

"I can go one better," David added. "How about I go down, let Dad come on up to take in the views, and I take Rip and Riley back to the VW? In that way, you can order the lobsters in a while, and I can drive around to the shack and meet up in an hour and a half or so. It will avoid having to carry the lobsters all the way back."

"Sounds like a plan to me, if you don't mind. I'll wait up here for John and enjoy the solitude for a while longer."

"On the condition that I can drive home," David replied as he eased himself back through the door. "I quite like driving the bus."

In due course John arrived up at the parapet, and the two stood leaning on the rail, quiet in thought, for half an hour. Eventually they descended the spiral, emerging onto terra firma, and made their way back to the shack. There they ordered three good-sized lobsters and told the owner that they would be back in about forty-five minutes.

"There's a bench seat at the end of the headland if we want to sit," John suggested.

"Sounds good," Bill agreed. "Standing up there was tiring."

They sat on the bench, feet resting on the metal rail fence placed at the edge of the bluff, presumably to avoid people tumbling over the brink, from where they had an unobstructed view out to sea. Now that the tide had gone out, a large flat island of rock, about twenty feet long by ten feet wide, was exposed off the tip of their headland, thirty feet below their vantage point, with its fringe of long fronds of green seaweed around its circumference being swept back and forth as the ocean waters swirled around it and through the passage between rock and mainland. Looking farther out at the expanse of the ocean, they saw that the water had started to sparkle now that the frothing white horses had been replaced with choppy waves that no longer broke but instead reflected the descending afternoon sun. The ocean had lost a lot of its earlier ferocity and had become a more tranquil vista to end the day.

"We have seen some different faces of the ocean today," John commented. "It looks fine now that the wind has died down, a gentle giant. But I did enjoy the wildness when we arrived. An enjoyable visit to your ocean?"

"Yes, John—days like this make me happy. Days to remember."

"Do you enjoy memories, Bill? Do you enjoy looking back over your life?"

"A thoughtful question. Had you asked me ten years ago, I would have answered no. No, I didn't always enjoy remembering, because like most people I was focused on trying to make the future what I wanted and did not necessarily like to dwell on the imperfections of the past— almost as if I was trying to persuade myself that some of the past had not happened."

"What changed your thinking?"

"I came to understand that all my life is true, John. It is all true. My boyhood life is true, my life as a youth growing into a man is true, and my later years are true. All my happy times, all the sadder times, all my successes, all my difficulties, and all my mistakes—they are all equally true. The paths I elected to take and also the opportunities I didn't recognize or chose to ignore—they are all true, and they all brought me to where I ended up. It is easier to remember the more recent events in my life and therefore easier to persuade myself that the more recent events are more true—but it isn't so; they are all equally true and equally what made my life. You can be led to believe that the family you created as an adult with your wife and your own children is all that your life is about. But you have been part of another family, when you were young those many, many years ago; you were part of somebody else's family, and those memories and times are also true, John. They are true and deserve remembering because they were happy times made by people trying to give you a happy life. We shouldn't dismiss them as not true times."

"But you are happy with what you have created at the inn. Happy that the inn is also true?"

"Definitely happy, John."

They sat quietly for a while, watching the ocean before them. The gulls were out in force, now that the wind had subsided, shadowing the lobster fishermen as they checked their pots before nightfall. Finally it was time to return to the shack for their dinners and to find David and the dogs.

The drive back to their lake was a pleasant affair, taking them into the now-setting sun, which alternately bathed them in weaker red sunlight or dark, cool shadows cast by the increasing hills of New Hampshire. David was enjoying himself at the wheel, leaving Bill to pick the soundtrack for their journey, starting with Simon and Garfunkel before moving onto Don McLean, both of whom received a lot of vocal accompaniment. They stopped at a small general store to buy essential supplies, including wine, fresh bread, and some more bundles of wood.

It was already dark by the time they arrived back at their camp. Their fellow campers had been joined by some new arrivals because there were three fires burning away as the VW maneuvered over to their site. John got the fire going while David and Bill prepared their lobster feast, complete with melted butter and a large container of cole-slaw and local cheese from the general store. Rip and Riley had their own dinners and then meandered off into the dark to check out their new territory.

Dinner was more of a drawn-out affair. They were in no rush—the food was all cold—and so they enjoyed reflecting on a good day at the ocean, sipping their wine and steadily extracting the lobsters from their already cracked shells. The beauty of eating outdoors was that they didn't have to worry about making the inevitable mess with the lobsters.

John didn't fall asleep that evening, but neither he nor Bill objected when David offered to clean up the few dishes and track down the dogs, who could be heard occasionally but not seen. The older two admitted to being tired after the day of exercise and fresh sea air, maybe compounded a little by the wine.

"I was reflecting on what you asked me earlier as we watched the ocean this afternoon, John," Bill said, while David was off attending to his chores. "You asked me if I am happy with what has been created at the inn."

"I remember the conversation—you said that you were happy."

"Very happy, yes. But sometimes I know that I am too happy," Bill said reflectively.

"In what way too happy?" John questioned.

"You remember when we first met that I told you about my father telling me that if I had the ability and got the opportunity, I should choose the life that I wanted? That if I lived a life of my choosing, then I would have had a good life? Well, I found that advice to be good advice, but what my father failed to mention was how hard it can be to face leaving that life of your choosing. I have built a life that I love at the inn. I have found a life and a place where I am truly happy again, and the thought of leaving this life saddens me so much, John. I don't know, but I would believe that many people end up in situations not of their choosing, and the thought of leaving might not sadden them in the same way—I don't know. But my father never explained that I would end up wanting so much to never leave."

They sat and listened to David calling the dogs and watched the black night over the lake and the flitting fireflies in the wooded shoreline.

CHAPTER 21

Biplane in the Clouds

THE NEXT DAY THEY STAYED at the lake. On Bill's previous camping trips, mornings usually consisted of a hike with Rip and Riley or canoeing out on the water; whereas afternoons by the lake tended to be more relaxing affairs. During the morning, John and David went off for a four-hour hike while Bill took a canoe out to explore the lake—the two dogs sitting quietly on one of the cross thwarts, seeming to know not to rock the boat. After a couple of hours, Bill returned toward his point of origin and, at about a hundred feet off the shore, gave Rip and Riley the go-ahead to jump in and swim to shore—that was all they had been waiting for.

On that third afternoon, John was determined to catch their dinner, so, after a light lunch, he carried his chair and fishing equipment about a hundred yards farther along the lakeside, away from the other campers, setting himself up in a shaded spot between two pine trees at the water's edge, making sure the branches were high enough not to interfere with his casting. Luckily for the fish, John took a rest after about fifteen minutes and promptly nodded off in his chair, the line floating lazily in the sunshine. Luckily for the three campers, they had bought hot dogs and rolls the previous afternoon to make up for the lack of fish for supper.

Bill and David stayed close to their camp and watched John from afar. Bill was laid out on the grass at the edge of the lake, his head resting on a rolled-up blanket for a pillow, and David sat in a camp chair, legs outstretched, reading and resting in the late-spring sunshine.

Bill squinted up into the bright May sky through half-closed eyes, watching the occasional bird of prey circling high above and small cumulus clouds drifting across his view.

Bill broke the long period of silence. "Have you ever thought about those puffy white clouds, David?"

The question surprised David a little as he broke away from his book. "In what way, Bill?"

"It was just something posed to me a long time ago by my mother. The question has stayed with me, I suppose."

David didn't say anything.

"Looking back, it was probably one of the last carefree conversations that I can remember having with my mother," Bill said reflectively. "I left for college the next year, and life seemed to get busier; 'things' took on more importance and complications. After that, although we had good conversations, the conversations had a purpose, and we didn't seem to have the time to just chat like we did that afternoon. Anyway, I remember this particular day. It was a Sunday in mid-September, so the heat of the summer had gone, and large cumulus clouds were drifting across the fall sky on light winds that blew through the trees, rustling the leaves that were beginning to turn color but not willing to fall from the branches yet. I must have been seventeen. Had been out golfing with friends from school and came home to find Mom sitting out on the stone patio with a light sweater on, half-reading and half-watching the afternoon float by. I sat with her for a while, eyes closed, resting after the exertions of golf.

"Have you ever thought what it would be like to fly through one of those white puffy clouds? In an open-cockpit plane, I mean," Mom asked, suddenly dragging me out of my relaxation. "What it would feel like to be sort of inside one?"

"You have asked me that before, Mom. I know that the idea fascinates you a little," I replied. "Yes, I have sometimes thought about it—I have sometimes thought that it would be warm. I suppose that I am thinking of steam, but mostly I think that it would be chilly, damp on your face, and pleasantly quiet. Why, how do you imagine it to be, Mom?"

"Oh, I just think that it would be so peaceful. Nothing to trouble you, nothing to worry about—just tranquil."

We sat and watched the sky float by for a while. "What makes you think about the clouds, Mom?"

"Not wanting to sound morbid, William—but sometimes, in quiet moments, when I think about Brian, my mind wanders, and I think about the clouds and what they feel like."

"Do you somehow imagine that Brian might be sort of up there in the clouds, Mom?"

She watched the sky some more before replying, "It would be a nice thought, William—nice to imagine."

We didn't talk about the clouds anymore, but I remember the afternoon well.

Bill and David remained quiet for a long time, watching a still-stationary John and enjoying the absolute quiet of a sunny afternoon.

Eventually David asked, "Do you often reflect back on those you have lost, Bill? I ask only because I have never lost a close family member. I have been lucky in that regard."

Bill contemplated before replying. "As you reach your later years, you start reflecting more on your life and inevitably remember more and more of the people you have known, might have loved, who are no longer with you. Your parents, maybe siblings, good friends, and sometimes people you came across only fleetingly but whose memory stays with you. When those people left you, yes, you were sad. 'Grief-stricken' is a common phrase, and you do lament that they had to leave us. Sometimes wonder why they were taken so young. The question that does not surface when you are younger, at least it didn't to me, is 'Why am I still here?' But the older you get, the more you reflect on the fact that the majority of the people from your younger days are no longer alive. They are all gone, and those times are gone. And inevitably the question that sneaks up on me is 'Why am I still here when all those good people are gone? What did I do to deserve to have outlived them?'

You look at photos from younger days and come to the realization that you are the only one left! All gone—and sometimes long ago. That is the sadness, David. Sadness that you will not see those people or those times again. I can best describe it as an ache, a heartache that persists and gets more pronounced.

"I suppose that you remember your brother, Peter, in a different way to how you remember Brian, although I know that you do not really remember meeting Brian.

"Peter died before he was sixty-five, the age I am now. I have come to recognize that he was a good man. He was probably a better man than myself, because he lived life you see, lived life to the fullest; whereas I know that I just try to live. Lived life versus living? To me, at least, David, a good man is not one who doesn't do wrong…it is a man who doesn't do bad things."

"My dad has sometimes told me that what hurts him is that it is rare you get to say good-bye in a way that you would like," David said.

"I definitely understand that sentiment, David. I would never say that I have wanted to die—that would not be true—but yes, I have often wished that I could be with some, or all, of those people whom I once knew again. Just to hug them or shake their hand one more time. Would that diminish the ache? I don't know—but I do think that it would."

After thinking about it for a moment longer, Bill added, "I once read somewhere that when you die and go to heaven, all the cats and dogs that you have ever known are waiting at the gates to greet you. I am not the firmest believer, but I do hope that that thought is true for the people whom you have known and loved—it makes me happy to imagine that."

They again sat late into the evening after their hot dogs for dinner, cooked over the open fire, accompanied by sauerkraut and the usual fixings. They didn't discuss a great deal, happy to enjoy the quiet and contemplate.

"Do we have a plan for our last day, Bill?" John asked when they had all started yawning, indicating that their beds were calling.

"I was thinking that we can head up to the north and take a drive to one of the higher mountains," Bill answered. "Spectacular scenery and good hiking if you feel like getting a last one in."

"I am sure that David would like to hike," John said, getting a nodded agreement from David, "and I would like to take a drive up to the higher elevations—I do like the views of endless forest."

They watched the fire die down for another fifteen minutes before Bill and David called it a night. John sat on his own for a while, his mind wandering idly over the last year since he and David had first set eyes on the inn. He thought about that chance encounter and tried to remember the Robert Frost poem about the paths you took in your life. When he felt his head begin to nod and could no longer focus his thoughts about the roads in a yellow wood, he reluctantly dragged himself out of the chair, made sure that the fire was safe, the bus was all closed up, and then quietly crawled into his tent without disturbing a snoring David.

CHAPTER 22

1967

DAVID WOKE UP FIRST THE following morning and was delighted to find, when he went to grab a quick shower, that the hot water had arrived. Bill had just emerged from his tent when David made it back to their camp.

"We have hot water, Bill," David announced. "If you want to grab a shower, I will awaken Dad and then we can go down to the little diner in town for breakfast. My treat."

"I don't need asking twice when it comes to a diner breakfast." Bill laughed, grabbing his towel.

David woke up John, gave him the plan, and within half an hour, the three hungry campers were ready to go.

"Should we take Rip and Riley with us?" David asked.

"Yes, there are tables outside on a front patio at the diner, so we can eat out there and the dogs should behave and lie quietly."

Breakfast was the relaxing affair that Bill enjoyed, complete with plenty of coffee and the day's newspapers. As usual, it took longer than anticipated, but they were on vacation with nowhere to be. Nevertheless by around nine thirty, they were well fed, had caught up on the day's news, David had settled the bill, and they were heading north in the VW.

They intentionally stayed on the smaller, less-traveled roads, with John driving, David in the passenger seat, and Bill in the rear relaying navigation instructions as he consulted the maps. The route initially followed the course of a river and then headed into the hills, rising and falling gently as it headed generally northward, deviating to follow the contours around the higher peaks rather than traversing over the top. The elevation increased slowly and steadily as their drive progressed, indicated by occasional roadside markers, and the higher they climbed, the greater the preponderance of conifers covering the endless vista. On two occasions John pulled over at small rest areas so that they could jump out and enjoy the views, particularly the sight of the mountains they were bound for.

"Great ski areas in the winter," Bill said, "but I love the isolation and vastness at this time of year. Feels like you are on top of the world."

About an hour and a half into the drive, after passing the four-thousand-feet elevation marker, Bill slowed them down before pointing out a sharp left-hand turn signposted "Mountain Summit." The road narrowed and snaked upward through the pines for about another two miles before emerging above the tree line. The forest setting was replaced by an open landscape consisting of moss-covered granite, with intermittent stretches of grass and just the occasional solitary tree trying to survive against the odds as they approached what appeared to be the roof of the world. After they had driven for another mile, the road dropped down to the right and terminated in an expansive circular cobblestoned parking area bordered on one side by a rising grass bank cut into the side of the mountain, while the other side of the lot looked out on the endless panorama below and was demarcated by an extensive wooden railed fence. John pulled across the lot and parked the nose of the bus close to the fence rails, giving the three occupants an exceptional view of the vista spread before and below them. The color of the carpet started as bright green in the foreground and transitioned into pale gray away on a horizon that looked to be fifty or more miles away.

Bill, John, and David climbed out somewhat slower than the two dogs, who leaped out and scampered around expectantly. They walked over to the fence at the edge of the parking area and stood admiring the impressive view for a few minutes.

"It feels special up here, Bill," John said. "*Majestic* is probably the description that comes to mind."

"Everything always looks unspoiled to me," Bill agreed. "I imagine that the view has hardly ever changed."

"Can you actually get up to the top?" David asked, turning and looking up at the granite summit rising above the grassy bank on the opposite side of the parking area.

"Yes, I was going to give you the options," Bill replied. "You can either trek up to the top there by taking a rough pathway that starts upward at the point where the road drops down to enter the parking lot. The hike is steep in places and would probably take you about two hours to get there and back. It is interesting. When you get to the top, there is a small brass monument marking the summit and some metal markers set into the granite describing the landmarks that you can see. Or the other option is to take the pathway leading off through the gap in the fence on the far side of the lot over there. It leads partway around to the other side of the mountain—has great views. I think that I will take a walk on the pathway—not as strenuous, but good exercise—but feel free to head up if you want, David."

"I think I will if that is OK with you," David said. "Seems a pity to have come this far and not actually reach the top."

John opted to tag along with Bill; whereas Rip and Ripley didn't think twice, running ahead of David, assuming that was where the excitement was.

"See you in a while," John called back to David as he and Bill headed for the opening in the fence, and David was reaching the entrance to the parking lot.

"Enjoy," David shouted back as he started up the rocky path to the top and gestured for the terriers to follow.

Bill and John's path, which was signposted to the Scenic Observation Area, was a well-maintained trail, natural terrain in places, and in others manmade endeavor had assisted with steps, wooden railroad ties, and the occasional handrail to keep the walkers safe. As they traversed around the mountaintop, more and more breathtaking views were revealed. In some respects, the views were a continuation of the magnificent scene of forest, hills, and mountains that seemed to stretch on without end. They were looking out to the north now—the green cover was broken occasionally by the twinkling of a lake set within the trees of a valley— but apart from that, it seemed as though it must stretch to Canada. It wasn't any particular snapshot of the view that was spectacular. It was the enormity of it all.

Bill and John talked about their lives in general but tended to work on a backward time line. They started out discussing their adult kids and their families when the children were growing up. Their discussion moved further back to the time when they themselves were still single and the world was their world, eventually ending up in their own youth.

"I don't feel it is our world, or at least my world, anymore, John," Bill said. "It didn't go away in a day, but it definitely left."

"If the truth be told, Bill, I felt that it stopped being my world more or less the day David went off to college. There were periods when it would flicker back into focus—there still are periods—but it wasn't my world anymore. It was someone else's."

Bill nodded. "You could be right; you could just be right."

By now they were approaching the advertised Observation Area, complete with a wooden fenced perimeter and some small wooden picnic tables complete with built-in bench seats. Strolling across to the furthest table, they sat down the wrong way on the table's bench so that they could lean with their backs against the edge of the planked tabletop and their feet outstretched. They both sat in silence for a while, taking in the tranquility and the vastness of the scene before them.

Eventually it was John who broke their quiet contemplation. "Do you remember last summer when you mentioned something to the effect that they should have paused time in 1967?"

"Yes, that is a thought that I have frequently sensed. Although I probably added that I am not dogmatic on the date, just strong on my belief that time should have been suspended back before computerization invaded and dictated every facet of our lives."

"Well, I have found myself dwelling on your conviction a lot during the past months and more and more empathize with the premise and find myself agreeing more and more with your feelings," John said.

"Does your understanding stem from what I expressed, or have you harbored such frustrations and irritation of your own, albeit subconsciously?"

"When I stopped to think about it, I recognized a lot of the feelings you expressed were in my own life, and deep down I agreed with your sentiments. The frustrations and sadness must have been with me for quite a time, but I either suppressed them or failed to recognize them. Of late, though, I have found myself identifying with such aggravations, and the resulting disappointments, on a very regular basis. And the phrase you used, that they should have paused time in 1967, echoes through my mind frequently, and it gives me a lot of pause for thought."

"What causes your exasperation, John? What type of experiences?"

"Oh, there have been many sources—and the frequency has increased alarmingly, probably because it is on my mind these days. The core of my dismay, if that is a good description, is how what was simple and straightforward can be made complicated. How the introduction of modern technology and communications can complicate what was a simple task. The example that you gave of no longer being able to make a phone call is perfect, and it is that sort of thing that irritates me." John paused for a moment before continuing, after thinking through an example. "What I am most aware of is the sheer frustration, bordering on anger to be truthful, that I regularly come across when trying to accomplish what should be simple transactions on the computer or smartphone. Something that is depicted as a convenience in the age of the computer. All I want to do is buy tickets to an event, as an example. First I have to jump through hoops to prove that I am, in fact, a person and not some computer robot. I am then allowed to pick tickets, which are held for fifteen minutes so that I can complete the transaction. So I try to check out. To do that I have to log on to my account, but find that my password is no longer secure enough. So before I can proceed, I have to enter a new, more complex password, including symbols and capitals and numerals, and the site sends an e-mail to my registered e-mail address to confirm that the password has been changed. E-mail arrives and I have to confirm authenticity. I can now log into my account, only to find that the registered credit card is no longer valid, so I have to find the new card and edit online—and confirm changes to the account via e-mail authorization again. You can guess the outcome: by the time I get to buy the tickets, my fifteen minutes have expired, and I am back to square one, proving that I am not a robot. It is irrational, but I just want to scream or to reach into the computer and grab something or somebody. It would help if I could talk to somebody to vent my annoyance, but I know that talking to a real person is a fantasy unto itself. And talking to somebody who even cares in the least let alone who can effect a change is a dream that I have had to abandon long ago. And that realization saddens me, Bill."

Bill nodded and smiled a little. "I do know how infuriating it can be, not intending to make light of it."

Having got his thoughts in his head, John continued. "I know that your Internet activity has been limited for the last few years, but you would find the experience much more upsetting than you ever used to. The extent to which increasingly invasive websites and the people behind them can intrude and corrupt my Internet browsing is infuriating. You cannot appreciate how much worse the violations have become. The computer geniuses are doubtless very proud of their accomplishments, but to me it is insulting and exasperating to the point of wishing I had an alternative to their search engines. Those geniuses must love the fact that they can tailor the advertising on every page I am looking at to mirror the products that I have recently searched for or purchased, but I find it insulting and sort of arrogant of people wanting to extricate even more money out of me. But I feel powerless to stop it—it is exasperating."

Bill nodded but didn't say anything.

"I have often recalled your reference to 1967, and although I would err more toward the mid-to-late seventies, the sentiment in what you said rings true to me. Life was good, we understood life, and it moved at a pace we could keep track of and enjoy at the same time. There seems to be a commonly held belief that the faster life moves, the faster new innovations can be introduced; the better off we are, the more enjoyable life is, and the more productive we are. But the premise feels wrong to me. If life and changes move too fast, then we can neither appreciate nor enjoy it, Bill, and I don't believe that it is age talking. I feel that it is a desire for quality of life rather than how fast we can skim through the surface of a lot of life. I will stop there."

Bill smiled again. "I do firmly believe, and maybe even have expressed to David, that the commonly held notion that change is a good thing is very wrong—maybe improvement is a good thing, but you shouldn't believe that change is necessarily improvement. Change for the sake of change is a poor thing. And I believe that subconsciously everybody eventually wants consistency; they want to be able to visit their yesterdays."

They sat thoughtfully for a while before John concluded, "I reflected last fall, how when theme parks were developed, over the past thirty years or so, they featured futuristic worlds but also showcased the life and times we were losing. And I figured that the reason why the parks took us back there was because those times made people happy. You could say that the visitors preferred those times to what they had been replaced with, Bill. I was telling David while we were at the inn over Christmas that we had good times in those years, and they were taken away. I sometimes wonder how it came to be that the settings and the world that we had can be experienced now only in theme parks. Those settings were real, and we allowed them to be ruined and relegated to memories that we can walk around in theme parks and describe as quaint. But we had them, Bill—we had them to enjoy."

"We should be glad that we knew the times, John. Glad that we have the memories."

Their thoughts were interrupted by a very faint sound way up to their left. Looking upward and shielding their eyes against the sun, they could make out a faint figure waving its arms at what they presumed to be the summit. John and Bill assumed that it must be David, and waved their arms in response, figuring that it didn't really matter if it wasn't him. It was too far away to spot Rip and Riley, who were too low to the ground anyway.

Their reflective mood broken, they arose slowly, stretched their limbs, and started on the path back to the parking lot and their friend, the bus.

CHAPTER 23

Going Home

DAVID ACTUALLY BEAT THEM BACK to the VW, the trek down obviously a lot easier than the upward hike. The dogs were eagerly lapping at their well-earned water, and David was leaning against the rounded bulb that was the front of the bus, admiring the views. After John and Bill had been teased for their slowness, and all three had caught their breaths and also had drinks of water, they headed the bus back down from the mountain. Before loading a cassette into the player, Bill put the radio on for a couple of news cycles to catch up with the world. The local forecast called for probable thunderstorms along with some stronger winds to roll through in the early hours of the next morning.

"My suggestion would be to take down the tents when we get back, let the bottoms dry out in the afternoon sun, and then pack them away before nightfall," Bill said as they reached the main road at the base of the narrower mountain roadway, "and then we can flatten out the bench seats in the bus and sleep on those beds in our sleeping bags tonight. Otherwise, it could be wet and messy trying to pack up soaked tents in the morning."

"Sounds like a good idea to me," John agreed. "No point in making things difficult if we have an alternative."

As they passed through the small township, built along the river closer to their lake, Bill pulled over at the Country Store to collect some provisions for their last dinner. David picked out steaks, which had worked out well on their first evening, and some Italian sausage along with onions and peppers. Bill got a large loaf of freshly baked bread, while John busied himself across the road, picking out some more wine and locally brewed beer. Bill also pulled into the town's small service station to fill up, check the oil, and give the engine a quick check in readiness for their drive the next day.

"Everything looks OK to my untrained eye. Touch wood, she has behaved very well."

It was already midafternoon by the time they got back to camp. Bill made sure to park the bus a little further from the pine trees and then all three quickly took the tents down and turned them over to dry on the warm grass. David took Rip and Riley for a lakeside walk for an hour while Bill and John sat and relaxed in the afternoon sun, both with hats pulled down to shield their eyes. There wasn't much sign of movement when he and the dogs returned, so David packed up the tents as quietly as he could and stowed most of the gear safely inside the bus while enjoying a beer for his efforts. The two relaxing campers pulled their hats up at around five o'clock, claimed that they hadn't been asleep, yawned, and roused themselves.

The evening largely mirrored their previous three dinners, a similarly relaxing affair. By the time the sun had set, the food was well roasted over the fire, and they sat eating quietly as night followed twilight across the lake. The temperature dropped, the wind increased, and there was a sense of if not foreboding, then definitely of weather approaching.

"Rip and Riley can sleep up on the front seats," Bill said aloud but to nobody in particular. "We don't want them clambering over us in the night."

The wind made the logs blaze more fiercely and picked up some of the embers as sparks and carried them far, luckily out over the black waters. David told them about his trek up the mountain and about the view from the top. John was interested, as was Bill, even though he had made the same climb three years ago during one of his early excursions with Eddie.

"Standing right on the granite top was a good feeling," David assured them. "Very satisfying and probably even more so because there wasn't anybody else up there. The solitude was something. What were you two doing down there when I shouted?"

"We were lamenting how fast and how much life has changed, David," Bill answered. "Your dad was yearning for the times gone by."

David laughed a little. "You are definitely rubbing off on Dad, Bill. He has always been nostalgic, but your life at the inn definitely resonates with him. You have a convert, doesn't he, Dad?"

John smiled but didn't say anything immediately.

"You have been very quiet tonight, John," Bill said. "Very mellow."

"The wine is deepening my thinking. Some people get loud and obnoxious when they drink. Me, I get thoughtful. Maybe it is the wine, maybe it is the nighttime, I don't know—but I tend to get thoughtful— in a meaningful way."

"About what?" Bill asked.

"To be honest, I was actually thinking back to that conversation, about 1967, Bill," John said, "and was wondering if it is a mistake to dream. If I should let it go because dreaming can eventually bring discontentment."

"I'm not sure, John—I have never thought it a mistake to dream. As long as you know that dreams can be unfulfilled because the dreams might be unattainable—and that is OK. But I have always thought that you should never let the dreams go unfulfilled because you never tried to achieve them."

"Why is 1967 special, Dad?" David asked. "It can't have been that good because I wasn't even born."

"That is why I would never truly want to go back there, David. It is a sentiment, I suppose. A sentiment to go back to the lifestyle, not the year." John smiled. "Don't worry. I will always have you."

"You dream, John, and if you ever seriously want to come back, you are always welcome," Bill concluded. "But don't just dream until it is too late to act."

Eventually there were no more flames, just the remnants of the last logs looking gray on the outside and somehow glowing orange on the inside. One by one they made their walk over to the bathrooms, and while Bill was away, Rip and Riley wandered off into the darkness. David put some water on the remaining embers, even though the rain was approaching, and the five weary campers agreed to call it a night.

Bill put blankets on the front seats and the dogs obediently jumped in, Rip driving while Riley curled up on the passenger seat. Bill also opened the angled front windscreens, the quarter lights in the front, and the cabin windows on the leeward side so that the cool breeze blew freely and steadily through the bus as the three lay looking up at the night sky. Bill had explained that this model was called "the twenty-one-window edition" and included four smaller windows on each side curving between the side panels of the bus and the roof, giving the occupants a good view of the heavens. An almost full moon provided sufficient illumination to see the clouds scudding across the sky, heading toward the east and steadily increasing in their coverage as the hours passed into early morning. By the time the thunderstorm arrived, all three were sleeping, but they were awakened by the thunder and managed to see some of the lightning over the distant mountains across the lake before falling back into their slumbers.

They awoke early to a very wet campsite, although the rain had ended.

"Good call to pack everything up yesterday, Bill," John said as he opened up the double rear doors.

"Should we retrieve the fire tub and head back to the diner?" Bill asked and received a positive response.

And so it was that the trip ended more abruptly than planned. But they enjoyed their diner breakfast and turned back toward Vermont in good spirits, even though they had not showered and were unshaven. Whereas on the way out all three had been keen to drive, their fatigue was kicking in a little, and John and Bill were happy to let David take the bus.

Once over the border into Vermont, they stopped for a coffee break, and they sat outside the small coffee shop, reflecting on their trip.

"Thanks for inviting us, Bill," David said. "I enjoyed it all, but most of all, the bus and driving the bus."

'Thank you for coming along, David. Thanks to both of you for the company."

"We enjoyed it, Bill, very much. Although you have made me dream," John replied.

"Just remember, John, that if you want to act on your dreams, you are very welcome up at the inn whenever you want," Bill said. "And if you want those dreams to take root, you are welcome to stay for as long as you want."

After a few minutes of enjoying their coffees, Bill asked, "Did either of you plan on coming back later in the summer?"

"I was definitely intending to," John replied first, "but it will probably be closer to September, because I have commitments to cover some golf and tennis tournaments in August."

"And I will try to make it for a few days while Dad is up here," David added. "I don't have as much flexibility as Dad but can hopefully manage some time in that first week of September."

"For as long as you want," Bill said as they rose up from their seats, stretched, and made their way back to the VW.

"So what music do you have planned for the last leg, Bill?" David asked, grinning.

"I think that we should go back to something older, David. I will introduce you to Frank Sinatra."

So they got back under way to the sound of "Love's Been Good to Me." All three stayed in their own thoughts until they were getting close to the inn and the end of their trip. Frank was singing about the summer wind.

"Do you remember me telling you that music can bring back the feelings and the memories of your life like nothing else can, David? Well, this song takes me back to a car trip in the summer of 1966, when

I was home from college. I am back in the back seat of that car. I can see my parents and my brother and can feel again the excitement of those days. My father decided that we could drive down to Florida, a daunting adventure in those days. As we drove, we listened to the ever-changing radio stations as we went down through the eastern states. And Frank would come on fairly regularly, and 'Summer Wind' would resonate through the car. I can hear my father singing along with Frank, and I can see out of the car's windows at the summer winds and countryside of Virginia, the Carolinas, Georgia, and into Florida of the sixties. I can see my mother and can laugh with my brother. We were happy together, and they were happy days that, at that moment, we knew wouldn't end. The thing is, David, when I hear Frank sing now, yes, I am back in that car heading for a vacation that I didn't think would end—but I sometimes stop and wonder why I am the only one left. They were all good people in that car, and I wonder why I had to outlive them all. I sometimes wish that I hadn't outlived them—that I could have departed, imagining the family car trip to the sand and sea of paradise didn't have to end."

"I understand what you say," David replied, "and I know that when I hear this song, maybe forty years from now, it will take me back to a VW bus and four enjoyable days in a peaceful world with yourselves and two terriers. Thank you, Bill."

"It is somewhat ironic that it was a summer wind that brought us to the inn in the first place," John added reflectively.

The three campers arrived back at the inn by midafternoon, weary but happy after an enjoyable trip. Bill backed their trusty bus into the barn, where John and David offered to empty out all the gear so that Bill could go down and catch up with Annie, Eddie, and their helpers. The terriers scampered on ahead, seemingly glad to be home.

They recounted their trip to Eddie and Annie in the bar following a much-appreciated home-cooked dinner and, after a good and long night's rest, John and David bade their farewells the following morning, assuring their hosts that they would return later that summer.

Part 4:
Contented

CHAPTER 24

The Cottage

AUGUST RETURNED, AND TRUE TO his word, John turned up three days before the end of the month. It was a blustery late-summer day when he dropped down to the inn, overcast but with temperatures still up in the low seventies. Looking over toward the stables as he climbed out of the Jeep and stretched his limbs, John could see the horses sheltering inside but with their heads poking out and their manes blowing forward over their eyes.

"Hello, stranger," Bill called as he approached from the direction of the barn.

"Checking everything is secure?" John asked as they shook hands.

"Yes, it's expected to be a breezy evening," Bill acknowledged as they headed toward the front door.

Bill got John installed in another room, the fourth different one in the twelve months since he had first arrived at the inn. They agreed to catch up and have a drink together out on the deck after Bill had finished with his dinner duties in the restaurant.

"I have been thinking things over, Bill, since our conversations at the lake in May, and would like to talk something through a bit," John said before heading upstairs with his bag.

"Plenty of time," Bill said as the door opened and two more arriving guests entered out of the windy afternoon.

Soon after ten o'clock, dinner was all finished. John had enjoyed his pork chop with roast potatoes and applesauce, followed by some blueberry pie with cream, and was now settled on the deck, as he had been during his first evening at the inn, feeling the warm wind gust around the end of the building and off across the pasture. Bill came out to join him, bringing another glass of wine for John and an evening whisky for himself, along with Rip and Riley, who dawdled off the deck into the night for an evening forage.

"So how has the writing been? Is the book nearing completion?" Bill asked when he was settled.

"The regular articles have been good, thanks. I am slowly reducing the number of articles and publications, out of choice really. I seem to be drawn more toward tennis, golf, and some baseball now. Tending to write pieces around the major tournaments, either the current event or a historical slant on past editions. And more and more I collaborate with half a dozen monthly or bimonthly publications rather than the weekly magazines. I have even done a couple of articles about boxing from decades ago. I used to cover boxing a lot toward the end of its heyday, but it is probably fifteen years since I saw my last fight in person. That was a sport where the athletes' careers were either on the ascent or were descending rapidly. There were not many true comebacks once they were past their prime, once they had shown fallibility."

"And the book?"

"It is finally finished, thanks. Well, finished from my standpoint and is now going through the long editing process."

"And David—how is he doing?"

"Getting on very well, thanks, seems to be learning all about life at school. Spent a few weeks this summer out in Colorado with friends, fly-fishing, hiking, and white-water rafting. Goes back to school in three weeks, I think, but he will be up next week for about a week."

"Yes, he called to book a room. He is good boy; you should be proud."

"Thanks, Bill. But it isn't me; it's all him. I cannot take credit."

"So what is on your mind, John? You said that you have been thinking about things since our camping trip."

"Dwelling on a few things really, but probably all being generated from the same origin. I have been considering where my life will go when it comes to retirement. In a way how I want to retire and where I want to retire. And I got to reflect on a number of things you said on our trip and wondering what exactly you were referring to or sort of hinting at."

"You are thinking about retiring?" Bill asked, a little surprised.

"Well, that is the thing really. I am lucky to have a job where I am somewhat independent and can elect to half-retire in a way. I work from home anyway, just me and the computer and the traveling, and I have been thinking about transitioning increasingly into the retrospective pieces, which I do enjoy very much, and away from the more current articles. And then I have my books. I have started another one, with a couple more fleshed out in notebooks but mainly in my mind. So the long and short of it is that I can sort of retire but also keep active, to the extent that I want."

"And where do our camping conversations come into the equation?"

John took a moment before broaching what had been on his mind. "When we were talking seriously about life and the past, you alluded to the fact that I was always welcome at the inn, could come up whenever I wanted, and, if I remember correctly, that I could stay for as long as I would like if I wanted my dreams to materialize."

"I can remember a conversation to that effect." Bill nodded. "Cannot remember the words, but the conversation, yes."

"Well, as I said, I got to imagining semiretirement and what that could look like and inevitably started thinking about where I could retire to," John continued. "And to ask the direct question, Bill, I started to imagine moving up here, to the inn, and wanted to know if you would be at all amenable to such an arrangement."

"Do you mean as a permanent guest?" Bill asked, clearly interested.

"No, not really. I don't think that I could be content being a resident guest. No, what I got to thinking about was whether you would be willing to allow me to buy the larger cottage from you. For me to sell up and move into the cottage. To make my home there."

Bill was quiet for a few minutes, and John gave him time to digest what had been thrown out there.

After a short while, John added some more flavor to what he had been considering. "And if it suits you, Bill, I would be more than happy to help out here at the inn. In a way lend a hand to yourself, Eddie, or Annie if you get busy or need a break."

"I am definitely receptive to the idea," Bill said, after he had been able to initially think it through. "I am just not sure exactly how we should think of structuring such an arrangement—to safeguard you, me, and the inn."

"Oh, I wasn't thinking that we have to reach a decision here and now. I just wanted to throw it out there for you to consider. Please take some time. Like I said originally, I am not committed to retirement or even semiretirement yet, but I did want to explore some possibilities in the hope that might crystallize my thoughts so that I can make a decision. So that I know what I need to decide."

"Thanks, John, nothing like some thought-provoking conversation before bed," Bill said jokingly. "I will definitely sleep on it, and we can brainstorm some more tomorrow."

"Sorry. Maybe I should have waited until the morning before raising the question," John acknowledged. "Please don't lose any sleep.

Bill smiled. "Don't worry about me. I never lose sleep, thankfully. And it is a pleasant issue to think through. Actually, getting more pleasant as I think about it. But it is getting late, so if it is OK with you, I will take the pups for a quick walk around and then head to bed."

"Thanks, Bill," John said, rising up and collecting their glasses. "I will pop these on the bar and see you in the morning. Not too early, as I am on vacation."

"'Night, John," Bill replied, heading off the deck into the warm wind of the moonless night.

The following day was much more summery. The wind had decreased significantly, and the overcast outlook had given way to a mixture of blue sky mixed with some higher stratus cloud. The temperature was probably around the same, but the day looked warmer.

In between serving breakfasts, Bill did chat briefly to John. "I have been pondering about it, and I think that there is a good way for this to work out. Will keep working on it."

John smiled. "No rush, Bill. I am not going anywhere."

Bill went into the larger town, approximately fifteen miles away, to run some errands for the morning while John did some work on the computer up in his room. It was afternoon before the two got to chat again, in the bar after lunch was over.

"So what I have been thinking," Bill started, "is for you to effectively buy into a share of the inn but not necessarily own a specific part, such as the cottage."

Bill allowed his initial thought to sink in before continuing. "You can definitely have the cottage as your own, and carry out any remodeling that you might want. But I was trying to arrange a way whereby you can have an interest in the property but you cannot sell it and disrupt life at the inn, if we ever do not see eye to eye somewhere down the road. Can't see it happening, but you never know. Except that obviously you can sell your share back to me. In a way, I think we should be partners, but neither one can sell out except to the other. And both Annie and Eddie are partners in a way—they both have a home for life."

"I think that I could go along with something along those lines, Bill," John said. "It wouldn't be my intention to ever disrupt what you have created; that is exactly why I want to come here. But I take your point that nobody ever knows how things evolve, so we should structure something to safeguard you, me, Eddie, and Annie. On the face of it buying a share of the property sounds good to me. It would give me the reassurance of owning something rather than being a permanent guest."

"Let's give it some more thought," Bill suggested, "and I can mention it to Annie and Eddie, just to make sure that they are comfortable with the concept."

So after dinner that evening, Bill asked Annie and Eddie to come out onto the deck for a glass of wine before Annie headed home. He laid out the idea that John and he had been thinking through and explained that they had not sorted out any details yet and that John had not actually decided whether or not to semiretire. Nevertheless, Bill asked Annie and Eddie if such an arrangement would be agreeable to them.

Annie spoke but Eddie nodded the same sentiment. "You know that you don't have to ask us, Bill. It is nice that you do ask, but there really is no need."

"In a way I know that, Annie," Bill replied. "But I also want you to know that this is your home, and you have a right to be comfortable in your home."

"I know, Bill," Annie continued, "and I appreciate the consideration. But it is a moot point, because I for one would be delighted to have John live at the inn permanently."

Eddie nodded and added, "To some extent, Bill, it is something that people don't often get to appreciate. In some ways we all begin life as part of a family, then leave home to start our own families and as such are not often alone for a long period. But eventually, through one of life's circumstances, the person's own family dissolves, and their original family is sadly gone, so the latter part of life can bring loneliness. You live the majority of your life with your families but can end your life alone. I know that the loneliness can be continuous and difficult. We three are good examples of people who would have grown old alone. What we have at the inn is a chance to grow old together as our last family maybe—and I would be very happy to have a new member of our family."

Even though John again tried to explain that he had not absolutely decided on the plan, the four toasted their union.

"So what has made you want to make such a move, John?" Annie asked. "I mean, Eddie and I were not giving up too much to make the move, but it must be a harder decision for you. Don't get me wrong—there isn't a day that I don't wake up and appreciate where I am and the life I have—but I'm just wondering what drove you."

Eddie couldn't help smiling when Annie had said that he had not given up too much.

"It wasn't really one single thing per se," John answered. "In truth, I liked the thought of the inn, and what Bill had tried to create, during that first visit a year ago, during the storm. And Bill's description, his reasoning for wanting to establish a haven from a world that wouldn't rest, caused me to pause and made me think. And each time I visited, I loved to arrive, and each time I left, I was a little miserable. Part of me wished that I didn't have to leave and wondered why, in fact, I did have to leave. But I am not sure that there was one specific reason, Annie."

"But something must have been on your mind over the summer for you to approach the subject so soon after returning," Bill asked, pushing John a little. "Nothing triggered your decision?"

John thought for a few moments. "Well, see if you can relate to this feeling," he said to none of the three in particular. "It has been going around in my head for a few months now, actually since that night when we slept out in the bus on the last night of our trip. I was awakened in the early hours by the thunder, and I lay there, drifting in and out of sleep, watching the rain occasionally lash the VW and the lightning fork across the sky. The thought crept into my mind that in some respects, life was a circle insofar as what made you happy all those years ago when you were young is what still makes you happy today, that eventually you come back to your childhood. What occurred to me during that night, and I cannot shake, is that although my life has taken me down many roads—and I have experienced many wonderful things, accomplished a lot, and life has blessed me with a family that I would not change for anything—it dawned on me that I have never been happier than when I was a boy. As I say it, it sounds somewhat heartless of me and unappreciative toward all those I have loved and who have loved me through my life, but I don't mean it in that way. On that night, I remembered how happy I had been as a boy, around ten or eleven maybe, safe and happy in my world. It was a world that I understood and a world that didn't present me with problems I couldn't solve or show me the sadness and fear that existed. My memories went back to my boyhood. I specifically remembered cycling to the small local library, getting another book in the series of schoolboy adventures that I was reading, getting home, and being able to spend hours in my fictional world. No real responsibility and the unappreciated luxury of no demands. Simple pleasures that could be repeated and did not disappoint. I reasoned that why I was so fulfilled with so little was that nobody, and nothing, had tried to persuade me that there was more to life, that I should, in fact, be dissatisfied with just a book. You see nobody had yet said there is more to life, so you need to abandon your safe haven and go and experience it all. And, more importantly, nobody had told me, ever did tell me, to be careful, John, because once you do leave your haven and your happiness, you can never have it back. You can never have it back."

John paused. Because of the darkness, he couldn't see the others' faces, nor could they see his.

"And then along came youth, and girls, and college, and a job, and family, and a career. And roughly, in the same order, so they all went away again. But when they had all gone, nobody came along and said you can go back now, John. Nobody ever said it, and I never have."

John took a couple of sips of his wine, collecting his thoughts from the bus. "What made me happy all those years ago still makes me happy. For all the things that I have done and accomplished and experienced, I am still that ten-year-old boy and deep down still want exactly what I wanted then. I have experienced so much and had such highs in my life, but I desire nothing more than my own company, a good book, and no responsibility. It is almost as if I came to the understanding that I have seen it all, have had it all, have tasted it all, but I want to go back to where I started, to what made me happy all those years ago. And I asked myself, why have you never gone back? Why, after you had seen life, did you not elect to simplify things again? And the answer I arrived at was that I had been persuaded there was so much to do in this world, so much to see, to experience, so much to acquire that needed an ever-increasing source of funds that I couldn't go back to my enjoyment. The habit of keeping going and the pressures of needing to keep going are difficult to ignore. You are afraid that if you allow the car to stop, and get out to take a look around, it might not restart again, and you might not like where you are, so you keep driving."

John continued after another wine break. "When the thought wouldn't leave me, I tried to rationalize, and I think I understand the reason why I was happy then and have never been as truly contented since. I think it is that I didn't know the bad things in life, didn't know the sad things in life, and once I knew those things, I could never be as untroubled as I was in those days—inside I wanted to be untroubled again. I think that I have risen to the challenges of my life and have been rewarded for my efforts. But I don't want to be challenged anymore; I don't need to be rewarded anymore. I want the happiness that I knew before my eyes were opened to the unhappiness. We don't really change. We grow, we experience, we become worldly, but inside I am the boy who is happy with a book—safe and happy in my room, without somebody telling me that I should want more. In a way I wish that I hadn't learned everything that I have learned in my life—it sounds strange, but that is the truth. I want my happy boyhood again, my happy uncomplicated boyhood and my innocence, my happy innocence."

John fell silent, and it was Eddie who spoke up. "Somewhere inside, I think we all feel that way at times, John. I know that I cannot always articulate it, and often we do not recognize it in sufficient time to do anything about it, but I think we all feel much of what you just expressed—feel it before it is our time."

"It is difficult to convey your feelings, I know, John," Bill said, "and equally difficult to recognize your own feelings, but I think that I understand."

"The path of your life can sometimes be interrupted," Eddie added, "but the desire to regain the innocence, and hopefully your happiness, from your boyhood resonates with me—had never thought quite in those terms, but I see it, John."

"To innocence," Bill toasted as he emptied his glass.

A short while later, after Annie and Eddie had said their good-nights and headed off up the lane to their cottages, and Bill was getting ready to take the dogs for their late-night stroll, he turned to John, fishing for the cigar in his pocket, and said, "You can have it back, John—you cannot have the years, but you can have the happiness."

CHAPTER 25

Out of the Race

─────────

The calendar had turned into September when David arrived for his few days before getting ready to go back to college. It was only a week after John had come up, but the feeling in the air was fall now. Summer had departed for that year.

After bustling into reception around noon, David quickly unpacked his belongings, and then he and John grabbed a beer and a sandwich out on the deck, where David recounted his three weeks in Colorado with various friends from college. The fly-fishing particularly interested John; it always seemed the perfect pastime, a beautiful natural setting, absolute quiet and solitude, and you were participating in an outdoor activity, so you could even feel good about yourself. But David seemed to have been taken by the white-water rafting even more than the fishing, both of which were planned, and golfing, which was unplanned, but some of them had managed to play a couple of rounds up on mountain courses. As David was recounting Colorado, he referred to a few of his friends, some of whom John had met over the last couple of years, but mentioned Jane on a few occasions, which raised John's eyebrows a bit.

"Jane?" John asked. "Is she at college?"

"Yes, she has been there the same time as me," David confirmed. "I have known her for about the last year, and she wanted to go out to Colorado. There were four girls on the trip; some were there all the time, others joined while we were there."

"But you only mentioned Jane."

"Maybe," David said in a noncommittal manner. "Actually, I said that I would pick her up on my way back to college, so I have to leave Mom's a bit earlier than planned."

John smiled but left it alone.

"I was going to tell you about my summer. Interested in a walk?" John asked.

"It would either be a walk or a snooze, so let's get some fresh air," David volunteered.

John took David for a walk up toward the lone cottage, and on the way, he started to explain what he and Bill had been thinking about and discussing over the last week.

"That is what you want to do, Dad?" David asked. "I know that you have been thinking things through since the first day we arrived here, but this is what you really want?"

"I have always found that if you reach a decision, sleep on it, and still feel content with your thinking the next morning, then that is the right decision for you. And I feel happy with what I have decided."

"You have thought it all through? What I mean is, do you think that you will be OK here at the inn for the long haul? Not a passing phase?"

"Yes. I have been thinking it through for quite a long time, and I know it is the right move. The right move for me, that is," John said thoughtfully. "I want to be out of the race, David. It is a race that I don't enjoy; it is a race that I cannot win, that I don't really think anybody can win—and I just don't want to do it anymore. I know that you are younger, and to you the race probably feels necessary—so I will not demean it—but if truth be told, it is a race that people are forced to participate in because it benefits the few. I have run long enough, and I want to rest now—enjoy the world as I think it should be. I'm going back to my yesterdays, where I was happy."

"I have listened to what distresses Bill, Dad, but is your desire to recapture your yesterdays spurred by the same frustrations?"

"I don't know that it is practical to try to define everything that frustrates somebody or the actual source of those frustrations. Impractical for most people, including Bill and myself. But you do know the constant irritations and that you would love to remedy them," John reasoned. "When I say I want to rest, I am not necessarily meaning in a physical way but more from a mental standpoint. I want to stop worrying about life, stop worrying about how life might turn out. I want to feel that life has turned out well."

"Don't get me wrong, Dad. I have no problem with your decision. In fact, I can see the appeal of the inn and the life up here. It makes me rest, but I also know that I feel out of the loop when I am up here. It sounds silly, but I feel guilty about not keeping up with everything. Can I ask one thing, Dad?" and David continued, without waiting for an answer. "Is your decision somewhat a result of getting divorced from Mom? Is there something that I could have done differently to help you feel contented? Could I have been more thoughtful?"

"Never think that, David. It is nothing to do with you or your mother or the divorce. You have to understand that my feelings have absolutely no reflection on an unhappy life. I would not change any aspect of my life," John insisted. "It is really a reflection on my unhappiness in how the world has gone—not how my life has gone."

David nodded an understanding.

They were passing the row of cottages. Eddie was coming down the path from Annie's cottage, preceded by Rip and Riley. Eddie welcomed David, explained that he was busy fitting out a new bathroom for Annie but had to be getting back to the inn to fix a problem with one of the guests' showers while they were out for the afternoon. Eddie continued down the roadway while Rip and Riley changed allegiances and headed up, leading the way for their friend David.

John continued. "You have done the one thing I ever really wanted you to do, David, and that is to understand the world and understand life. It didn't really matter to me how successful you were, especially from a monetary standpoint. But the world can be a cruel and hard place. To have had to leave you floundering in life would have saddened me more than I can imagine. It would have ripped my heart out knowing that I would not have been able to help. I do thank you for that, David."

"Am I right in imagining that you see yourself as having finished your job in some ways, Dad?"

"Hadn't really thought of it like that. But yes, there is some truth there. You have grown into a good person, David, and I know that you will be just fine. You never know what turns life will take, but I know that things will not go the wrong way because of you."

"I will always try."

"You shouldn't assume that you are born a good man. It was you who elected to live as a good man, and I am very grateful for that."

The pair had reached the cottage. John's cottage.

As a matter of course, the dogs dashed around to the back patio bar-becue pit to retrieve their personal tennis balls and bring them across to David. There then ensued the usual fifteen minutes of "throw and fetch" directed by David while John successfully located the cottage door key, under a potted plant by the side of the barbecue pit, as Bill had described, and let himself into the cottage. Eventually David left the dogs lying panting in the sunshine on the patio and went indoors to find John looking around the cottage. It was the first time that David had been inside the cottage, John having taken a look around on his own two days earlier.

The cottage had been built soon after the main building in the early twentieth century. The interior was cool, probably as a result of the thick stone walls of the ground floor and the fact that all the windows were on the smaller size by modern standards. All the woodwork remained in its natural state, lightly stained, including all the heavy solid-wood doors, which clunked closed in a reassuring manner. The ground floor consisted of a large kitchen, with a back door out onto the patio at the rear, and a dining area complete with farmhouse table, a living room dominated by a stone-built fireplace, a smaller study-cum-library room, and a glassed-in conservatory facing roughly south to catch the sunshine. There was also an entrance hallway, with beautiful polished wooden floors and a wide curved stairway leading up to the second floor, where they found a good-sized master bedroom complete with en suite bathroom and two smaller bedrooms, which shared a decent bathroom between them. Finally, on the ground floor, there was a door between the study and kitchen, leading down to a small basement, which did not extend across the full area of the property and was carved out of the natural rock on which the cottage had been built. The basement was dry with no sign of any dampness but definitely cooled by the surrounding rock and with only small windows high up on the walls.

"With Eddie's help I was hoping to make this into a wine cellar," John said as he and David were inspecting the basement. "I have always fancied having one."

"So what are your plans, Dad? Have you thought through when you will make the move?"

"Only a sketchy idea in my mind," John replied. "I will take my time getting sorted out at home, talking with the various publications, and selling the town house. But I figured that by the springtime I could be in a position to take the plunge. Maybe the timing will depend on how easy it is to sell the house, but I don't think that that should be too difficult, because it is a moderately priced property when all is said and done."

"So you could be up at the inn before next summer. But what about the cottage? Will you move in and then make any renovations you might want?"

"That is what I was thinking. To be honest, I don't think I will need to do too much work. Eddie has completely redone the bathrooms and kitchen, and I love all the old-time original features of the cottage. I will ask for Eddie's help on the wine cellar and ask him how I could put a large bay window in the master bedroom, overlooking the pasture down to the inn. I would like going to sleep and waking up to a view of the fields."

John and David locked up and went back around to the patio, where Rip and Riley were now fast asleep—trusting that they would not be left alone up there.

"And I will see if I can renovate the barbecue pit out here," John added. "It will be good to cook and eat out here on summer evenings."

Calling the dogs awake, they set off to walk back down the roadway toward the inn.

"I will be sorry to have you further away, Dad. And sorry that you will be moving away from Mom. But I understand the pull of the place and know that I will be up here often—maybe to stay with Bill or maybe you. I will see who provides the best accommodation," David said, smiling.

"Don't worry, David. I will be OK, and you will be just fine on your own now," John replied. "But if I am honest, cutting ties with the life we had and moving away from where we grew up as a family does bring sadness. Deep down I know that I still want to take care of you, although I know that I cannot and that you don't need me."

"I will always need you, Dad," David assured John, putting his arm around his shoulder.

"In some ways I wish that was true—but that isn't really the case."

They walked on toward the row of cottages again, where Rip and Riley checked the front gardens to see if Annie was out pottering.

"You know that I am happy for you, Dad. Don't worry about Mom and me. Mom obviously has Keith, and she will be all right. And as for me, I am a big boy now and need to finally take care of myself fully. Although in a way I have never wanted to make the final break."

"I know, David, I know. Not wanting to leave what has been a good time in your life is understandable and actually makes me feel good," John reflected. "Throughout your life I have wished that I could protect you. That wish has never lessened. Even now that you are an adult, I wish that somehow I can shelter you from a life that can be very harsh, very unfair—but I know that cannot be. I have never wanted the world to hurt my boy, never wanted anybody to break your heart—but I cannot prevent it—you have to see the ugliness of the world for yourself and experience the world as it is. I cannot stop it.

"I will be OK Dad"

"I believe you will," John said, smiling "But as we are having a semi-heartfelt discussion could I ask you to remember one thing, before I have to let you go."

David nodded, adding "Don't feel that you are letting go. I will always need you."

"When we walked in the snow covered pasture last Christmas here at the inn, the discussion was difficult but it is still the truth. Life will give you setbacks, David. I'm afraid it will hurt you at times and probably the most painful experiences that you will suffer are when you lose people. You will lose me. I wish that it wasn't so, but I know it has to be. And when you lose me there will be questions in your mind. But as I tried to tell you that day—know that I am happy now—have had a happy life and above all am proud of my son. That happiness is all you should remember. This is the real me me...And that doesn't change when I die—that memory cannot change because it is true. Always know that, David."

David was quiet for a time. He was visibly moved.

"I suppose that a father always wishes he could have taught his children more. I just hope that I taught you well." John added as an afterthought.

You taught me everything I know, Dad. You were a good teacher."

"Don't think that, David. I only ever tried to teach you the important things, of which there are very few. You learned everything else yourself."

"A deep discussion, Dad."

"Not easy to say, which is why I have never managed in the past."

It was still only four o'clock as they approached the inn, so John suggested a drive in one of the cars before dinner. He had been looking around the Citroen 2CV the day before, intrigued by the basic interior and loving the novelty of the layout being so individual, before uniformity commandeered car design. Having checked with Bill that it was OK to take the little car for a drive, they headed over to the barn—the dogs for once preferring to stay at the inn, maybe because it was getting closer to their dinnertime.

"Here you have a car with less than half the power of Eddie's ride-on lawn mower," John said as he introduced David to the little pale-blue curved car after they had entered the dim, cool interior of the barn. "I would guess that the acceleration to sixty will be impressive if it is under a minute."

"It is almost more basic than the bus," David remarked as he took a look around the little car, at the spindly steering wheel, the very strange-looking gear shift coming out of where a dashboard normally resides, the front bench seat that looked to offer about as much comfort and support as a wooden bench, and the front side windows, which opened simply by flipping up the bottom half.

They both took a few minutes to fathom out the gear change, unlike anything they had driven before, and then rolled back the soft canvas top, which had ties to secure the roll at the back. John set off driving and, unlike some of the other cars that could be described as roaring up the driveway, the Citroen puttered up the hill at seemingly little more than a walking pace.

They both enjoyed the driving experience so much that they lost track of time and ended up a good hour away from the inn by six thirty and elected to grab dinner at a modest German restaurant on the outskirts of a small town to the northeast of the inn. They elected to eat out on a deck, overlooking the river running parallel to the main street of the town, where they enjoyed a delicious, if relatively simple, meal. David happily agreed to be the driver going back, so John enjoyed a stein of the German beer. They didn't talk too much during their dinner, preferring to sit back and watch the river flowing along and some of the locals, parents and children, fishing from the banks.

"It is good to see you comfortable with your decision, Dad," David said as he turned his chair a bit and stretched himself out at the end of their meal. "There don't seem to be any doubts in your mind."

"No, I don't have any doubts about the decision as such."

"Doubts about other things?" David pursued in response to John's inflection.

"I sometimes dwell on how it will all turn out. I wonder if I will be allowed to grow old gracefully and can then leave life quickly when it is time."

"I know that you have always thought deeply about how people's lives end. How their lives play out. And I understand how much you would like a peaceful conclusion when it is your time, Dad?"

"I do hope that such things come true; sometimes I hope very much and sometimes I have hoped all my life. But I am not sure that hope is belief, David. Hope is easier because you don't have to face whether you believe."

CHAPTER 26

Spring Dreams

THE TIMETABLE PROGRESSED ROUGHLY ALONG the lines that John had envisaged. He spent the rest of that year and into the New Year getting his affairs sorted—including selling his town house in the following March. He took a week's break over Christmas and the New Year to travel up to the inn, not to really further his move but to simply relax and revisit the spirit of Christmas. The weather cooperated by snowing periodically with temperatures in the midtwenties throughout, ensuring a white holiday at the inn and great excitement among the visitors who had come up in anticipation of the winter sports in the area.

By early April, John had finished taking care of the seemingly endless tasks associated with moving his life and was ready to make the transition. The town house was empty, the final details surrounding the sale being left in the hands of his lawyer, and with his belongings on a moving truck, John said good-bye to Connecticut and the Tri-State area and headed to Vermont, hopefully for good.

John had made earlier arrangements with Bill to stay in one of the inn's rooms for the first month after his arrival. This allowed Eddie and him three weeks of freedom to paint the rooms in the cottage that needed a fresh coat, prior to John's furniture being delivered, and then a further week for John to unpack at a more leisurely pace. They purposely left the master bedroom and the study empty of furniture because Eddie had happily agreed to install John's requested bay window in the bedroom, with the help of one of his friends who was a local contractor, and had also suggested that they fit some additional shelving in the study, which John intended to use as his office.

Because Eddie's familiarity with the required home improvement skills far surpassed John's abilities, it was agreed between the two that during John's first two weeks, he would learn and take on the majority of Eddie's regular tasks around the inn, which would, in turn, allow Eddie to dedicate more time at the cottage. John actually thrived on a lot of the tasks that Eddie temporarily handed over to him. He welcomed the opportunity to interact with the guests in the restaurant and bar during the afternoons and evenings and also very much enjoyed his time working with Annie in the kitchen, preparing the meals.

By the second week of May, John had officially moved into the cottage, albeit into one of the smaller guest bedrooms. By the end of July, Eddie had finished remodeling the master bedroom and study, and by the end of August, the wine cellar was fitted out and John was realizing a long-held fantasy and was busy stocking his collection.

Soon after moving in, John spent an afternoon mounting a number of bird feeders of varying designs intended to appeal to different species, around the south-facing side of the cottage, making them visible from the conservatory, master bedroom bay window, and from out on the patio. The number and variety of visitors that the feeders instantly attracted soon initiated a request from Annie for John to mount a few feeders in her own back garden, followed by a couple outside the kitchen window at the inn.

The one element of John's unwritten plan that actually happened a lot quicker than he had originally anticipated was his intention of getting a dog, maybe a year or so, after moving up to the inn. As a family Melinda, David, and he had had a lovable Labrador as David was growing up. The dog lived a good life, dying at the decent age of thirteen, when David was fourteen, about a year before the divorce. Later John had wanted to get another dog, but living on his own in the town house, coupled with the frequent traveling, was not really conducive to taking on a companion. So he had determined, in his mind at least, that the move to Vermont and the inn, with all the surrounding space, would present a perfect opportunity to become a dog owner once again. The part of the process that he had not predicted was the timing. Within a month of making the move, while idly talking to Jenny down at the stables as she groomed her horse one Saturday morning, the conversation turned to dogs as Rip and Riley chased around the paddock. She mentioned that her friend's border collie was having a litter in a few weeks and that Jenny was actively trying to persuade her parents to get one. This was one of the breeds John had always admired but never owned because of the amount of exercise and space to run that they needed. Inevitably, the idle conversation translated into John visiting Jenny's friend, who lived on a farm barely five miles away, falling in love with the expectant mother and one of her pups from a previous litter and, before he knew it, gratefully agreeing to take a male puppy from the pending litter.

So in the last week of July, John arrived back from the farm to introduce an eight-week-old puppy to Rip, Riley, and everybody else at the inn.

"Say hello to Spot, you two," John said as he put the small furry black-and-white ball down on the grass, below the deck, at the rear of the inn. The two terriers sniffed him all over, nudging him as he rolled around in the sunshine before getting clumsily to his feet and gamboling gamely after Rip and Riley, but not being able to keep up.

"I think that he will enjoy it here, plenty of the space that he needs," Bill said.

And enjoy it he did. Through that summer the terriers showed Spot the ropes. Initially they could outrun the collie as he still half-hopped and half-ran after them. But by the time the geese arrived in September, Rip and Riley were struggling to match Spot's speed. And that was the last time they could hope to keep up with the young newcomer. The two brothers were ten years old at that stage and no longer had Spot's limitless endurance, or maybe they understood by that time that trying to catch the geese was a fruitless exercise. In the years to come, after a couple of token sprints toward the geese, they were happy to lie and watch bemused as Spot did the running for them, never tiring of tormenting the birds.

"Why Spot, though?" Bill asked John as they watched the dogs on that first afternoon. "Not being difficult, but there really isn't a spot on him. Some large patches, yes, but nothing that I would think of as a spot."

"Spot used to come with me to the library, Bill. He would run alongside my bike, rest outside the library while I browsed the books, and then, fully refreshed, happily run back home with me. Mom and Dad got him as my puppy when I was two. He was always there for me, and it was the only thing that he ever asked of me—that I let him come with me."

As it turned out, John and Spot weren't the only new arrivals at the inn that year.

As part of one of his regular internships, with established veterinarians, David had been working at a practice in northern New Jersey. The practice was strictly in the town of Roselle Park, although in David's eyes all the towns in the northern part of New Jersey ran into each other with no differentiation, so he never actually knew when he was going from one town into another. Being very much in the suburbs, David fully expected that he would get to gain only small-animal experience during the entirety of the three-month internship. He envisaged that a Rottweiler, or possibly a Great Dane, would be the largest creature that he could get to practice on. So it was quite a surprise to David when, toward the end of the three months, the resident vet, with whom he was interning, asked him to make a house call to take a look at a donkey in one of the adjacent towns. David half-expected there to be a practical joke involved but turned up at the old, large Victorian house to find not one but two donkeys, although to be fair they were miniature donkeys, about four feet high. The animals were housed in a decent-sized stable toward the rear of the house at the end of the driveway. The stables faced away from the road, out onto a fenced-in area of field grasses that encompassed approximately half an acre. The owner of the donkeys was a lady named Carol in her midsixties, only about five feet tall herself, with thinning gray hair and dressed comfortably in jeans and what looked to be a man's shirt—comfortably, as if she didn't plan on going out of the house that day. The donkeys themselves seemed to be in good health, their living conditions quite decent except that they looked somewhat sad. But there again, donkeys always looked a little sad, David reflected. One of the animals was gray and one was pale brown, but with a lot of age gray particularly around his face. They were introduced as Salt and Pepper. The purpose of the visit was explained by Carol but was self-evident when David went into the stable. One of the donkeys, Salt, had lacerated one of his front legs, evidently on a splintered fence rail-ing out in their enclosure, and although the bleeding had stopped, Carol wanted to be sure there was no chance of an infection. Although he was not a donkey expert, a lacerated leg was well within David's range—he reasoned that it could not be that much different to a Great Dane—and he soon treated and bandaged the wound. Having com-pleted his official duties, David went into the large house to wash his hands, whereupon Carol asked if he would like a coffee. Sensing that she was a little lonely and would appreciate the company, David gladly accepted and sat down at the kitchen table with his cup of coffee and took an offered cookie. The conversation quickly turned to how two donkeys came to be housed behind a Victorian house in the suburbs of New Jersey. The abbreviated story, because Carol did like to chatter, was that her husband had been in the carnival business for the last forty years of his life—he had died the previous summer at the age of sixty-nine, never having managed to retire. The donkeys had been part of the carnival for the previous fourteen years; they were around seventeen years old, although they looked older to David. Most of the time the donkeys would be traveling with the carnival, as far afield as Georgia and Massachusetts, but occasionally would come home to the house during breaks in the carnival schedule. Carol used to often travel with the carnival, and in fact, Salt and Pepper had sort of been hers, as a petting attraction and sometimes also giving rides to small children if the area set aside for the carnival offered sufficient land. She did admit that her desire to be on the road had diminished with age, and she had probably been spending around half of her time at home in New Jersey over the last few years. Carol regretted that her husband never actually got to rest toward the end of his life. When her husband had passed away the previous year, her heart was no longer in the carnival, so she sold her 50 percent share of the business to her husband's partner of more than thirty years. The partner was a little younger than her husband, but he was still over sixty and had to continue his life on the road—he knew nothing else. The value of the business was nowhere near what it had been when they had been young entrepreneurs—the world had moved on—but she received sufficient compensation from the partner to keep her reasonably comfortable in her later years. Sitting there at the kitchen table, Carol reflected that maybe it had been a wasted life, starting out so promising and ending with something that few people wanted anymore. "Maybe like a TV repairman from decades ago or the Good Humor ice-cream man from when I grew up in rural Pennsylvania," she reasoned. But there again she acknowledged that it had given her and her husband a decent living, even an exciting life during their first ten years or so on the road. "But when the enjoyment is over, it is difficult to get out of such a life," she said. "The carnival gave us good times—but you have to keep paying back long after the good times are over." So the partner took the carnival business, but he didn't want the donkeys. Times had changed, and between children not wanting to ride donkeys nearly as much and the animal rights groups, there was no place in the carnival for Salt and Pepper anymore. Carol did have a lot of affection for her donkeys and feared what might become of them if it was left to their partner to find a new owner for them. So she brought them home to New Jersey as a temporary measure, nine months ago. "But they are not really happy here," she said. "It is not practical for me to get them any real exercise, besides which I am getting too old. They are looked after, but they don't have much of a life."

David didn't decide anything there and then, but over the next couple of days, he spoke with Bill, who in turn spoke with Jenny and Sarah. Once he had everybody's buy-in, David returned to the Victorian house and discussed the idea with Carol. Yes, she would be more than happy for David to take Salt and Pepper as soon as she was assured that they would be going to a good place—a place that would be good for them. "They will be going back to their younger days," David said, "going back to your yesterdays." But she didn't fully appreciate his meaning. And so it was that, at the end of his internship two weeks later, David drove up to Vermont, drove back to New Jersey, with Jenny, in a local farmer's truck with a horse box behind and finally back to Vermont with two donkeys.

Salt and Pepper moved into their own stall in mid-August, some two weeks after Spot's arrival. They spent all the warm days that they could out in the paddock area, enjoying the fresh air and constantly nibbling on the grass. It amused Bill and David to see the donkeys pay due deference to the horses, as if they knew they were guests there, while Rip and Riley, who had usually stayed well clear of the horses, paid the same respect to the donkeys; they seemed to feel safer with them and had the confidence to get reasonably close. David wasn't sure, but the donkeys looked happy to him.

Having chauffeured two donkeys to their new home, David managed to stay over for almost a week, spending a few days in the inn and a few days with his dad and Spot. He hadn't been able to get up to the inn since John moved up there, and he enjoyed seeing how the cottage had turned out and was pleased to see the developing dynamic between the four residents of the inn. John was the youngest of the men, being five years younger than Bill and seven years younger than the elder statesman, Eddie. Annie was the youngest of them all, almost five years younger than John, and although she tended to defer to Bill and Eddie when it came to running the inn, David got the impression that Annie was growing to be the mother of the family and enjoyed looking after her three elders.

CHAPTER 27

Flight to Remember

IT WAS THREE YEARS LATER when Bill celebrated his seventieth birthday at the beginning of fall—and by that time running the inn had become a collaborative effort between the three men and Annie. When Annie jokingly described how the inn was run, she would claim that Bill, Eddie, and John spent more time talking to each other and the guests than actually getting down to some work. She sometimes claimed that between the three of them, after all their socializing, they probably accomplished about as much in a day as one capable woman could. But she knew deep down that was what the guests wanted, what they came to the inn for. They wanted to feel like they were visitors to somebody's house rather than a revenue source for the hotel and hoped that their hosts enjoyed having them there as guests as opposed to the visitors being a responsibility that the three innkeepers had to endure.

And Annie knew that time marched on and didn't pause, even at Yesterday's Inn. Eddie was in his seventies while the youngster of the trio, John, had passed sixty-five that year. The four of them were all reasonably healthy, thankfully, but that didn't mean that they could or wanted to work like they did at forty. They still had plenty of help that came in regularly from the town on an unofficial rotation basis, whereas Sarah's mother, Helen, had evolved into a full-time employee. Sarah's father had passed away unexpectedly the previous year, and Helen had asked if she could work on a more regular basis, not really out of financial need but more out of wanting a purpose, because both of her girls were in college now—Sarah a senior and her sister, Rebecca, a freshman. Bill and Annie had offered Helen the middle cottage if she wanted to move in, but she preferred to keep her house at least for the time being as long as the two girls would be coming home from college. It was good for the four innkeepers to have a young fifty-year-old to lean on.

David came up to stay for a few days over Bill's birthday, which they celebrated with a special dinner, including all the inn's guests, on the actual Saturday evening that marked the landmark day. Jill and Stephen both came in on the Friday but had to leave by Sunday afternoon. The celebration and the wine extended long into the night, but it was not a raucous party of their younger days, but more of a family gathering, appreciating that they could all be there.

The inn was back to normal by Monday—a bright, cool September Monday.

After lunch, when nobody would take him up on his offer of help with the chores, David set off for a walk accompanied, as usual, by the two dogs. He initially went past the front of the barn and then, instead of taking the track leading westward up the pasture, he kept strolling in a more southerly direction, where the incline was more gradual across the field, until eventually reaching the trees along the southern edge of the property. At that point, he elected to stay on the property heading up to the right, and followed the slowly curving tree line for probably half a mile before arriving at the spot where he and the dogs had emerged from the fields of the adjacent farm at the end of their hike along the river during his and John's initial visit to the inn years ago. He sat for a few minutes, with his back against a large tree, looking down on the horse pasture, stables, and beyond to a few guests on the deck at the back of the inn. He watched somebody, presumably Bill, walk across from the inn to the barn and disappear inside for a while. David rose up slowly, whistled for Rip and Riley, and headed leisurely down the field toward the buildings.

Three horses were out in the fenced-off paddock, grazing away in the afternoon sunshine, occasionally taking short sprints across their pasture as if appreciating the cooler temperatures now that the summer heat was gone. Salt and Pepper were standing across on their far side of the enclosure, nibbling on the still-lush grass and quietly observing the afternoon. David leaned against the fencing close to the stables and watched the animals for a while, eventually being joined by Bill, who had finished up in the barn.

"Are these still the same horses, Bill? Still belonging to Jenny and Sarah?"

"Yes, still the same. The girls are off at college now, so they have younger friends and siblings take care of the horses and exercise them daily, but the girls are here every day during the holidays."

The two stood quietly, watching the impressive animals for a while. Rip and Riley made their own way back to the inn deck to get some water and rest in the shade.

While looking up into the blue of the sky, Bill's attention was taken by the vapor trails of two planes. He could see the silver glint of one plane, while the other was simply a vapor trail with the assumption that a plane was up there making it. "Strange, David—I would look at those trails as a young man and be envious of where in the world they were going, would be envious that they were going to exciting places. Now I feel sorry that they have to go somewhere. I am grateful that at seventy I can enjoy the life I have created down here, no longer envious of somebody doing something more exciting than me."

"Seventy, Bill. Does it feel different? Do you think of yourself as old?"

"I have thought of myself as old for quite a while now, David."

"For how long?" David asked. "Not wanting to pry, but I have sometimes wondered how people see themselves as they age."

Bill nodded, considered for a moment, and then explained. "I found the realization of old age comes very unexpectedly. You grow old in your mind suddenly. You shouldn't imagine that life has youth, middle age, and old age as a nice progression. You see yourself as young, as having your future ahead of you—you see it that way for a long time, perceive yourself to be young—until you are suddenly old. I never saw middle age come and go. You don't concede your age in a single day or moment—but the recognition does come in a relatively brief span of time. And above all, remember that such acknowledgment is troubling and disappointing. You were young, still with dreams of the young...and then you are old—the dreams unattainable."

"What triggered the recognition that you are no longer young? Why do you say that it happens somewhat suddenly?"

"I have to believe that everybody comes to the realization in a similar manner. Maybe men and women differ in when they recognize age; I am not sure. But what I experienced was that the recognition comes without any fanfare, such as a specific birthday, and consists of only a few isolated comments or incidents that serve to tell you that you are on that downside of life—that you are old now. For me it happened over maybe three months as I came to see that people were no longer looking to me but were looking past me now. It saddened me to accept and definitely caused anguish. It happens because a small series of occurrences, actions, or maybe comments make you realize that your best days are behind you, that you are no longer the relevant person you once were. Time has passed you by—you are old now."

When David didn't interject, Bill continued. "I have sometimes likened getting older to losing some of your confidence. The confidence that you can change things. You come into the world confident that you can make a difference, that you will be remembered, sure that you will impact life. And that feeling remains through your youth and through your life for a long, long time. But when that feeling dissipates—it dissipates very fast—you are old. You haven't changed the world—and you are old."

"Is growing old a sad thing, Bill?"

Bill thought about the question. "There are elements that bring sadness, David. It isn't growing old that brings sadness but growing old alone without the friends of your life, without the friends of your youth, without those who shared your life—that can break your heart. I have sometimes wished that life had a final scene, allowing you to say good-bye or to thank those who played a role in your life. But if you have lived long enough, most of those people have long gone, and you feel alone, and there is nobody to remember with. That is the sad part, David."

"Is getting old hard, Bill? I mean, is it difficult?"

"Not really. Getting old is relatively easy, because in many ways you are grateful to have got that far, knowing that many didn't. Life isn't easy, and as you get into your later years, you recognize that you have managed to stay the course, have in a way triumphed over the challenges of life, and you know that the finish line is nearing—where the need for you to answer the challenges will no longer be there. I sort of imagine that having lived out your life and not given in will enable you to rest peacefully. No, getting old isn't the difficult part, David; it is remembering your youth that is hard—and remembering a happy youth is very hard."

They watched the horses grazing and occasionally flicking their tails, presumably at insects invisible to the watchers.

"Now that we have established you are old, to celebrate your birthday, I have a surprise for you tomorrow. It will mean about an hour's drive but hopefully well worth it. The forecast is good, high fifties, some clouds but mainly a bright fall sky. Can we take one of the cars?"

"What's the surprise first, David?"

"For your seventieth. But, believe me, you will enjoy it more if I keep it as a surprise."

"Open or closed top for the car then?"

"Probably open top would be more in the spirit of the day. Just need a hat, scarf, and jacket."

"The E-Type it is then, but I don't need a hat or a scarf."

"No, you don't, Bill, but humor me a little."

"OK," Bill said in conclusion, smiling at being instructed by somebody forty-plus years his junior.

John stayed behind to take care of things at the inn while Bill and David set off in the open-topped E-Type about two hours after breakfast the following day. David drove, heading south on a gorgeous morning, toward the Vermont/Massachusetts border. The drive took nearer to an hour and a half, but just before noon, they turned in at the entrance of a small airfield and pulled up in front of the only building. There were a number of signs on the gray-shingled exterior, by the door, but David tapped the one that read Brannigan's Air Tours before opening the creaking door and heading into the cool interior.

"Bill, this is Art Brannigan," David said, by way of an introduction to one of the two occupants of the airfield office. Art was a short, stocky man, in his midfifties with a mainly bald scalp, but what little hair remained was very white. He beamed broadly at the sight of his two visitors.

"Pleased to meet you, Bill," Art said, extending his hand. "And this is Peggy, whom David met when he came in a couple of days ago," gesturing to a dark-haired middle-aged lady at another one of the four desks in the office. "Without her, we pilots would struggle to stay in business."

Bill shook hands with Art and Peggy and then looked toward David expectantly.

"I wanted to surprise you for your birthday, Bill, and after a little research online, I got in touch with Art here—actually with Peggy. He runs charter flights in a beautiful 1940s biplane and is all set to take you up for a couple of hours."

Bill nodded and smiled but was a little lost for words. "Thank you—I have thought about taking a flight many, many times but never did get around to it. Thank you for remembering."

"Can we show Bill the plane, Art?" David asked.

"Sure," Art said. "I am all ready to go, so if you want to take a quick bathroom visit, we can drive over and get the show on the road, so to speak."

Bill took Art's advice, and five minutes later they were heading across the airfield in Art's battered old Jeep Wrangler toward a bright-yellow biplane that stood shining on the grass in the sunshine.

When they had climbed out of the Jeep, Art presented his pride and joy. "A Boeing Stearman built in 1942. She has been mine for fifteen years now. A hobby really."

Bill and David spent a few minutes looking around the plane; both seemed fascinated with the wings and fuselage and stroked it repeatedly. It seemed very flimsy by today's standards. Bill's smile didn't stop.

"Whenever you're ready, we can get going, Bill."

"Ready as I will ever be, Art. Just show me how to get in," Bill replied and added, turning toward David, "Thank you—it means a lot."

Under Art's guidance, Bill clambered up into the cockpit and took a further few minutes of instruction about various aspects of his cockpit seat, generally what to expect on the flight, how to fit the seat harness, and, as importantly, how to get out of it quickly, in the hopefully unlikely event of an emergency. Bill listened intently but later admitted that not too much actually sank in. Art then secured himself into his pilot's seat, which took a lot less time and, after tapping Bill on the shoulder, turned the engine, which coughed, spluttered, and roared into life. After that nobody, especially David, could hear anything, and he backed well out of the way of the throbbing machine. Communication consisted of some thumbs-ups between the two aviators and across at David. Then the Stearman started to trundle slowly from its grassy spot out onto the runway.

And so it was that early one afternoon in September, Bill took off into a duck-egg-blue fall sky. He smiled broadly from the front passenger seat and sported a checkered scarf that trailed and flapped behind him. David imagined that he was smiling because of both the excitement of the flight but also because of the puffy cumulus clouds drifting low and white across those skies.

As they had been climbing up into their respective seats, Bill had asked, "How high are those clouds, Art?"

"I would guess around three to four thousand feet," Art answered. "Why's that, Bill?"

"Can we fly that high?"

"Yes, we can easily get up there if that is what you'd like."

"That would be nice. I have wanted to feel the clouds for a long time now," Bill said, looking up as they floated on by.

After taking off, the Boeing circled the airfield and flew relatively low over David's vantage point at the edge of the runway. Bill waved enthusiastically from the cockpit before the plane droned away in a westerly direction climbing steadily. David watched them as far as the eyes could see and then took the Jeep back to the office to await the fliers' return.

After sitting in the office for about three-quarters of an hour, chatting with Peggy, David eventually took his second mug of coffee outside and sat in one of the lawn chairs on the grass at the rear of the office, enjoying the afternoon and waiting for the biplane to return. About an hour and twenty minutes after its departure, David first heard and then, in time, made out the little plane returning to the airfield on a reciprocal course. As it got closer, the plane again took a wide circle around the airfield, disappearing from sight for a while, before approaching the runway from behind David's seat, gliding in and bumping lightly a couple of times before settling on the ground.

David jumped back into the Jeep and followed the Boeing over to the far side, where Art swung the plane around on the grass before killing the eager engine. Both fliers took their time disembarking, but from the happy, excited chatter between the two, and down to David, it was obvious that the afternoon's flight had been a success. When he reached terra firma, Bill was beaming broadly. The three stood talking for quite a while before Bill, with David's help, remembered to take a lot of photos of the Stearman, Art, and Bill himself. Bill continued his discussions with Art and descriptions to David on the return Jeep ride and for a while back at the offices of Brannigan's Air Tours. It had been an enjoyable adventure.

"Could I ask a favor of you, Bill?" Art asked as Bill and David were saying their good-byes and getting ready to leave.

"You can ask, Art, and I will try to oblige if I can."

"I have always wanted to drive such a car. Do you mind if I take it for a quick drive?"

"Be my guest, Art, and I can go one better. Why don't you take it down the runway and get a real feel for what she could do in her day?"

They quickly checked with the little control room that no planes were intending to land, and then Art and his copilot Bill roared off on their second jaunt of the day, their scant hair blowing wildly. Their first trip down the runway was so enjoyable that they promptly did a wide U-turn on the asphalt and set off on a repeat run, this time even faster.

"She hasn't been that fast in quite a while," Bill said as he climbed out.

"Exhilarating." Art smiled. "Probably faster than our takeoff."

"Do you want to take a run, David? You won't get many such chances," Bill asked.

David couldn't resist the opportunity, so he offered to take Peggy for a trip down the strip, which she seemed to enjoy immensely, although her hairstyle suffered a lot more than the men's.

Eventually Bill and David bade Art and Peggy good-bye at around four o'clock, and the E-Type headed north again. David was driving, but a lot slower.

In due course David said, "Good day, Bill?"

"Very good." Bill smiled. "I will not keep thanking you, but thank you. One of the more unimagined surprises I've had."

After another minute of quiet, Bill added, "I suppose that you want to ask me about the clouds."

"And?"

"It was peaceful in there. I know that the engine was still loud, but it felt calm and serene, if that makes sense. And I felt to be on my own. It was nice to be on my own with my thoughts."

Another period of quiet ensued before Bill continued his reflections. "I can't claim that I physically saw anybody, if that is what you were wondering. But in a strange way, when I was alone with my thoughts, I could remember very clearly—more clearly than I have for decades now. It has been a long time since I have been able to remember my mother as she was, David. My father died relatively young, and I always remember him that way, as he was in my twenties. But my mother lived to a good age, and I have struggled to remember her as my young mother when I was growing up. She has been old in my memory for a long time now. But I remembered her as young today. She was sat on the patio today. We were all young today."

The two continued to talk, on and off, during the drive home to the inn, recounting their day, but they were somewhat quieter than usual. Happy to be in their own thoughts, accompanied by Bob Seger's reminiscences on the freedoms and innocence of youth and his yearning for what was lost in the passage of the years.

On his walk with Rip and Riley late that evening, crunching along the road toward the cottages, Bill paused and looked up at the starlit, moonless sky and murmured, "I have always tried to remember Brian, Dad." The dogs heard him in the darkness.

CHAPTER 28

Reflections-the Dreams of Yesterday

RIP AND RILEY

A YEAR AFTER BILL'S SEVENTIETH, David came up to the inn in late September. He tried very hard to come up either two or three times a year, but this year his summer visit was later than usual. He admitted, more readily as the years passed, that he liked the setting that was the inn. To John he sometimes remarked that he found the inn to be a restful place, and more and more he enjoyed the rest. John smiled to himself and thought, "That is exactly what the inn is about, but it is harder to appreciate when you are young."

He headed the car down the driveway with a heavier heart this time, and as he walked up the path toward the front door, there was only one nose pressed to the window. Rip had left Riley on his own during the past spring. He was almost fourteen years old and had developed a tumor that, the vet explained to Bill, was inoperable from a practical standpoint and would become increasingly painful during the next couple of months as it grew. Bill waited for almost three weeks, after being given the news, but when he could see that Rip was in noticeable discomfort and not even wanting to chase his beloved tennis balls anymore, he took him back to the vet. For the first time since they were puppies in the litter together, Riley stayed in the car outside the vet's and seemed to be accepting when Bill returned alone with a leash.

"How's Riley doing?" David asked as Bill greeted him in the entrance.

"He's fine but definitely a little quieter than before. I've noticed that he tends to stay closer to me now. Goes out on his own but seems to not be gone nearly as long as when he and Rip would go off exploring. I sometimes imagine that he is expecting Rip to come back."

Riley jumped back up onto his window seat, after greeting David, to resume watching the world go by.

"On the seat there, Riley has free reign now, but he will not sit anywhere other than the spot where he has always sat. Even if I put him at the opposite end, he immediately goes to his seat, as if out of respect to Rip. And when we visit John's cottage, Riley will always go and get Rip's tennis ball first and bring that to me—he won't chase Rip's ball, but he likes me to have that one before he goes and fetches his own. I imagine that he must wonder where his friend has gone and, maybe, wonder if something will happen to him."

After a moment Bill added, "I used to envy dogs going through their lives never worrying about what happens to them, about how life turns out. But now I look at Riley and see that same lack of understanding results in him yearning for his friend to return and not being able to comprehend."

"Seems like only yesterday that they both sat out on the deck with us in the aftermath of the hurricane, Bill," David said and then asked, "What will you do when young Riley has to leave as well? Will you get another puppy, or haven't you contemplated that far yet?"

"Yes, I have considered it. I suppose it is an inevitable train of thought. I guess that I might change my mind, but at the moment, I don't think that I will get another dog, David. Deep down I would always worry and wonder if somebody would take care of him when I was gone. But we don't have to cross that bridge just now," Bill reflected before changing the subject. "But how are things with you, David? It must be almost two years since you started working at the practice in Connecticut—how are you enjoying working full-time for a living?"

"Things are good. Thanks, Bill. Jane and I have been in the house for eight months now, and she has a full-time job at a law firm in Greenwich,

Yesterday's Inn

as a paralegal. She is happy there but doesn't get as much vacation, which is why she couldn't come up this time. All being well she wants to come up at Christmas—and stay with you at the inn."

"Look forward to it—tell her she is always welcome. Are you going to walk up to see your dad?"

"Yes—is he at the cottage?"

"Popped up there after lunch. Should be heading back soon, I would think."

"Do you want to come with me, Riley?" David asked, patting his thigh. "Shall we go and see Spot?"

Riley jumped down from his seat, more than happy to accompany his longtime walking partner.

"I am not sure whether you will find Spot up there; he might be staying close to his friend Annie, outside the kitchen on the deck, possibly. He alternates his affections between John and Annie but knows who will be cooking and baking in the afternoons. But go ahead and take Riley. He will enjoy the walk. See you at dinner," Bill said and then, remembering, called to David as he headed down the pathway. "If you see Eddie, could you let him know that Annie was looking for him? Something to do with the kitchen door hinges squeaking a bit."

"Will do, Bill. See you later."

EDDIE

David and Riley passed Eddie as he was heading back toward the inn from his cottage and gave him Bill's message.

"No rest for the weary," Eddie joked. "I will go around and see her. Good to see you David—John will be happy."

Eddie relished the fall. He was seventy-three now, and the older he got, the less he liked the heat of midsummer or the bitter cold of winter in Vermont. But the spring and the fall were the seasons he looked forward to. He imagined these were the seasons that the inn enjoyed. He, Bill, and Annie had been at the inn for fourteen years now, and his role had changed bit by bit over those years. He still enjoyed looking after the inn, still enjoyed that everybody came to him when things needed doing, but whereas a decade ago he would take on renovations himself, now he would use some of the local contractors to do the heavy lifting parts. John had happily adopted many of Eddie's daily routines, and sometimes Bill jokingly referred to Eddie as a gentleman of leisure, but in reality Eddie was still up and about by six thirty each morning and remained an integral part of the daily life of the inn.

Eddie found Annie taking a break, drinking a cup of tea on the deck outside the old kitchen door, on the side of the inn overlooking the barn. The area of the deck was shaded from the September sun, which was pleasant on that afternoon, though getting lower in the shortening days, with a gentle, warm breeze blowing across the pastures from the south. Spot was stretched out further along the deck, at the rear corner, where he could catch the sun and still keep close enough to the cook. As soon as Eddie approached, Spot jumped up and trotted over, wagging his long-haired tail in greeting.

"What do you have cooking today?" Eddie asked, climbing the couple of steps onto the deck.

"There's a meatloaf and some short ribs in the oven," Annie replied. "Spot is sniffing the air and hoping to taste test before long. Do you want some tea?"

"Love some, while I take a look at the door. I think I know what it is—same thing happened a couple of years ago after a hot summer."

Eddie grabbed a few tools from his closet inside the kitchen and worked on the hinges of the heavy door.

"David is visiting. Did you see him?" Eddie asked, stopping to sip his tea.

"Bill mentioned, but no, I haven't seen him yet. I was busy when he arrived. It's always good to have him around for a few days. Good to have somebody younger than you three old-timers around," Annie joked.

"Good to be young, Annie." Eddie nodded. "But I am never certain whether I would like to relive all those years, the good and the not-so-good. I know that I am in a happy place now."

Annie smiled. "It could be good to feel young again sometimes—assuming that you didn't know the heartaches that go with living your life, Eddie."

ANNIE

After finishing her tea, Annie went back inside the kitchen to attend to her dinners and put two prepared loaves of bread into the oven to bake. Eddie finished off adjusting the door, tested that it was squeak free, thanked Annie for the tea, and went through into the restaurant and bar to get everything ready for dinner and the evening. Spot got to taste a piece of short rib, gave it his blessing, and then, knowing there would only be the one treat, ran off freely across the fields, parallel to the gravel roadway, toward John's cottage. As he approached the cottage, Spot caught sight of John and David starting on their way down the road toward the inn and altered course to greet them. David made his usual fuss over Spot, who ran wildly around in large circles before calming down.

It was approaching five by the time John and David arrived back at the inn. Bill was attending to guests in the bar while Eddie and Annie were busying themselves in the kitchen and waiting on one family of early diners. John joined in the process seamlessly, initially helping Annie in the kitchen, until Helen arrived about fifteen minutes later, and then looking after guests out on the deck as they started arriving for predinner drinks.

David made himself scarce by taking a beer out onto the far end of the deck for a while and then going into the library, where he caught the evening news before a dinner that included the short ribs Spot had sampled earlier.

John took the helm in the kitchen at around eight thirty, as things were quieting down, and Annie emerged out onto the deck, with the one glass of wine that she allowed herself most evenings, to catch up with David.

"You look good, Annie. You look contented," David greeted her. "Bill gave me the happy news of your second grandchild."

"At long last." Annie smiled. "Sam and Alan have been trying for a long time, almost given up hope I think. But now I have a grandson, Timothy. Yes, I am very contented."

"Have you managed to meet Timothy yet?"

"Yes, I've met him once. The four of them came up for a very short visit in July, but they hope to come back for a week at Christmas. That will be nice, and Tess will enjoy Christmas up here in Vermont."

"Hopefully, Jane and I will be up. We look forward to it. So how do you enjoy looking after your three men, Annie? The four of you seem to get closer every time I come up, as if you have spent a lifetime together."

"We do seem to get on very well. It probably helps that we all have our own places to escape to when we need it, but yes, I think that we enjoy each other and make a good team. If I am honest, the three men are very similar to three kids—but I love looking after all of them." Annie laughed.

"And Dad seems very happy, seems to thrive on living up here. He has never seemed unhappy, not that I have known, but he seems care-free now. Genuinely at peace with his life. My sense is that he made a good move for himself."

"Oh, I think it was a very good move, David. He just loves the inn, he is getting increasingly comfortable interacting with the guests, and he Bill and Eddie have a great understanding on sharing the workload and each taking time off," Annie confirmed. "And John loves to dabble in the kitchen, loves to try his hand at cooking."

"So I believe," David replied. "Is he cooking on his own or under your supervision?"

"At first he liked me to keep an eye on him, but now he takes it upon himself to cook, on his own, two or three afternoons a week. He tells me in the previous evening that he is going to try making this, that, or the other for dinner the next night, and I take a few hours off the next morning and let him have free run of the kitchen. He comes and gets me if he needs help or advice."

"And exactly what sort of dishes does Dad like to make?"

"He keeps trying various different dishes, but I would say his preference is anything involving the word *pie*," Annie said, smiling. "He has tried steak-and-ale pie, chicken pot pie, and shepherd's pie many times."

"And I would think that he likes to eat his fair share of those pies." David laughed.

"With John's help and Helen coming in almost every day, I can take it a lot easier than a few years ago," Annie reflected.

"Good for you, Annie," David replied. "I suppose you want the inn to be busy, but you don't want to work long hours every day, seven days a week."

"Most of it doesn't really seem like work. More like taking care of a family. But it is nice to be able to put your feet up when you want to," Annie admitted.

"Can you ever see yourself stopping working?" David asked after a few moments. "It doesn't seem that the four of you have any intention of ending anything."

Annie considered the question before replying. "Retirement is a worry we don't have, David. I think that the decision to retire must be very difficult, especially if it is from a place that you have enjoyed for decades. If there was a way to take six months off from a job and then return, that might be OK—get to travel and enjoy a well-earned long break, but then be allowed to go back to familiarity. But to have to abandon the life you have lived for all those years so suddenly, permanently, and irreversibly—I am sure for some it can be a lonely experience. Bill has unknowingly created a place that we don't retire from; we don't have to retire from our home. Not to say that we have to keep working as much or keep working at all, but we don't have to go away. So far that is very reassuring."

"You say it as if you imagine the reassurance won't last, Annie."

"I am a creature of habit, always have been. I like to do the same things and in the same way and get quiet comfort out of the repetition. But the flip side is that I get upset when my routine comes to an end. When I realize that time has moved on, as it must do, I know, then I look back at the routines I had. Often I don't appreciate routines until they are no more. I get saddened by the change."

David looked quizzically over at Annie.

"You see, I know that my routines will change; they have to end. I know that things come to an end for everybody, but I fear that I will be left to remember, to remember these happy times, and I wish it didn't have to be so. That is why deep down I am troubled by being the youngest here at the inn. I understand that I am old, but I am the youngest of the old, and that worries me, David, because I know what the outcome might well be. I don't know what alternative outcome I would wish for, but I know that it could be a sad outcome and sometimes wish I didn't have to face it."

"I understand how you feel. I have come to understand that the happier your existence, the more you fear the outcome, as you describe it," David reflected and then continued. "But you shouldn't fear what has to be. There are other younger people around, and they will be here to help you through when those changes come. Will help you when your routines are taken away from you. Because they will be taken away from all of us."

"I know that one given day will start like all the other days that I have enjoyed; everything will be the same. But the next day will not start the same. It is unavoidable, I know. But I fear the next day, David."

David and Annie sat and finished their drinks in quiet contemplation, looking out past the stables and the pastures to the distant trees on the ridge, silhouetted against the night sky, illuminated by the setting moon. Only the occasional snort from the stables broke the quiet.

Annie yawned and got ready to say good-night. "I often look out at Salt and Pepper. They are a lot like me in many ways. Put out to pasture, so to speak. And they enjoy every day up here, as do I. Couldn't be happier. But I wish I had their blissful ignorance of not fearing the next day."

"You know that you will be OK, Annie."

"I know, David. And thank you for letting us have John up here now."

SALT AND PEPPER

Salt and Pepper did enjoy their life at the inn, watching the world go by. Riley would still come and lie close by the donkeys and bask in the sunshine on warm days, never seeming to fear being stepped on. When the donkeys very occasionally lay down on the grass—and if one did, they both did—Riley would go over and sit propped against one of them. When he was very young, Spot didn't have time for Salt and Pepper, but now that he was a getting a bit older, he would also come and lie by them in the paddock sometimes, but never for too long; his rest lasted for maybe ten minutes before something more interesting called.

Maybe the donkeys were different to the other residents of the inn. The other residents were trying to recapture some of the pleasures of their younger years in one way or another. But these were the best times the donkeys had ever known. They were just happy to amble out of their stable every morning and enjoy the day, never spending time dwelling on how they had ended up here. They didn't ask for much—never had.

JOHN

John didn't have any regrets over his decision to move up to the inn. From his perspective, he had everything that he wanted now. He had good friends, his independence in a comfortable cottage, his writing, and a setting that allowed them all to appreciate their later years. He more than did his fair share of work around the inn, but he never looked on it as work, and if he stopped to rationalize why, he concluded that it wasn't really work if you didn't "have" to do it. Melinda and her husband, Keith, had come to stay for a few days the previous summer. They had stayed at the inn, rather than with John, and had seemingly had a good time, promising to come back often.

Depending on whether he had any deadlines to meet, which was rarely the case, or if he was feeling in a particularly creative writing mood, John would normally spend parts of three or four days a week writing. Sometimes he would write for publications, but increasingly he would put his efforts and creativity into writing books. He normally had two or more under way at any given time. Once or twice a month, he would drive across to the bigger town, about fifteen miles away, and spend an afternoon in the library or coffee shop, on the Internet, reading e-mails, and uploading his work as need be. When the weather was good, John would often jump into a car with Spot and his computer and would spend the afternoon in a hay field, sitting against a large tree, and let his creative juices flow, taking an occasional break to appreciate the peace and quiet. Even Spot seemed to enjoy dozing with the warmth of the sun on his coat.

On the day after David had come up that September, John asked him if he would like to come up to the field with him.

"You will like it up there, David," John said. "Beautiful views, particularly at this time of year, and we can take the Thunderbird, if you like. I don't think you have ever taken a drive in that one."

"As long as I can drive," David replied, "at least some of the time."

Eddie was more than happy to take care of the late lunch crowd, so by one thirty John and David made their way across to the barn and the Thunderbird, leaving Spot to rest on the deck outside Annie's kitchen. After carefully removing the fiberglass roof and storing it safely in the barn, John let David ease the beautiful, shining, cream-colored two-seater out of the barn into the bright, fresh September afternoon. It was the first time that fall when the color of the afternoon could be described as orange as opposed to the green of summer. The foliage glowed orange in the afternoon sun. The leaves were not fluttering down in large numbers yet, but the various hues on the trees gave the clear message that they were all getting ready to drift down. The scent indicated fall was approaching, and it smelled to John to be from his childhood.

John directed David down to the bridge, where he had taken Rip and Riley for their hike those many years ago, when the dogs had still been young. Then they headed up to the right, through the woods and out into the hay fields beyond. John always remembered when he first chanced upon the field, and he had reflected that nothing would ever change in this setting—the field of grasses would be there each year. He was glad that he had been right. The field was no longer populated with the swaying grasses, having been harvested about a month earlier, replaced now with the beige stubble in readiness for the winter. But the tree looked the same, still standing on its own, imposing and with its full complement of leaves—although some were starting to pale from their summer deep green. David admired the views as he stood by the trunk of the tree—it was an impressive spectacle down and across the valley.

John did get his laptop out but didn't actually accomplish much work that afternoon. He was infected by David's appreciation of the scenery and his occasional desire just to talk. They both sat with their back to the tree, legs outstretched.

"Last night Annie was telling me about how much she enjoys it at the inn, how much she enjoys having the three of you to look after but also the occasional fear she has, stemming from you all getting older and the inevitable outcome, as she put it," David said, after a time.

"I saw you two out there for a while, was wondering what you were chatting about," John answered. "I suppose it crosses all of our minds occasionally, David, but there are just some things not worth worrying about. Nothing you can do to stop the inevitable."

"I think it is because she is a little younger. Wonders about what will happen—because logically she might be left here when something does happen."

"I can see that." John nodded. "Do you worry, David?"

"Not really worry, Dad. Yes, I wonder but not worry. I see you as being very happy here, see you as having done what you wanted to do in your later years, and it has worked out well," David said. "And I see you as having had a fulfilling life, which I hope goes on forever—know it cannot—but hope it does. But I know you will not begrudge how long your life is—if it isn't forever."

"Be careful about the forever part. You need to know that when I leave you and you are left behind, so to speak, know that I am happy. Understand that you are making me happy by outliving me. Yes, this way might be sad for you, but recognize that the opposite is beyond my imagination. It is the greatest fear I ever had since you were a boy. It haunts me still."

After a moment John added, "It doesn't need to last forever, you see—I know now that all a father really wants to achieve is to give his child a happy childhood. I hope I did."

David hugged his father, but they were quiet for a while. There were no hawks searching for prey today, so John guessed that the rodents must also be foraging away from the now-bare field.

"Strange the paths life takes, David," John said after a while. "I never would have dreamed I would be living in Vermont at sixty-six years old."

"What did you dream, Dad?"

"I suppose I was being a little figurative. In truth, I often used to be wary about dreaming too much, David, maybe because I worried that the dreams would be unattainable. But when I dreamed, the dreams would be about you and Mom and the family. Maybe the breakup with Mom stopped my dreaming; I'm not certain."

"But you still dream, Dad?"

"Dream. No, I don't think that I dream like I used to, but I do remember. I imagine now how things might turn out, but I don't think that imagining is dreaming. When you are young, you dream, but as you age, remembering takes the place of your dreams. If the memories are good memories, if what you remember makes you happy, then maybe, just maybe, your dreams came true, David."

They sat quietly for a moment before David asked, "Did your dreams come true, Dad?"

John considered for a few moments.

"They all did, David—every one."

David smiled, and they sat quietly for a long time before reluctantly rousing themselves and heading down the field to the patiently waiting Thunderbird.

After his visits to the hay field, John tended to drive home to Don Henley and "The End of the Innocence." He didn't understand all the lyrics, but the song sounded like his field. John put the song on after introducing David to the field—and they drove through September with the top down.

John had told David that he didn't dream anymore, but he knew that he wasn't being entirely truthful. He did sometimes dream. He dreamed late on summer afternoons when he was out on the deck or on his patio, looking out over the green fields, with the sun setting to the west and the long, long shadows creeping over the grass. He sometimes dreamed as he lay in bed, looking out in the direction of those same fields, with the windows open and the summer scents wafting into his room. He dreamed of a late-summer afternoon in Scotland with those same long shadows dancing across the expanses of seaside grassland. And he dreamed that Tom Watson's putt did fall into the hole late on that day and that he did witness the most improbable feat in sports history. And he dreamed that Tom Watson ended that day knowing that the impossible had happened and he would forever be remembered for what he had done on that afternoon in Scotland. The dream made him smile, and he wondered if Tom would have ever played another competitive round if he had won on that afternoon. But he inevitably came back to the question that saddened him: Why hadn't the sporting gods just allowed the putt to drop so that the story ended as it was intended to end? The story should have ended with everybody knowing they had seen history that day.

BILL AND DAVID

Years later, by the time David had been around long enough to be able to look back on his life, he would try to look back on his many visits to the inn during those years, and he would be unable to remember all of them. But for some reason, he could always remember his visit to the inn during that September. He remembered it as an extremely contented time. There would be other contented times, before and after that visit, but he remembered the four of them and the animals and the cars, and it was a good memory. He supposed that he wished Rip had been there, but when he recalled that time, Rip was there—sort of digitally imposed in by his memory. He would smile when he sat out there on the patio on his own. The people had all gone now—but the times had never gone—the times had remained.

David had been there as they left the inn one by one. He would recall his father saying years earlier that they would be happy that he, David, was around when they left—but the thought never brought comfort to David on those occasions.

After he had been left alone at the inn, he would make a point of occasionally venturing across to the Maine Coast, but he preferred to go there in late fall or early winter on a gray, overcast day, when the wind would be blowing strong and fresh off the ocean. He would like to stand on those headlands, bracing against the cold wind and remembering a good time and the summer wind.

David readily remembered his September visit, and he could always recall and listen in his head to the afternoon he spent with Bill—strolling and sitting and talking about nothing in particular. It wasn't the conversation he remembered; it was the time.

Three days after John had taken David out to the hay field, David and Bill took an afternoon walk up to John's cottage. John was busy preparing a Yankee pot roast for dinner, and Eddie was taking the afternoon to replace a few of the older wooden boards on the stables. The horses and donkeys were looking on with interest and hopefully appreciating that their abode would be secure for the winter.

The temperature had been dropping a little each day, and the freshening wind made it almost chilly. They did not need a jacket or sweater yet, but it was no longer warm. They walked up past the row of cottages, the wind bringing down more of the leaves now and whipping up the drying colorful ones on the ground.

"You all seem to be very happy up here," David said, breaking the silence. "Not that everybody doesn't usually seem to be enjoying life, but there just seems to be an air of contentment this fall."

"I must admit that we have become a very happy family, and comfortable in the routines that have evolved. Maybe it is a mistake to be so set in our ways, but we do enjoy ourselves."

"You always seemed a very even-keel person, Bill, never seem to get upset with anything or anybody. Have you always been that way, or is it the contentment of life at the inn that brings about the calm demeanor?" David asked.

Bill smiled. "I have come to realize one thing about the angry words we say. Come to realize much later in life, long after I have stopped getting angry. Whenever we get angry and frustrated with those we love and make those stupid threats in the heat of the moment, know that those threats are, in fact, the things we hope and wish will never happen. And I know now that they are the things I wish didn't have to happen eventually."

As they approached John's cottage, Bill paused, turning to look down over the property. Now that they were higher, moving out of the shelter of the hollow of the inn, the wind was stronger and blowing fresh into their faces.

"It is days like these that make you not want to leave, David—days like these that make you want to stay."

"Annie was explaining to me that none of you have to leave—that is what you have created together, Bill."

"Eventually we all have to," Bill said quietly, turning toward the cottage.

After a moment he added, "But I can tell you that I do think about all those times over the years I've been greeted innocuously with 'How are you?' 'How are you doing today?' never really appreciating the sentiment. Answering 'I'm fine, thanks,' 'I'm good, how about yourself?' I try to appreciate the greetings now, David, and really value being able to answer 'I'm good, thank you,' because I know there is a likelihood that one day I will have to answer differently. I am afraid of that day."

Although he could always remember that September clearly in the years to come, David recalled it, along with Annie's fear, about the inevitable outcome. He remembered that September but lamented that there was nobody left for him to remember with—they had all gone long ago and left David to relive those days on his own. The views from the deck remained as they had always been, but he so wished he had somebody to remember with, because they were good, good days.

He had three still photos from that visit he had retained over the years but no video—he had never taken any video at the inn. He didn't need to—it was all in his head. The one photo he had had printed many years later had been taken by Jenny, if he remembered correctly. They had called Annie to come down from her afternoon-tea break and were all leaning against the paddock fence. Riley sat by Bill's legs, and by chance Spot sat with Salt and Pepper out there in the paddock. Bill had once told John that if you could still remember times from your past, then you had not lost those things along the way—David had not lost that fall along the way.

When he reminisced, in those future days, it was difficult to remember occasions when the occupants of the inn were perhaps not as happy as they were in that September—maybe he didn't want to remember, he wasn't sure—but he could remember that they were happy then.

He could remember because they were all together and were all contented that fall. There would be later visits when they were all together at the inn in Vermont, but he knew for certain that they were all happy then—all understanding and all recognizing they were happy. And David knew, looking back, that probably none would have felt cheated if it had had to end that September. Salt and Pepper were examples of those who wouldn't have felt shortchanged had it had to end—they would have appreciated the times they had been given.

He had many of his own loved ones around in the future days—but only David was able to actually recall his friends at the inn during that September.

The bird feeders didn't seem as busy on those fall days; they were less frantic than in the spring and early summer, when the chicks were hatching.

Bill and David went around to the back of the cottage and sat out on the patio, surveying the fields of shadows in the fading autumn sun.

David had been thinking over what Bill had mentioned when he had arrived a few days earlier and commented, "Get another puppy when it is time, Bill—I promise to look after him if ever you have to leave."

"Thanks, David. I will give it some thought," Bill replied. "It pleases me to know that you plan on being around here after I have to go. Sort of heartens me."

After a few moments of contemplation, Bill asked, "Will you look after the cars? Will you keep them?"

"Why does that worry you, Bill? Why the cars?"

"Because they have never changed, you see. The cars have not changed from the day they were created. The world may have changed, but those cars have stayed the same, and it hurts me to think of them being abandoned after they have stayed true for some fifty years. That wouldn't be right."

David smiled broadly. "Of all the things you might think you have to worry about, that should be last on the list. When Dad and I first came across the inn, there were many aspects of the past that I did not really understand. Didn't fully grasp what you wanted back. But the cars made sense from the outset—I will make sure they are there in the barn."

"I can recall the difficulty I had when trying to explain what I had missed—what I was wanting to hang on to. I sort of know it in my head, but it is still difficult to put into words."

"Over the years, when I tried to rationalize it, Bill, I decided that you had come to see through all of the illusions of life and merely wanted your real world back. You wanted to know the good times again."

"You don't even know the good times are there, David—you don't recognize them until they are gone, and you are left wishing that you had appreciated them."

They sat, legs outstretched, savoring the afternoon, not talking for a long time.

After a while, looking away into the distance, Bill said quietly "It is a long road David - sometimes a difficult road. But boy when the end of the road is in sight you wish it was a little longer."

David looked over at Bill. He nodded an understanding but did not comment on the reflection.

"John has a grand view up here," Bill eventually said. "The original owner of the property knew what he was doing building a cottage up here on the hill."

"Like some coffee?" David asked as the wind started to gust a little stronger.

"Would be good—thanks."

David went inside to brew a fresh pot in his father's kitchen. Bill and Riley sat and looked back over many years at the inn. Bill could remember them, while Riley just seemed to appreciate the companionship.

David came back outside with the coffees and handed one to Bill before going over to stand on the edge of the old brick patio. He looked across the pasture to the stables, the inn, and beyond to the barn standing resplendent in the afternoon sunshine with one of the doors slid wide open. Steam rose briskly from the fresh, hot coffee in his mug. It had been over six years since that first August morning his father, Bill, and he had stood up here after the storm. Nothing had changed in the view, David reflected to himself.

Bill leaned back in the Adirondack with Riley sat propped against both his right calf and the leg of the chair. Riley tended to stay closer to him these days, no longer intent on following every scent that came his way. Looking up at the September sky, Bill watched a few small clouds drifting along on the strong southeasterly breeze. He watched the shadows that they cast move down the field by the driveway, across the roof of the inn, before clipping the edge of the stable's roof and then seeming to race up the pasture to the top of the rise in the west.

Bill looked down from the clouds at Riley and said, loud enough that David could hear, "That is where Rip is now, Riley—he'll be waiting for you."

Riley looked up at him, his tail wagging and tapping against the chair leg, not when he heard his own name but at the sound of Rip's name.

"Do you believe in heaven, Bill?"

"That thought definitely crosses your mind with increasing frequency as you get into your sixties. In your younger days, it is easy to dismiss the question, both outwardly and to yourself. But it becomes somewhat harder to ignore or put aside now. Knowing that you will discover the truth sooner rather than later makes the question real."

"So do you believe in heaven?"

Bill's look scanned across the bowl-shaped property of the inn— at the smoke curling up from one of the inn's chimneys; at the row of smaller cottages down the road, where he could see Annie resting from her gardening; at the old red barn inside which he could picture his beloved cars; at the stables where two of the horses were grazing in the paddock alongside and where the donkeys were just enjoying life.

Eventually Bill replied, "I believe that all you can know for sure is that you have tried to live a good life."

About the Author

Robert Geoffrey was born and raised in Yorkshire in Great Britain. After finishing college, he emigrated to the United States and has never found a reason to leave. Geoffrey has previously published A Letter to My Son, available through Amazon.com.

Geoffrey lives in Westchester County, New York, with his wife and son—and sometimes reflects on a time that was definitely simpler and maybe more enjoyable.

Made in the USA
Middletown, DE
09 January 2017